ENTHUSIASTIC PRAISE FOR *DogStar*

Canadian Children's Book Centre "Our Choice" Selection

New York Public Library's "Books for the Teen Age" List

Shortlisted for the Ontario Library Association Silver Birch Award

Shortlisted for the Dog Writers of America Fiction Award

"I was thoroughly entertained by
this captivating novel. It is a boy and his dog sto
a time travel tale and a grand adventure
all rolled into one book ..." VOYA

"... a beautifully resolved ending.
DogStar is a novel about the great love between
humans and animals." VANCOUVER SUN

"More plot twists than a Hardy Boys adventure
in cyberspace ... The authors expertly bring to life
a time and place for their readers with
fully-developed characters and lots of
background detail." NORTH SHORE NEWS

"... *DogStar* grows on the reader,
and Patsy Ann's doggy grin lingers long after
the book is done." QUILL & QUIRE

"A time-travel adventure story with
emotional appeal for dog lovers." BOOKLIST

A SIRIUS MYSTERY

DOGSTAR

BEVERLEY WOOD & CHRIS WOOD

POLESTAR
An Imprint of Raincoast Books

Polestar and Raincoast Books acknowledge the ongoing financial support of the Government of Canada through the Canada Council for the Arts and the Book Publishing Industry Development Program (BPIDP); and the Government of British Columbia through the BC Arts Council.

Design by Ingrid Paulson
Typeset by Teresa Bubela

NATIONAL LIBRARY OF CANADA CATALOGUING IN PUBLICATION DATA
Wood, Beverley, 1954–
    Dogstar
    ISBN 1-55192-638-5
Wood, Chris, 1953– II. Title.
PS8595.O624D63 1997   JC813'.54   C97-910818-7
PZ7.W66DO 1997

LIBRARY OF CONGRESS CATALOG NUMBER: 97-80427

First edition published in 1997

This edition published in 2004 by
Polestar/Raincoast Books
9050 Shaughnessy Street
Vancouver, British Columbia
Canada   V6P 6E5
www.raincoast.com

In the United States:
Publishers Group West
1700 Fourth Street
Berkeley, California
94710

At Raincoast Books we are committed to protecting the environment and to the responsible use of natural resources. We are acting on this commitment by working with suppliers and printers to phase out our use of paper produced from ancient forests. This book is one step towards that goal. It is printed on 100% ancient-forest-free paper (100% recycled, 40% post-consumer), processed chlorine- and acid-free, and supplied by New Leaf Paper. It is printed with vegetable-based inks. For further information, visit our website at www.raincoast.com. We are working with Markets Initiative (www.oldgrowthfree.com) on this project.

Printed in Canada by Webcom

10 9 8 7 6 5 4 3 2 1

For Piggy-Caesar, Luke and Pando, who wait for us at Dog Star.
And for Innis, whose courage inspires his father.

Table of Contents

W

one
THE BOY

JEFF BEACON and his parents left the check-in desk and walked along the wide corridor that led to Halifax International Airport's single security gate. With cameras slung over their shoulders and paperbacks parked under their arms, Ken and Frances Beacon looked every inch like two people setting out to enjoy a family holiday. Walking between them, the tall thirteen-year-old with the red brushcut looked like a convicted prisoner being led away for a lifetime or two of solitary confinement. His serious grey eyes held a faraway look and the shoulders inside his denim jacket sagged with an air of defeat.

"Who owns this backpack?"

Eh? The question snapped Jeff out of his reverie. He must have walked right through the metal-detector door without even noticing it. "Um, it's mine." He could feel his father tense up beside him. "Why?"

"Would you open it please," said the uniformed woman behind the big, boxy X-ray machine.

Jeff felt his chest constrict. He should have seen this coming; he'd flown enough to know the airport routine. He looked down at the dark green backpack lying where the endless black tongue of the X-ray machine's conveyor belt had lapped it onto a stainless steel counter. Glancing up at the screen he saw immediately what had alarmed the security guard. In the middle of the grey-and-white picture was a bright and highly suspicious blob, shaped vaguely like a hand grenade.

Buddy! His face warm, Jeff's fingers felt around for the zipper tab on his backpack and pulled it open.

The security guard rummaged methodically through the contents of Jeff's pack, sliding her hand deep inside. When she pulled her hand out, it held a polished brass cylinder a little bit smaller than a soft drink can. The cylinder had a narrow neck and a screw-on lid. Jeff heard his father's intake of breath. The woman turned the curious container over to read the writing engraved on one side.

"It's my dog," Jeff said. *Or at least it's what's left of him.* Even through his embarrassment he felt the hurt again and a part of him wanted to cry. *Not here, nerd-face, you're at the airport!* It was bad enough that people in line behind him were beginning to grumble about the hold-up.

"It's the dog's ashes." Dad's *lawyer voice.* The one he used to persuade juries in court. "He's a bit fixated with them." Jeff could hear the stinging disapproval in his father's words.

"It's only been a couple of months," Frances Beacon broke in, apologetic. "He's having trouble getting over it. That's why we're taking this trip, actually. We hope it'll take his mind off things."

"Mom!" *Jeez, can't she keep anything private*, Jeff wondered. *There are only about a hundred people here watching me squirm.*

The security guard twisted off the brass lid and peered

inside. Then she held the urn to her nose and sniffed at it. Jeff knew what she would find: dry grey powder and a dusty smell.

Oh Buddy, I'm sorry! Jeff squeezed his eyes tight against the tears. *Jeez, no!* They seemed to come every time Jeff was reminded that the white Bull Terrier who had been his best and closest friend since his first birthday was now just a half-cup of grey dust.

"Thank you, folks. Have a nice vacation." The security guard twisted the lid back onto the brass cylinder and handed it back to Jeff.

Yeah. Right! Still upset, Jeff thrust the canister back into his backpack and yanked the zipper shut.

"For God's sake, Jeff!" His father's lecture began as they rode the escalator up to the departure lounge. "What in heaven's name persuaded you to bring that with you? How often do I have to tell you: you've got to put the past away and get on with life!"

Jeff was silent. Inside, he promised himself once again, *No way am I letting go of Buddy. Ever! So get used to it, Dad.*

THE ENGINES whined to full power and the big jet lumbered down the uneven runway. Jeff felt the seat back push into his own and closed his eyes to wait for the little lift that meant they were flying.

On vacation. Oh wow.

The Beacon family had moved a lot, mostly following Mom's job changes from this hospital to that one. For vacation, Ken and Frances Beacon liked to take their only son to places like Jamaica and Cuba for a week or two of all-inclusive pampering. Nice sun, nice beach, lots of swimming, usually lots of good food. And perky baby-sitters pretending to be Youth Activity Counselors. Not bad. But with Buddy back home at a kennel, he'd always felt as though something were missing.

Last summer had been the exception. Buddy had come with him to Ontario to visit his grandparents for a month. *Now, that was what a holiday should be like.* Even now, Jeff found himself smiling at the memory of Buddy tearing around Grandad's big green lawn in that crazy way that made him look like a fifty-pound white jackrabbit.

His heart sank. *This trip will sure be different*, he thought unhappily. *No dog, no lawn, no beach. Not even my computer.* Lately, surfing around on the Net seemed to be the only activity that took his mind off Buddy. When you surfed, you never knew where you might end up and you got there in no time at all. There was a new adventure down every alley. It was almost magic.

Ten days offline, he thought. *Ten days on the good ship SS Boooorrring.*

The cruise to Alaska had been Dr. Doucet's idea. Jeff's parents had made him see a grief counsellor for some help "getting over" Buddy. Dr. Doucet was a small older man with a big nose and the quiet polite voice of an undertaker. *Dr. Pickleface, I hate you.*

Jeff stared sightlessly out the little oval window as the jet climbed up through layers of cloud. *This isn't really a holiday at all. It's a prescription!*

TEN HOURS, two airplane meals and one taxi ride later, they had crossed the continent and were climbing stiffly out of the cab in front of the cruise pier in Vancouver. It was right downtown, a gleaming white building with a futuristic roof that Jeff guessed was intended to look like sails filling in the wind.

As they crossed a gangplank onto the deck of a large blue passenger liner, he could see the harbour stretching away beyond the rail. It was busier than Halifax's. A huge grey ship stacked with containers the size of box-cars steamed past pretty white yachts and working boats painted in black, red and yellow. Beyond them, mountains rose almost straight up from the water, looking like a movie set painted on the sky.

Smiling crew members directed the Beacons to their cabin on the far side of the ship, away from the pier. The space was laid out like a compact hotel room, with two double beds and a tiny sitting area with two armchairs and a small coffee table. Jeff noticed that the table was bolted to the floor. There was a washroom to one side of the door.

Jeff's heart lifted at the sight of fresh-cut flowers on the table. *It was almost like they knew,* he thought. Avoiding his father's eyes, he pulled the brass canister out of his backpack and placed it beside the flowers. Reaching into the pack again, he removed a framed photograph and put it beside the urn. It was a picture of him and Buddy racing each other along a beach. He put his hand in again and came out with two smaller pictures, Buddy curled in his bed and the two of them lying on the floor reading comics. He arranged those on the table, too.

Jeff could feel Dad's glare-o-meter go up a notch with each picture. He braced himself for The Lecture on "putting Buddy away." But it was cut off before it could begin. A recorded announcement boomed through the ship, calling all passengers to Deck Eight for a lifeboat drill. Jeff looked at Buddy's urn, then shot a glance at his father. *Nah. It's only a drill.*

Following the disembodied instructions, the three Beacons found their life jackets in a rack in the closet and put them on. Then they left the cabin and set out to find Deck Eight.

As the ship pulled away from the dock, it passed a light-house on a rocky point. Beyond it, the land fell away into the dim blue distance where a vast inlet of the sea ran up into the mountains. Jeff saw snow on mountain peaks, coloured peach by the sinking sun. *The famous Whistler ski resort must be up there somewhere*, he reckoned.

Ken Beacon looked at Jeff, and then at his watch. "Time for a fast burger, then I think we should all hit the sack," he said. Jeff's body was still running four hours ahead on Atlantic Time, and he couldn't agree more. He was hungry and tired and bored. When the late August night finally closed in over the inky blue mountains beyond the cabin's big windows, he was already sound asleep.

THE NEXT MORNING, Jeff's eyes shot open at 5:37 a.m., according to the glowing face of his father's travel alarm clock. Outside the windows, empty squares of sea and sky had replaced the mountains. One or two bright stars still shone in the darkest arc just above the horizon. But as Jeff watched, the sky grew lighter and they twinkled out.

He felt wide awake.

He tugged on his jeans and shrugged into his T-shirt and then his denim jacket. He laced up his new Nikes. Tip-toeing past the double lump in his parents' bed he retrieved Buddy from the table and shoved the gleaming brass canister into his backpack.

Hey, boy, let's go explore this old tub! He slung the pack over his shoulder and slipped out into the corridor.

Not many other people were up. On the level where the arcade was, the gym was silent and the entrance to the movie theatre was dark and unattended. A few crew members moved quietly around the restaurant, setting out trays of sliced fruit and pastries for people who were mostly still in bed. *It's like walking through a mall on a holiday,* Jeff reflected, pushing open a door that led out to the deck.

The air was cool but fresh, and Jeff found himself on the side of the ship away from his cabin, squinting into the first rays of sun. The light was almost painfully bright as he gazed across a mile of blue-green water to a heavily forested shore.

No question, he thought, *the mountains here are pretty awesome.* Even the ones closest to him, rising out of the sea and folding back into dark green valleys, were bigger than anything back home. And beyond them were more peaks, soaring summits with sheets of snow hanging on their shoulders, the gap between each set of white fangs revealing others even more distant and mysterious.

As the ship steamed steadily north, the majestic coastline unrolled like an endless postcard of islands, bays and mountain valleys. Jeff imagined exploring each island with Buddy, finding new worlds on every one. *Sort of like Myst,* he thought, *only in real life.*

"Pretty neat, eh, Buddy?" he said over his shoulder to the backpack. "Just look at all those valleys! Bet we could find some adventures in there." *Unlike this stupid cruise.*

"Who are you talking to?"

Eh? Jeff spun around. The girl wasn't quite his height and maybe a year younger than himself. She wore a Boston Red Sox sweatshirt over baggy white pants, and had her reddish-brown hair in two pigtails. *Like Dorothy in the* Wizard of Oz *movie,* Jeff thought. "Eh? I'm sorry, what'd you say?"

"I asked who you were talking to," she said. She wasn't being smart-alecky, but her polite directness startled him. She sounded like she really wanted to know. Jeff felt his cheeks burn.

"Uhh … Well, actually I … I was talking to my dog."

The girl's face lit up. The strong morning sun danced in her large green eyes. "You have a dog in there? Oh, cool! Is it a Chihuahua?"

Now Jeff's whole head seemed to be burning up. "He's an English Bull Terrier," he said hotly. Then he realized how stupid *that* was going to sound.

The girl craned her neck to look past him skeptically at the backpack. "Is it a puppy? You should open that thing and let it stick its nose out. It could run out of air in there and die."

Oh jeez! Jeff looked away. "He's already dead."

"Huh?" A look of disgust began to creep over the girl's face.

"No, what I mean is," he slipped the backpack off his shoulder and fumbled it open, "it's just his ashes. He died a while ago. See?" He held up the brass canister. In the clear morning sun, the polished brass looked like gold.

The girl's face eased a bit. Now she only looked at Jeff like he was mildly crazy. *Not like I'm crazy* and *dangerous.* She cocked her head at him and stuck out her hand. "My name's Rosemary," she said.

"I'm Jeff," said Jeff, and hoped he wasn't blushing.

"You must have really loved him a lot," Rosemary said, nodding at the brass urn.

"Umm, yeah. Yeah, I did." *Now what?* Feeling very awkward, Jeff returned Buddy to his backpack. The silence got longer.

"There's a scavenger hunt after breakfast," the girl said at last. "Want to do it together?"

"Umm ... No. I mean, no thanks," Jeff stammered. "I ... I can't ... I'm busy."

Her green eyes opened in surprise, then rolled in exaggerated disbelief. *Good one, Jeff,* he thought, *you total nerd.*

"OK," the girl answered airily. "Whatever." She turned and started to walk away along the deck. Over her shoulder she called back, "So, have a nice day ... with your dog." She arched her eyebrows and turned away smiling.

The rest of that day seemed to Jeff to pass in a distracted blur of trying to keep busy and avoiding the girl. After breakfast a Youth Host led a tour of the ship, from the command bridge with its dials and gauges and radar screens, to the ear-splitting racket of the engine room. It took nearly three hours to explore the huge vessel's many decks. But somehow the tour seemed to cross paths with the scavenger hunt at every turn and corridor. Several times the girl from that morning managed to catch his eye and smile at him, despite his best efforts to avoid her. And once he felt himself go crimson when she called out to ask, "Where's your dog?"

Lunch was laid out on the same generous scale as breakfast. Jeff just had a couple of hot dogs. A news-sheet at the table advertised the afternoon's Youth Events: teen karaoke, a video game tournament and something called "Scattergories." *Whatever the heck that is!*

Half an hour later Jeff changed into swim trunks and tried to do some laps in the pool that occupied most of the ship's broad back deck. He liked to swim, and several school freestyle trophies occupied a shelf in his bedroom back in Halifax. But this pool wasn't really big enough for laps. It got even smaller when a clutch of mothers arrived with about three million screaming little kids in tow. Jeff gave up his workout in disgust. Dried off and dressed, he found his father one deck up from the pool at a small on-board driving range, plopping golf balls with fierce concentration into a billowing green net. Feeling Jeff's eyes on him, Ken Beacon dug into his pocket and pulled out a twenty-dollar American bill. "Here, son," he said. "If the scenery isn't doing it for you, why don't you check out that video game contest?"

But that girl was there again, pigtails flying as she worked the controls and threw herself into the galactic battle being fought on the flickering screen. Jeff wandered aimlessly away from the arcade. He passed a display of "Alaska's Gold Rush Days" and paused briefly to look at the relics being showcased: an old tin plate for panning gold, a large nugget of fool's gold and the twenty-dollar bill someone used to buy a famous gold claim. *Hmmph*, Jeff thought, *some relic. It looks like the twenty Dad just gave me.* He wound up back at the cabin, watching *E.T.* on the ship's closed-circuit TV. He'd seen it before, but still liked it.

Dinner was even more lavish than lunch. Jeff piled his plate high, balancing roast beef and chicken on heaps of mashed potato and macaroni salad, arranging just enough green stuff artfully around the edges to discourage Mom from giving the Nutrition Speech. But at first bite, he instinctively expected a nudge at his knee that didn't come. He remembered Buddy standing under the table at home, nose pushed between Jeff's legs, waiting more or less patiently for him to finish eating. Then sitting back on his haunches for the scrap he had come to expect after every meal. Guiltily, Jeff remembered how often he had been reluctant to part with the last bite of a burger or Mom's wonderful, but rare, deep-dish pizza. *I wish I had to save something for him every single meal for the rest of my life.*

The thought took away his appetite and left a tight knot in his stomach. He saw Mom and Dad exchange worried glances as he toyed with the food on his plate. But he didn't care. *This stupid cruise wasn't my idea in the first place.*

THE NEXT MORNING, Jeff slept in later, dozing until almost eight o'clock. But by noon Day Two on the Therapy Boat looked as lame as Day One. The kids' events listed on the ship's news-sheet offered a choice of face-painting, balloon animals and teen tanning time. *Teen tanning time?*

After so many hours of nonstop nature-special grandeur, each new majestic vista was beginning to look an awful lot like the last one. This morning he'd left the backpack behind when he slipped out of the cabin. Buddy was back on the little table. He could feel the lonely sadness settling over him again. *Some vacation!*

Without warning, a sound so loud and deep it made his lungs vibrate blasted out from above and behind him. *The ship's horn*, Jeff realized, in the long moment of near silence before his ears began working again.

two

THE DOG

THE DOG lay curled and asleep in the sunny corner of an unpainted wooden deck. Its long white muzzle ended at a black nose, tucked warmly under a skimpy white tail and two not-entirely-clean white back paws. Short white fur covered the barrel-like chest.

Under the fur, the dog's pink hide twitched. Whuffling noises emerged from beneath the tail and paws. Stubby legs jerked and eyelids fluttered as it followed something low-to-the-ground and scurrying, something smelling of cat or rat, down the backstreets of its Bull Terrier dreams.

Suddenly, the white head jerked up and beady dark eyes shot open, catching a ray of sun. Pinpoints of light danced in the black pupils, like stars in deep pools. Sharp white ears pointed to the sky. Black nostrils flared and twitched.

The dog stood and gave itself a short, businesslike shake. The deck it was standing on was a wooden platform, from which a ramp led down to a boat basin, visible over a low wooden rail.

An alert canine gaze passed over boats of every size and kind. It lingered for a moment on a human figure, small and spare in the distance, stepping from a teetering dock onto a weather-beaten old sailboat with two bare masts.

The dog's impassive gaze lifted again, until it was looking out over the tops of the two great breakwaters that protected the little harbour, to where a wide channel of white-flecked blue water led into the distance. On either side, steep walls of bare mountain came down to embrace the channel between high green banks. The white ears turned and twitched.

A moment later, the dog turned away from the water and trotted off the platform. Head down, thin tail straight out behind it, its short legs scissored back and forth in a blur beneath its barrel-shaped white body. As it followed a path along the edge of the boat basin, it looked like a dog with a mission.

A few minutes later, the dog's brisk trot brought it to a built-up area with stores and sidewalks and people. Several of them bent to greet the hurrying dog, extending a word or a treat. But the dog was not to be dissuaded. It carried on with scarcely an upward glance, leaving behind a string of puzzled-looking humans with food in their hands.

At length it came to a stop in front of an opening between two storefronts. The narrow, dirt-paved gap led away into musty darkness. The dog stopped and turned its thick white head to left and right, beady eyes scanning the sidewalk ahead and behind. Satisfied, the dog vanished into the dark alley.

Moments later it emerged back into bright sunlight. Across a small park, diamonds danced off the deep blue-green water of a long, narrow ship's harbour.

The dog chose a terrier-sized patch of sun that warmed a corner of the sidewalk and lay down. Its back legs stuck out behind, and the deep roman muzzle dropped to rest on forepaws stretched out in front. The dog breathed a heavy sigh and settled in to wait.

Dark eyes gazed intently down the empty channel.

three

THE STATUE

HALF AN HOUR after the blast of the ship's horn, Jeff was looking down onto a working area just behind the ship's bow. Members of the crew were laying out yellow ropes, as thick around as his arm, in long orderly loops across the deck.

"Ouch!"

The just-too-hard punch on the arm coincided with the forced enthusiasm in his father's voice: "First stop ... coming up!"

He really *is* trying, Jeff thought. *Very trying*, a little voice added inside his head, and he grinned. Mom and Dad looked pleased and Jeff didn't see any need to explain.

The land on either side of the ship had closed in to form a narrow channel. It seemed hardly wide enough to leave room for the big cruise liner. In the distance ahead, Jeff could see another ship already tied to a long grey wharf. Beyond it, the glass and cement of a few modest office towers raised their heads. Many smaller buildings ran out on either side of the wharf along the shore. Others climbed a little way up the very lowest slopes of the mountain that loomed above the whole inlet.

"Welcome to Juneau," a booming voice announced over the public address system. "We will be arriving shortly at Berth Two. Once the ship has docked, you will have just over five hours to explore Alaska's historic state capital. The ship's whistle will sound at six o'clock, one half-hour prior to our departure. Please return to the vessel at that time."

Before leaving the ship, Jeff and his parents returned briefly to their cabin. Jeff grabbed his denim jacket and checked to make sure his wallet was still in the left-hand back pocket of his jeans.

He shot a glance at the brass canister that gleamed softly on the little table. Then he flashed on the look of scorn in the eyes of the girl with the pigtails. With an effort, he put his hands in his jacket pockets. *I'll be back soon, Buddy*, he promised silently, and turned toward the door.

Then he led the way to where a steeply tilted gangplank ran down from the ship's deck to the Juneau waterfront. It was very different from the one in Vancouver. This wharf was functional rather than fancy, built from heavy squared timbers tarred like railway ties.

As Jeff and his parents stepped off the gangplank a crew member handed each of them a glossy tourist brochure. "There's a town map in the centre," she said, smiling. "And be sure to check out Juneau's Official Boat Greeter, just down the dock. In the 1930s, she was the most famous canine west of the Mississippi."

The word "canine" caught Jeff's attention. He looked down the dock and squinted. He could see a splash of that yellowy-green colour that bronze statues turn when they're left outside. But there was something about the shape of this particular statue ... He stuffed the brochure in a pocket and tore off down the dock.

It was a statue of a dog, somewhat bigger than life-size. The heavy head was turned his way, as though waiting just for him. The dog had sturdy square shoulders, a broad head and deep muzzle, a skimpy tail draped out behind. They were all as familiar to Jeff as Buddy's deep "woof."

Yes! It has to be!

"Look!" Jeff yelled at his parents, who were arriving at a more leisurely pace behind him. "It's a Bull Terrier!"

He sat on the edge of the weathered wooden sill that surrounded the statue and ran his fingers over the cold bronze shoulders. He swallowed hard, his fingers remembering the familiar shape.

"Her name is Patsy Ann," Frances Beacon said from behind a big "Welcome to Juneau" sign. Reading from a plaque, she went on: "*Although deaf from birth, somehow she 'heard' the whistle of ships from as far away as half a mile, and headed at a fast trot for the wharf, not to be dissuaded for any purpose whatsoever.*"

Jeff stroked the wide bronze forehead and tickled behind the pointed bronze ears.

"*Furthermore,*" his mother continued reading, "*somehow she knew which dock the ship would tie to.* Now, how do you suppose she knew that?"

"Oh, Mom," replied Jeff, "they just know!" *Just like Buddy always knew*, he thought.

"*Because of her unerring sense of the arrival of each ship that visited Juneau, and her faithful welcome at wharfside,*" Jeff's mom read on, "*the Mayor dubbed Patsy Ann 'Official Greeter of Juneau' in 1934.*"

Jeff's father was starting to fidget. He looked like he'd had quite enough of this Patsy Ann character.

"And listen to this," Mom went on. "It says that when she died, in 1942, her coffin was lowered into Gastineau Channel, *just a short distance from where the sculpture now sits, watching and waiting with eternal patience.*" She paused, then added a little dreamily, "My, what a wonderful story."

"Oh, come on, Frances," Dad erupted. "I hardly think the plan was to come all this way just so we could dwell on another dead dog." Lightening up a little, he added, "C'mon guys, let's go. We've got a whole town to explore ..."

Jeff looked pleadingly at his mother. "Aw, Mom. Can I stay here awhile ... Please? I'd like to see what else it says about Patsy Ann."

"Son," his father's deep baritone interrupted, "I really don't think that's a good idea."

"Oh, Dad ..." *They treat me like I'm a child,* he thought, his anger rising. He could hardly wait for the day when he wouldn't have to ask permission for anything ever again. "I'm big enough to stay out of trouble. And I'm not going to get lost." He pulled the ship's brochure from his jacket pocket. "See, I've even got a map."

Jeff's parents exchanged glances. Jeff knew he'd won even before Dad nodded reluctant agreement. "Have you got some money?" his mother asked. Without waiting for an answer, she dug into her fanny pack. "Here, maybe you'll find a sweatshirt you like or something." She looked away as she passed the bills into his hand.

Hey, this is OK, Jeff smiled secretly to himself, taking the two twenties and slipping them into his wallet alongside the one his father had given him the day before.

"But remember," it was Dad's listen-up voice. "It's almost one now. If we don't meet up in town, you find your own way back here no later than six o'clock. I don't want you holding up the ship. Or worse, not making it back aboard! You have your watch on?"

"Yes, Dad," Jeff sighed. "I've got the game plan. I'll probably catch up with you, anyway. This town doesn't look all that big."

"OK, son," his parents said in almost the same breath. Then, finally, they were gone, following the other tourists from the cruise ship as they set out to explore Juneau. Jeff was finally alone with Patsy Ann.

She looked a little skinnier than Buddy, Jeff thought. Her nose was definitely thinner. He sat back down and ran his hand up and down the smooth statue once again. It was cold to his touch. But, somehow, he thought he could feel a warmth, *like some kind of dog energy, flowing out of the metal.*

A gruff bark broke in on his thoughts. His heart leapt. He knew that bark! He stood up and looked around. Twice more the oh-so-familiar sound rang out, the note becoming sharper each time. *Just like when Buddy wants something and I don't figure it out fast enough*, he thought. The boy turned toward the sound.

There he is! A Bull Terrier was standing just across the street, beside some kind of store. He was watching Jeff, head down, his dark and piggy little eyes and black nose making a triangle in the white face. Between the alert pointed ears, Jeff could see a white tail waving back and forth. As he watched, the stocky white dog barked again, briefly flashing gleaming white teeth and a pink tongue.

Yes! Jeff felt like something was going to come apart in his chest. His eyes were smarting. *I knew you'd come back!* "Buddy!" he called, and began running.

For a moment, the dog stood in the same spot and watched him come. Then, without warning, it turned and bolted down an alleyway. "Buddy!" Jeff shouted again, piling on steam.

It was hard to see past the deep shadows between the buildings, but Jeff kept running. In the dimness ahead he could see flashes of white as the dog galloped away in front of him. "Buddy! Slow down, wait for me!" he called, but the white glimpses got no closer. He pumped hard, dodging trash bins and stacks of old junk as he went.

The alley was criss-crossed with others and didn't follow a straight course. It was all Jeff could do to stay on his feet and make sure he kept sight of the dog's retreating rear end. Soon, he had completely lost any sense of the direction in which they were running. The alley got narrower and darker. He skidded round a corner, bounced off the wall to the right and had to dodge fast to avoid bumping into a big upended barrel.

Suddenly he was out of the alley and pulling to a stop in the open air. The dog was there, sitting on the far edge of a wooden boardwalk, facing him. Its mouth was open in a wide, toothy grin. Jeff could swear it was laughing at him.

But now that he saw the dog close-up, he could also see that this sure wasn't Buddy. "Hiya girl," said Jeff, swallowing hard. He knelt and rubbed his fingers into the short fur behind her ears.

What have I been thinking? Dead dogs don't come back to life. He'd better stop this foolishness or he'd be back spending time with Dr. Pickleface. Buddy was in a brass urn back on the ship. And this dog might be a Bull Terrier, but she wasn't *his* bully. He reached around her to scratch the far side of her neck, noticing that she didn't have a collar on. When one grimy back foot began to lift and twitch in response, he laughed at the familiar reflex. The dog grinned even more widely, making little wrinkles in the fur at the corners of her mouth.

At last Jeff stood up and gave the stray one final pat. "You sure are cute," he said, "but I'm afraid I've gotta go." The dog's wide grin faded and she cocked her head, fixing beady eyes on him. "You be a good girl, now," he said finally, then turned back into the alley.

Blinding pain exploded between his nose and his forehead. His vision filled with brilliant blue sparklers, and he felt himself land hard on the ground.

"What the ... ??"

He opened his eyes. The alley was gone. In its place was a very solid, very hard, brick wall.

four

THE TOWN

IT COULDN'T BE! Just *could not* be! But there it was: rough red bricks filled the gap between the wooden plank walls on either side of the alley he'd just run through. At least, Jeff *thought* it was the same alley.

He took a couple of steps back and examined the area to either side. Nope. There *wasn't* anywhere else he could have come out. Just a narrow, bricked-over passage between a bookstore window under a green awning to his right and an insurance office on his left, with a matching awning in red.

Jeff put a finger to his nose and winced as he felt the rough moist skin of a bad scrape. Another sore patch over his left eye meant he'd banged his forehead too.

He turned to look again at the dog. Catching his glance, she wagged her skimpy tail and opened her mouth wide, exposing a lolling pink tongue and impressive white teeth. Jeff recognized the expression. It was the one Buddy used to wear whenever Jeff did something especially goofy. "You're *laughing* at me, aren't you?" he said aloud.

"Well, you'll have to do better than that," he added, looking up and down the street. There was no sign of the harbour, let alone the cruise ship. "You got me here. Now how do I get back?" *Fifteen minutes in Juneau and already I'm lost! Oh boy, Dad is going to kill me.*

And that wasn't the only thing. Maybe he *had* gotten confused about where the alleyway came out. Maybe he'd followed the dog further along the boardwalk than he'd thought. Or banged his head harder. But something just didn't *feel* right about this. It was … well, *weird.* But he couldn't put his finger on exactly what was wrong.

Whatever it was, it hadn't affected the dog any. Still grinning happily, she stood up and gave herself a shake that started at her nose and worked its way in stages down her thick white body all the way to the tip of her tail. Then she set off down the boardwalk, stopping after a few steps to look back at Jeff for a second before continuing on.

Jeez. Now what was he going to do? He looked around again. But nothing better came to him. Maybe *she* would take him back to the square by the harbour. "Wait up!" Jeff called, and set out in the dog's wake.

Following a few metres behind the white dog, Jeff kept his eyes peeled for a way back to the waterfront. It couldn't be that far away. A mountain wall rose steeply behind the buildings on his right. And over to his left another mountain loomed so close that there plainly wasn't much more city in that direction. In fact, there couldn't be more than a street or two between him and the water.

After the first block, cement replaced the wooden boardwalk planking. And at the next corner he had to step around three brightly painted totem poles set into the street. They advertised a souvenir store called the Nugget Shop. So this must be "Downtown Juneau," he thought, searching for the office towers he'd seen from the ship. But somehow they were nowhere in sight.

Instead a lot of buildings had elaborate false fronts painted like stage scenery to make them look bigger and grander than they really were. He could see several large swinging signs announcing "Saloon." Farther along, the windowless brick side of a building larger than most of its neighbours declared in large, white painted letters that it was the Gastineau Hotel.

Despite the false fronts, Juneau's buildings looked older and more weather-beaten than Jeff had imagined they would in a state capital. The few cars on the street were old, too. *Like ... really old!* They were like the classic autos that people brought out for parades back in Halifax. Except that Juneau's car collectors didn't seem to take very good care of their cars. *Most of these look pretty beaten up.*

And now that he was thinking about it, the other people he passed on the sidewalk were dressed oddly, too. Almost every man he saw wore some kind of hat — old-fashioned fedoras or those peaked tweed caps like English Cockneys were supposed to wear. Most of the girls he saw wore skirts or dresses. He hadn't seen one yet in jeans or a T-shirt. And all the colours seemed just a little dull. *Juneau sure doesn't go in for Day-Glo Spandex.* Jeff managed a private smile.

Still, his uneasy feeling was growing.

Maybe this is like Louisbourg. Each summer, the ancient fortress at the mouth of the St. Lawrence River was full of people dressed like the French colonists who had built it, doing for the tourists all the things they would have done 300 years ago.

With a start, Jeff realized that he hadn't yet seen anyone else who looked like they might have come off the cruise ship. Now that was *definitely* weird. There must have been a thousand other people coming ashore at the same time he and his parents had. And most of them had been wearing the universal tourist uniform: ball cap, T-shirt and video camera. Looking up and down the street, he realized with a shiver of alarm that there was nobody like that anywhere in sight. *Mom and Dad should be here somewhere.*

Ahead of him, the dog was still trotting confidently along, looking back now and again as though to make sure Jeff was keeping up. As she walked along, one passerby after another stopped to pat her or scratch behind her pointed ears. Several reached into pockets or purses to find her some treat. The dog accepted every one with a restraint Jeff had never seen in Buddy.

As they walked, he window-shopped. But soon he was struck by something else. *No T-shirt shops. What kind of tourist town has no T-shirt shops?* Jeff liked to buy a T-shirt everywhere he travelled. He had quite a collection by now. But it didn't look like he'd be adding to it in Juneau.

There were a lot of antique stores though. *At least, I hope they're antique stores.* The clothes and housewares in the store windows looked like they came from an earlier era. He hadn't seen a stereo or computer store yet, but he *had* spotted one of those old stand-up radios for sale. It was the size of a dresser and had a printed price tag on it that said 300 dollars. *Pretty expensive old radio. Bet it doesn't even work anymore.* Next door, though, a clothing store was selling leather jackets for ten dollars. *Got to be used,* he decided.

Or were they? He stopped. Ahead of him the dog also stopped and looked back at him, her expression watchful. He was standing in front of a cigar store, its windows paved with the coloured covers of magazines for sale inside. There were newspapers in a rack beside the door. The headline was something about Germany. Jeff's father watched CNN at breakfast, and he couldn't remember hearing anything about Germany lately. He frowned and stepped closer. He suddenly realized his heart was beating hard. His eyes travelled over the page in search of a date. *Tuesday, August 22, 1933.*

His vision swam. Fear washed over him like a tidal wave. Then he got a grip.

It has to be a novelty paper. It's part of the Louisbourg thing. He straightened up and looked around at the cars, the clothes, the colours.

A store bigger than the rest caught Jeff's eye. A sign over the window said "Amory's Outfitters and General Store." On an impulse, Jeff ran across the street and stepped in the door.

The store smelled of sawdust and tobacco and something he thought was molasses. The floors were bare wood. There were chocolate bars under a glass counter and loose candy in a jar beside the ornate steel cash register. A quick glance around turned up no soda cooler or ice cream freezer or snack food display.

On a shelf behind the counter was a double row of liquor bottles. At each end were bundles of metal objects Jeff thought he recognized as animal traps. To one side was a locked rack with rifles and shotguns. Further inside the store, he could see shelves of tinned groceries, sacks and crates, and coils of rope. At the back were shelves of work boots and clothing.

The feeling of something being very wrong with this picture came over him again, more powerfully than before. Suddenly, Jeff wished he'd never let his parents go on ahead without him.

A weird thought hit him and he reached into the pocket of his jeans for his wallet. Inside he still had the "phone home" card he'd been given last summer. "I don't want your grandparents paying your long distance bills," Dad had said. Mom had teased him, "Please, E.T., call home ..."

Well, I'm starting to feel a little like E.T. about now. I think it's time to "call home" and make sure there still is one ...

He walked up to the counter. A burly man dressed in a soiled white bib apron ran his eyes suspiciously over Jeff's clothes and grunted grudgingly, "Yeah, kid? Whadda ya want?"

"Do you have a pay phone?" Jeff asked.

The man's heavy brows rose in surprise.

"I need to call home," Jeff heard himself blurt.

"Yeah? And where's that?"

"Halifax."

The man looked at him blankly.

"In Nova Scotia ... That's in Canada." *Jeez, some people.*

"I know where Halifax is, kid. It's what planet *you're* from I'm wondering. I got a phone, but you sure as heck can't call *Halifax* from it. That's clear across the continent. You want to get in touch with Halifax, you better talk to the folks at the telegraph office."

He regarded Jeff skeptically for a moment. "Unless it's an emergency. Then they might put you through down at the Army Communications Center. But it better be a pretty *big* emergency. And it'll still take 'em a day to get a line."

The big man leaned out over the counter to give Jeff a closer look. His gaze lingered for a long time on Jeff's new high-tops. When it returned to Jeff's face, it had lost some of its friendliness. "What's a kid want to phone Halifax for, anyway?" the man asked, eyes narrowing.

Jeff felt dizzy and the floor seemed to tilt under his feet. He closed his eyes and shook his head hard. When he opened them again, things had settled down and the store had resumed its former everyday solidness. But the eerie sense of no longer being in his usual world, the feeling he had been unable to shake since he'd come out of the alley, was stronger than ever. "Never mind," he muttered.

Blinking, he walked back out into the late-afternoon sun. The white dog was lying in the precise centre of a patch of sunlight hardly any bigger than herself, back legs stuck out comically behind her.

At that instant a sharp bang, like a rifle shot, rang out somewhere off to the right. He turned in time to see a battered pickup truck burp blue exhaust and turn a corner. His heart slowed down a little. Then it almost stopped, as he realized what he had just seen. Or rather, not seen. The dog's white ears had not budged at the loud sound.

"Hey, you! Dog!" he yelled. There was no sign of a response.

Then, suddenly, he knew. It was like a faint electrical storm dancing all over his skin. He felt the bottom fall out of his stomach like a trapdoor swinging. *It couldn't possibly be …* His brain frantically searched for ways to make it not true.

The map from the cruise ship brochure! Jeff pulled it from his jacket pocket. He flipped past the whale watching ads, past the helicopter tours, past McDonald's, until he came to the map. It was a cartoony affair, with little drawings of town landmarks. A number identified Patsy Ann Square.

He tried to figure out where he was.

Downtown was off to the right somewhere. The nearer mountain was now at their backs. *That must be Mount Roberts,* he figured, reading the name from the map. The waterfront should be just ahead. *And so should Patsy Ann Square.*

Jeff took off, running. The white dog followed at his heels. He had sprinted only two blocks when the harbour came into view. Ahead of him was a wharf. There was even a ship tied up to the tarred timbers.

But it was no cruise liner. Rust and salt stained the ship's slab-like sides. Two floors of tiny cabins opened directly onto promenade decks that looked hardly bigger than catwalks. Forward of the cabins, squared timber and wooden crates were tied to the bare steel deck.

Beyond the tramp steamer, the harbour was empty across to the wall of the far mountainside. To the left and right sheds and metal buildings faced the water. Signs said fish were being canned. But there was no cruise liner in either direction. No tourists. And certainly no tidy square with a bronze dog.

But ... this is where the map says it is ... He knelt down and took the dog's muzzle in his hands. Dog and boy locked eyes. Hers radiated a calm intelligence that Jeff found soothing.

"You're Patsy Ann," Jeff whispered. "You're Patsy Ann and this ... this is 1933!" *That newspaper is real ...*

She held his gaze. He was shaking.

Holy cow! He really *was* lost! Funny thing though: his weird feeling of being in a dream had disappeared.

five

THE SANDWICH

JEFF PIVOTED on his heels and slumped into a sitting position beside Patsy Ann. *Wow! 1933! Holy Michael J. Fox, Batman. So now what? OK, just take it easy. Figure out how you got here and you'll be able to figure out how to get back.* Simple. *Yeah, right.* This was a moment when he sure wished he could just point to the "back" button on his Internet browser and click.

Patsy Ann moved closer, her dark eyes fixed on the boy. Soon she was leaning heavily against his legs, head resting on his knees, looking up at him. He stroked her ears absent-mindedly while his mind struggled to get his thoughts into some kind of order.

She brought you here, a voice in his head was saying. *She knows how to get you back.* He put his forehead down to the dog's own and looked her straight in the eye.

"You *are* Patsy Ann, aren't you?" he asked, his voice low and conspiratorial.

She barked a reply. "Ow!" Jeff yelled. Barking, she had banged her rock-like head hard under his chin, bringing his teeth painfully together on his tongue. He grinned, despite the pain. He'd learned long ago to avoid that Bull Terrier trick with Buddy. *How could I have forgotten it so soon?*

"It's OK," Jeff told Patsy Ann. "It's not your fault. You're just a dog. Eh, girl?" She turned her head, pushing her neck against the boy's fingers.

"But I really *do* have to get home," he went on, looking around. "I mean, I have to meet Mom and Dad at your statue in a few hours ..." Not hours, he thought with a jolt. *More like a few years. Sixty or so.*

What time is it, anyway? He looked at his watch. It was a digital one, with separate windows for the day and date. But it seemed to have stopped: the seconds appeared to be frozen. It still said 1:00:45. And that was around the time that his parents had left Patsy Ann Square.

But I've been here for at least an hour ... I think. Jeff looked up at the sky. It was deep blue over the mountains on his side of the harbour. *It must be getting on to late afternoon.*

Across the water, a faded white sky was turning pink where the sun was sinking towards the mountain. *Jeez, this is confusing ... I've gone back in time to the 1930s, but I've skipped forward through most of the day.*

A wild thought hit him. "Hey, Patsy Ann!" he burst out. "I'm not even born yet!" *Wow.* Then came an even weirder thought: *Neither are my parents.*

He looked down at the dog, her muzzle still resting calmly in his lap. Leaning over, he spoke directly into her ears: "I know you can't hear me, Patsy Ann. But I don't belong here, I really don't," he said. "I need to get home, girl, back to Buddy. He's waiting for me. Can you take me back there?"

Suddenly pulling away from him, Patsy Ann backed up until she was crouched at his feet, tail tucked around her haunches and head low, her grubby ears back in apology. "Oh no, you don't!" he said hotly. "You're not backing out now. You brought me here ... You get me home!"

Patsy Ann's white muzzle lifted and she looked up at him, meeting Jeff's gaze with her own. *I trust a dog that looks you in the eye.* For a long moment, Patsy Ann stared evenly at him, not letting his eyes leave her own.

Then the searching expression relaxed, as though Patsy Ann had found what she was looking for. Her rough tongue flicked out and slapped warmly across the scraped tip of his nose. *I will.*

"It doesn't have to be right away," he said quickly, *now that things are going to be OK.* "But pretty soon. I mean, I *do* have to get back before the ship sails, OK?" The dog's skinny tail was whipping back and forth in a white blur.

On the other hand, Jeff had to admit that he was enjoying himself more than he had for a very long time ... for months, it seemed. *Since Buddy died, to be exact.*

He laughed suddenly at the silliness of the idea. If he wasn't born yet, then *neither was Buddy.* Which meant Buddy wasn't *dead* yet, either. Whew. This could take some serious getting used to! *Well*, he thought with growing amusement, *the cruise line promised a visit to "Historic" Juneau.* He was sure getting the deluxe, authentic version. At his feet, Patsy Ann wagged her tail, grinning widely.

"I'm hungry," Jeff said to Patsy Ann. "Whatever time it is

now, they've got to have places to eat. I wonder if they let kids in the saloons."

He didn't have to find out. Heading further into downtown Juneau, he quickly came to something called the Gold Dust Cafe. Patsy Ann followed him to the door, but stayed outside while he went in.

A lunch counter with stools ran along one side of the cafe, with booths on the other. At the booth by the door, a couple were tucking into thick sourdough sandwiches and tall, velvety milkshakes. Down at the far end of the counter, three girls of about his own age were finishing off ice-cream sundaes. A few other diners were dotted around the place. Jeff was suddenly ravenous.

He took a stool at the counter and examined the choices listed beside a pass-through window to the kitchen. A skinny man, with strands of grey hair plastered over a bare sweating scalp, appeared behind the counter. "What'll it be, kid?"

"I'll take two of the biggest sandwiches you've got, mister," said Jeff.

"That'll be two Klondikes." The man made a note on an order pad. Then he looked up sharply. "Two? You got a date I don't see?"

"They're to go — one's for Patsy Ann," Jeff said, watching for a reaction..

But there was none. All the guy said was, "Oh. OK," and turned back to the counter. He replaced the pad in a stained apron pocket and began briskly to assemble bread, sliced meat and garnishes. "I'll leave the peppers off hers," he said over his shoulder to Jeff. "Peppers give her gas so bad you wouldn't believe it. You don't want to be within a mile of her when she gets into some peppers."

Jeff could hear his stomach growling as the counterman layered cheese with slices of ham and beef on thick slabs of sourdough. He and Patsy Ann would eat their sandwiches, hang out for a bit, she could show him around town, show him the 1930s, and then she'd take him back to the alley and he'd go home.

Yeah, that works. He would be back in time to meet his parents and maybe even grab a souvenir T-shirt in Patsy Ann Square before they got back on the ship. *Not that anyone will believe me when I say I'm a personal friend of Patsy Ann herself,* he thought with a chuckle.

The counterman broke into his thoughts, standing with two truly heroic sandwiches wrapped in paper. Placing both in front of Jeff, he said: "Eighty cents."

Eighty cents! Wow, there's something to be said for living in the past. Jeff reached into his jeans for his wallet. "I'm afraid all I've got is a twenty," he apologized, holding out one of the bills his parents had given him. *Maybe I should get fries, too,* he thought, eyeing the food hungrily.

Thin eyebrows zoomed upward in the counter man's skinny face. He put down the sandwiches and took the bill in both hands. He looked it over closely, carefully examining both sides of the paper. He looked sharply at Jeff, then back at the bill. Then he said, "Just a minute, I ... I gotta go see if I can make change."

"Sure," Jeff agreed, "OK." Senses full of the sharp tang of sourdough and the waxy smell of cheese, he reached out for the sandwiches. The counterman's thin hand got there first, whisking the paper packages off the counter. Avoiding the boy's eyes, the man put both sandwiches down out of Jeff's reach on the rear counter. Then he ducked through the swinging door that led to the kitchen. Through the pass-through window, Jeff watched him lift the earpiece from a large, black, box telephone on the far wall of the kitchen and crank a handle.

What the ...? Jeff looked around. No one else seemed to be picking up on the counterman's odd behaviour. At the far end of the counter the three girls were whispering together, stealing looks at him and giggling. Jeff had seen girls in his own grade act the same way. From behind him came gurgling sounds, as the couple in the booth drained the last of their milkshakes through straws.

But what's taking the guy so long? Jeff could see his sandwich. *Jeez, I can smell it.* He longed to sink his teeth into it. The thought set his tummy grumbling again. A sharp bark broke Jeff's trance. He tore his eyes from the forbidden sandwiches and turned toward the sound. It came from the back of the cafe.

Looking past the giggling girls, he saw Patsy Ann framed in the small building's open rear door. She stood with her feet planted on the ground, head down, staring directly at him with those beady dark eyes. Lifting her muzzle she barked again, loudly.

"In a minute," Jeff mouthed at her, pointing to the sandwiches on the counter. But Patsy Ann simply barked some more, this time putting a new note of urgency into the sound. For an instant, the dog's gaze lifted to look past Jeff toward the street. He turned his head to follow her look.

Two burly police officers were crossing the street and making for the Gold Dust Cafe on the double. Jeff looked back just in time to see the counterman return from the kitchen. He still had Jeff's twenty-dollar bill in his hand, but he seemed to have lost any interest in serving the sandwiches. His face was fixed in an anxious scowl and his eyes were turned toward the fast-approaching police.

Holy doodle, Jeff thought. *I don't know why … but they're coming for ME!*

Patsy Ann was now barking nonstop. Making up his mind, Jeff dropped from the stool and ran for the back door. He had a brief impression of surprised faces turned toward him in the booths and bodies spinning on the stools to get a better view. Then he was out in the alley, following Patsy Ann once again.

This time he had to run for all he was worth to keep up with her. Behind him, pandemonium broke out, with confused shouts and a ringing metallic crash as something collided with a trash can. He could hear heavy feet pounding behind him.

Once again, Patsy Ann led him through a maze of narrow alleys and passageways. Some led steeply up or down the beginnings of the mountain and were even equipped with wooden steps. As Patsy Ann came to the foot of one flight of stairs, she made a sharp left turn. Jeff was going too fast to make the same turn. He lost his footing and fell to the ground. He scrambled up and kept running, blood pounding in his ears and a stitch forming in his side. Whoever was chasing him, *the cops probably*, they were noticeably closer now.

But the race was almost over. Ahead of him, Jeff saw Patsy Ann's stubby white stick of a tail dodge to the right around a low wire coop with chickens in it, then deke back left and vanish into what looked like a bare grey wall of wide weathered planks.

Coming fast around the corner of the chicken coop, Jeff saw where she had gone. Half hidden behind an old wagon wheel was a place where one of the planks had rotted away at the bottom, leaving a rough square hole at ground level just big enough for a dog to crawl through. Or a boy. Jeff glanced back. His pursuers were still out of sight, but he could hear them closing fast. Desperately, he threw himself to the ground and wriggled into the blackness.

A pungent animal smell unlike anything he had ever encountered before surrounded him like a suffocating blanket. He heard grunts and whuffling sounds. A pair of feet thumped past outside, followed moments later by a second pair. Then it was quiet. Quiet and dark.

Jeff was in a narrow space between the barn's rough wooden planks and another wall that appeared to be made entirely of straw. Patsy Ann's solid warmth pressed tightly against his side, the two of them filling the small space. She was panting with the exertion of the chase and his own heart was beating fast.

A dim light came from the gap through which they had entered. There was more straw underneath him, Jeff noticed, making a soft but spiky mattress. Looking up, he saw still more straw that formed a roof over them, creating a warm, dry, dusty-smelling secret cave. Deep-throated grunts and that overpowering aroma, so sharp and strong it burned his nose, made Jeff suspect they must be sharing the barn with a family of pigs.

It was a perfect spot to hide out and try to come up with a plan. But his chest ached and his legs were trembling from his frantic race through the back alleys of Juneau. As the energy of his panicked exertion drained from his body and Patsy Ann settled beside him in the straw, Jeff's thoughts drifted. It felt good to have one arm draped around the warmth of the little dog's white coat. It was the texture of coarse velvet but Jeff could feel the hard terrier muscle beneath the skin. He thought of Buddy, and it brought a sharp stab of painful memory. The hurt faded when he pulled Patsy Ann closer and buried his face in her fur. In the musty darkness, the living dog beside him was a reassuring presence. He knew he was in serious trouble but his brain refused to think about it.

For now, all that mattered was how safe and warm he was, lying here wrapped around this familiar shape. *It's been so long since I've held you like this ... I've missed you, Buddy.* Jeff's thoughts faded as his waking mind shut down and he drifted off to sleep.

six

POP-FLIES FOR BREAKFAST

PATSY ANN began her morning rounds early. Slipping from under the sleeping boy's arm, she poked her nose out the door of her secret den. The sky over the mountains was just beginning to be light. She sniffed the air. Cool. Rain not too far off. Cats. A recent raccoon. Bacon frying somewhere.

She pulled the rest of her thick white self through the gap in the planks and stepped out from behind the wagon wheel into the empty alley. There she stopped to stretch herself like a dancer getting ready for the day, front legs first and then the hind ones, arching her back and neck for the fullest effect. She finished with an extended all-over shake, then set off.

First stop was the Gold Dust Cafe. Men with big appetites put down giant breakfasts of flapjacks and eggs there every morning, before they went off to labour in the Alaska-Juneau gold mine, whose thundering machinery climbed the mountain-side at the south end of town. In the summer, Danny the cook and owner kept the back door open for her.

It was the moment most everyone in the place waited for. "Heck," Danny sometimes swore, "Patsy Ann's the reason half these fellers eat breakfast here at all, 'stead of waking up the wives to cook for 'em at home."

Patsy Ann trotted a few paces to a spot midpoint between the Gold Dust's booths and its long counter. There she stood, four legs planted firmly, shoulders squared, watching. Only her head moved, ears up, turning to look from one table to the next for the signal.

It might be Jake Earness, tearing a corner off that thick slab of buttered toast, his eye on Patsy Ann instead of his plate. Or Elwyn Harris, breaking a piece of bacon in two, the stubble on his face crinkling into a half-smile and his eyes turned down, trying not to tip her off.

But Patsy Ann was hard to fool in the matter of handouts. This morning she caught Cletis Connors first, knifing a sausage into pieces, spearing a section with his fork, then just looking at it … waving it back and forth in front of his face. Patsy Ann's nose twitched. She scuffled her back end around until her whole body faced Cletis. She got her front paws set properly, then slowly lowered her neck and shoulders until she was in a half-crouch, muscles quivering. There she froze, eyes fixed on the glistening, golden morsel.

Cletis broke first. He pulled the sausage off his fork with thick fingers and turned to face Patsy Ann. "One," he said, faking a toss.

"Two," another fake.

"Three!" This time the slice of sausage went sailing. Up it went … up … up … and Patsy Ann watched it. She didn't budge. Only her eyes moved, following the spinning sausage until it started down again. Then she went for it, all four feet off the ground, jaws wide open. A sound like a car door closing and the bite of sausage was gone. There was laughter and the hubbub of conversation resumed. Patsy Ann licked her chops, then took up her position again, waiting to field another succulent pop-fly.

No one in Juneau remembered her ever missing a catch. Or outstaying her welcome, for that matter. She always left while one or two people were still trying to interest her in a bit of steak gristle or ham rind. Danny claimed it was her way of making sure there'd always be more breakfast tomorrow. Barking her thanks at the Gold Dust door, Patsy Ann turned down Franklin Street and trotted in the direction of the Baranof Hotel. It was Juneau's fanciest, and its manager George Williams — an oily man who smelled of cigars — professed to disapprove of dogs on the premises.

Patsy Ann slipped through the kitchen to a spot near the swinging half-doors that led to the dining room. Two bowls waited for her, a Baranof soup tureen with a chip out of one side and a water dish. Overhead, brisk figures in white jackets and tall hats slung pots and pans around. Patsy Ann tucked herself into the space underneath a counter, keeping her nose close to the chipped Baranof china but the rest of herself out of the way.

Two waitresses bustled back and forth from the dining room. Every few trips, one or the other leaned over to scrape some scraps into the tureen. There were usually plenty of scraps, too. The Baranof was where Juneau's fanciest and most powerful men and women liked to come to eat. But they seldom did much eating — they were usually too busy talking. From her post under the swinging half-doors, Patsy Ann could keep an eye on most of the conversations.

The Baranof dining room was quieter than usual this morning. Apart from a handful of tables where single gentlemen in suits tried to keep the morning *Empire* out of their coffee and eggs while they read and ate, there was only one familiar face in the place. His Honour J. Samuel Shrite, Mayor of Juneau, sat alone at a large corner table, his broad round back turned to the wall and his circular pink face looking out over the rest of the room.

Shrite lifted his left arm and shot back the smooth pin-striped cuff of his suit to look at his gold wristwatch. Then he ran his hand over his shiny, almost-bald head as if there was still hair there needing to be smoothed out. In front of him, the table was already in disarray. A half-eaten roll, slathered in rhubarb jam, lay in a bed of crumbs at his elbow. Pulp from his freshly squeezed orange juice clung to the sides of his drained glass. He looked up as someone approached the table.

"Made up your mind yet?" asked Sylvia, the older of the two waitresses. A few threads of silver were beginning to show in the gold hair she kept secured beneath a starched uniform cap. Her blue eyes sparkled with good humour.

"What's good this morning, Syl?"

"Well, gee, Mr. Mayor," Sylvia smiled, "you've eaten here more times than I have."

Shrite gave her a sharp look. "Then gimme the Gold Digger Platter," he said curtly and dismissed her, picking up the *Empire* and burying his nose in the financial page.

Sylvia made a note on her pad, retrieved Shrite's menu and headed for the kitchen. As soon as her back was to him, Shrite glanced slyly up from his paper to eye her retreat.

Patsy Ann caught sight of movement near the dining room entrance. A moment later, a tall figure in a dark uniform was striding toward the corner table. Shrite's eyes returned to his newspaper. Carter Beggs, Juneau's Chief of Police, thrust a ham-sized fist under Shrite's pug nose. In his thick fingers, he brandished a banknote. "This turned up yesterday at the Gold Dust."

The mayor continued reading. "So?" he grunted, and reached, without looking, for his coffee cup.

Beggs leaned over close to Shrite's ear.

"So ... it's not one of ours," he said, his voice low.

That seemed to get Shrite's attention. His hand twitched and coffee splashed onto the Baranof's linen tablecloth. Shrite's sharp blue eyes widened for a moment and then narrowed again, disappearing into the fleshy folds of his face. "What do you mean?"

"It's ... not ... one ... of ours," Beggs repeated in a half-whisper, emphasizing each word as he pulled up a chair.

The mayor reached out and grabbed the bill from Beggs' hand. He held the banknote up to the light of the crystal chandelier over his head. Then he reached into his vest pocket and removed a jeweler's magnifying glass. Screwing it into his left eye, he bent closer to the bill.

Finally he put it down on the table in front of him, slowly shaking his large head. "Who caught it?" Shrite asked.

"Danny's counter man, guy named Earl," Beggs answered.

"I'm surprised he did. This is impressive, darn impressive. Frankly, it's better than our own stuff." Shrite picked the bill up again, fondling it between soft pink fingertips. "This paper feels like it came direct from the Treasury Department. And the print job could fool J. Edgar Hoover himself."

"Look here," Beggs pointed to a picture of the White House on one face of the bill. "Those trees don't come up nearly that far on a real twenty. And this signature — we've never had a Treasury Secretary named Bentson."

"But that's nothing," insisted the mayor. "Whoever made these plates is an artist, Beggs." Shrite's eyes gleamed moistly in their paunchy folds. "An artist! More than an artist … He is a genius!"

The mayor's fat face took on a rapt look. "I want to meet him. If this isn't just a fluke bill, if someone's printing these here in Juneau, I have to know!"

"A kid passed it," Beggs offered. "Earl said he hadn't seen him around before."

"But you picked him up, of course."

Beggs looked up at the ceiling, then down at the floor. He shifted his weight from one hip to the other. Then he rumbled, "Well, not exactly."

"Not exactly?" Shrite's colour darkened. "And what does 'not exactly' mean … exactly?"

"He, well …" Beggs shuffled his spit-polished shoes on the Baranof's carpet. "That is … I'm afraid he gave us the slip, Mr. Mayor."

"Gave you the slip," Shrite glowered. "Gave you the slip." He fingered Jeff's twenty-dollar bill. "Well, I'll make it simple for you, Beggs. You find that boy, I don't care what it takes. Do I make myself clear?"

"I get the idea," Beggs' deep voice grumbled.

"This bill is perfect, Beggs," Shrite hissed. "I want the plates, and I want that paper."

Sylvia reappeared with fresh coffee, a cup and a menu for Beggs, and a steaming platter of pancakes, sausage, ham and eggs for the mayor.

Both men straightened up. "Just coffee for him this morning, Syl," Shrite instructed. Shooting Beggs a look, Sylvia took back the menu. Both men were silent as they watched her walk back to the kitchen.

Shrite leaned forward again. Beggs watched him. His big square face had the eagerness of a puppy anxious to please its first human.

"Let's be logical about this, Chief," Shrite said. "Where could the kid have gone? There hasn't been a boat out of Juneau since yesterday."

Beggs' square face showed bafflement. "I can't figure it out. My guys chased him down the alley. Then, *poof*, he disappeared."

Shrite bit his tongue. "We're not in one of your Frank Capra movies, Beggs. Magic is a trick with mirrors and people don't just go *poof*. I'll tell ya where he is." Shrite shoveled a forkful of flapjacks into his mouth. Golden droplets of maple syrup clung to his coarse moustache.

After a pause he went on. "He's hidin' out with the rest of Juneau's garbage, down on the waterfront. What you do, Chief," the mayor speared a sausage and brought it whole to his lips, "is get a dozen or so of those layabouts of yours away from the squad-room coffee pot for a day. You take 'em on down and you start at one end of the waterfront and you work your way to the other. And you knock down every door that don't open up until you find that kid." Grease glistened in the corners of Shrite's fleshy lips and the fat on his neck jiggled when he chewed. "And just to give your lads some incentive, the city will put up a 200-dollar reward to the man who finds him!"

Beggs shifted uneasily in his chair. "I can't just go busting down doors without some kind of authority."

"You're the *Chief of Police* for heaven's sake!" Shrite's fork made an angry stab at his eggs. His little blue eyes blazed in their pink pillows of cheek. "If you must have these qualms of conscience, Beggs," he said grudgingly, "call Judge Burns and get a warrant. That's what he's there for. In fact, Beggs," the mayor grinned, showing large yellow teeth, "you can tell him you're finally on the trail of these counterfeiters he's been complaining about!" Shrite's round shoulders shook. He laughed with a sound like some large animal burping.

"Get on it," he said, dismissing the chief.

Beggs rose heavily and returned his chair to its place. "I'll do that."

"And Beggs …" Shrite drawled out the name. "Don't you think this would be a good time to clean out the waterfront?

While your boys are down there, show a few of those idle fishermen where the door is, why don't you." His voice got hard. "Start with that old fool Harper." He turned back to his newspaper.

Sylvia caught Shrite's final words as she came up to clear away his breakfast dishes. She pursed her mouth in disapproval. Back in the kitchen a moment later, Sylvia knelt to scrape the remains of Shrite's Gold Digger Platter into the chipped china bowl. "I don't know why they can't just leave Captain Harper be," she said to Patsy Ann, as though the attentive white dog could hear her. "That poor old man feels punished enough by losing a ship. They don't need to make him feel worse, spreading all their rumours and suspicions again after all these years."

Patsy Ann thumped her tail and thrust her nose out to sniff at the bowl. But then her muzzle wrinkled and she pulled back. The short white fur just above her tail stood up.

"Patsy Ann?" Sylvia looked at her. Juneau's First Dog wasn't known for turning up her nose at food.

The long warm tongue flicked lightly across Sylvia's wrist. But Patsy Ann had had enough of the company at the Baranof for one morning. Without touching Shrite's scraps, she slipped out through the kitchen door.

Back in the fresh air, Patsy Ann stood for a moment at the corner where Gold Street met Sixth, nose pointed to the sky. Her dark little eyes searched the heavy grey clouds that hung low over the town. Mist in ghostly streamers drifted across the green walls of mountain enclosing the harbour.

The rain smell was stronger. A moment later she was trotting purposefully down the hill. Soon she came to a large rectangular building even larger than the Baranof and, like the hotel, made of bricks and mortar. She left the street and slipped along the side, barking twice as she passed the barred and grimy glass of a basement window. By the time she reached a wooden door thick with layers of green paint, someone was already holding it open for her.

Jefferson, the janitor who took care of the Federal Building in Juneau, pulled the door firmly shut behind Patsy Ann. Officially no doors were supposed to be open in the Federal Building before 8:00 a.m. Jefferson rummaged in his coveralls and brought out something wrapped in newspaper. Unfolding the paper, he produced two molasses cookies. Patsy Ann dropped her tail to the floor and sat, looking up. Crumpling the ball of paper into his pocket, Jefferson planted one cookie in his own mouth, then held the other down for Patsy Ann. Gently, she removed it from his fingers.

She let him scratch her ears for a bit, then stepped away. It was still early and the tap-tap-tap of Patsy Ann's nails on the polished floor echoed in the empty corridor. She went down one hallway and along another, then up two flights of wide stairs. Across another hallway was a door with a frosted glass window and words written on it in square gold letters: "U.S. District Court: Southeast Alaska Division." The door wasn't quite shut. Patsy Ann nosed it open and walked through the outer office to a second door that stood wide open.

Inside, a lean, leathery fellow in shirt sleeves and baggy trousers sat at a desk, bent over the spread-out contents of a beige file folder. He had a fountain pen in one hand and was making notes. Beside a pot-bellied stove, an old blanket lay in a tousled heap on the bare floor. Patsy Ann stood in the doorway and watched him. After a few moments, Judge Henry Burns felt her gaze and looked up.

"Well, good morning, girl," he said. Burns' voice was cheerful and clear, comfortable with itself. "You're awfully early. What brings you up to see me at this fine hour?"

Patsy Ann's mouth widened in a grin and she wagged her tail.

"Well, come on in, then." Judge Burns nodded his head toward the blanket.

The dog ambled across the room and stepped onto the blanket. She circled it, pushing with her paws at the cloth as she did, getting it just right. When at last it was, Patsy Ann dropped heavily onto the nest she'd made and curled up. Her back feet tucked up under her porky little body and her nose rested on her tail. But her eyes stayed on the hawklike face behind the desk, as Judge Henry Burns turned back to his papers.

When the phone rang, Judge Burns straightened up and looked at it with distaste. Then he picked it up. "Burns," he said crisply.

Patsy Ann's eyes narrowed but she didn't move. There was silence.

The judge leaned back in his chair. "An arrest warrant,

I suppose you mean, Chief," he said patiently, reaching into a drawer. "In what name?"

Patsy Ann lifted her head to get a better view of the judge.

"A search warrant, then," he said, closing one drawer and opening another. "For what address?"

Henry Burns listened a bit more, then removed the handset from his ear and stared at it as though he hadn't seen one before. Then he put it back to his ear.

"Are you sure you wouldn't just prefer the whole territory?" he asked in a voice laced with sarcasm.

"No, Chief," he said after a moment. "That was a joke." He listened some more and then spoke sharply. "Chief Beggs, what you're asking is my leave to force your way into every law-abiding home in Juneau on the off chance that a crook is sitting down to flapjacks at the breakfast table. Well, that happens to violate the United States Constitution, Beggs. Which it also happens to be my job to uphold and defend. You do remember the Constitution, don't you, Beggs?"

The phone squawked in his hand. Henry pulled it further away from his ear, then told the mouthpiece: "You should read it sometime. It's got some interesting ideas. But without a shred of evidence, Chief, you'll get no warrant from me!" He banged the phone down in its cradle.

The judge rested a fierce look on Patsy Ann and shook his head back and forth in disapproval. "Darn it, young lady, you wonder where fools like that one get their half-baked ideas."

He frowned and picked up his unread morning *Empire*. His voice took on a gloomy tone. "I tell you, my dear, too many more like that in this country and we'll be marching down the same bad trail as Mr. Hitler over in Europe." He tossed the paper aside with a grunt of scorn and returned to his notes.

Patsy Ann's tail thumped the floor.

seven

PIGS & PILINGS

JEFF WOKE with a start and reached out for Buddy. *He was just here.* What was this pokey stuff in his bed? He blinked in the gloom. Where was his big *Lord of the Rings* poster? His red swimming ribbons? Buddy? *Buddy ...*

Oh, yeah. It felt like a punch in the stomach each time he remembered. *Buddy is dead.* But Buddy's collar should be there, right beside the bed where it hung over the lampshade ...

Jeff turned his head and saw rough grey planks. Then the rest of it came back to him in a rush. The alley, the dates on the newspapers, the police! He looked around for the dog — for Patsy Ann.

He was alone. Panic clutched at his throat but he fought it down. *Stay cool*, Jeff told himself, *she'll be back.*

In the gloom, sounds were very clear. The pigs were quieter, whuffling and grunting softly, shifting themselves heavily now and again, making the whole barn creak. From outside, he heard the sound of a car horn. Distant machinery pounded away. An engine chugged and chuffed. Someone far away yelled muffled words to someone else.

Sooner or later Jeff would have to venture outside. But it didn't have to be right now. Patsy Ann's cave in the straw made a perfect hideout. Besides, he still didn't have any idea what he was going to do next. If Patsy Ann had been able to bring him to 1933, he felt pretty sure she could get him back to his own time. *But when? For that matter, how long have I been gone already?* Jeff rolled over in the straw, put his wrist up to his face and groped for the button that turned on the little light in his watch. The digital window read "1:15 p.m." And it still said, "Tues Aug 22."

Can't be, he thought. It was just about one o'clock when he'd left the ship with his parents. And that was a long time ago. *At least, it sure feels like a long time ago.*

Judging from the square of pale daylight coming in through the gap in the boards, it was too light to be one in the morning and too dark to be one in the afternoon. Jeff shook his watch. *Maybe time travel isn't good for watches,* he thought. And what about his parents? *Mom and Dad must be going mental.* He wondered how long they had waited by Patsy Ann's statue for him. *Would they leave with the ship? Report me as missing?* A cramp seized his stomach. He didn't know whether it meant he was afraid or just hungry.

Whatever time it was, it had been a very long while since his last meal. Jeff thought about the sandwiches he'd left behind at the cafe, soft layers of bread and cheese and roast beef and mustard and ... The long, rumbling gurgle that issued from inside him was startling in the confined space. He hoped it wasn't loud enough to hear through the boards. He was ravenous. But if he left the hideout and tried to buy some food, he might get in trouble again because of his money. He could try stealing food, but that was wrong. And besides, he might get caught that way too, only for something he really *did* do. On the other hand, if he stayed here he'd be safe, but he'd starve.

He heard a soft "ping" somewhere above his head. Then another. They were like dry peas falling on a tin plate. *Rain?* More pings. A pause. A rattle like a whole spoonful of peas on the plate and a moist smell wafted in through the gap in the boards. The rattle became a steady downpour.

Stay in the barn, stay dry, get hungry. Jeff weighed his options. *Leave, get wet, get caught. Great choices.* He was still thinking when a scuffling noise announced Patsy Ann's return. Suddenly the small space was uncomfortably stuffed with boy and wet Bull Terrier. Smelly white fur filled Jeff's vision, dog breath wafted over him and a hot tongue slapped across the scrape on his nose. He could hear Patsy Ann's tail thumping hard against the barn wall.

"You're going to hurt your tail, old girl," Jeff laughed. But the beat just got faster, so much like Buddy that Jeff grinned in the dusty half-light. He reached out to put his arm around the dog, then yelped as twenty kilos of wiry muscle did a power spin in his lap. "Careful!" he squealed. "You're like a sack of cement in a fur coat." *Only with legs! Ow!* Jeff gasped as a strong white foot jabbed into him.

Patsy Ann had managed to turn around in the narrow space. Now her tail was thumping back and forth in Jeff's face and her nose pointed to the gap in the wall. She looked back at him and barked. It wasn't a loud bark, but in the tiny space it made Jeff jump.

"But it's raining," Jeff protested. Then a thought occurred to him: *Maybe it's time to go home!* His heart leapt. Patsy Ann gave him another growling half-bark, then crawled back out through the hole.

As quickly as he could in the narrow space, Jeff squirmed and wriggled until he, too, had turned around and faced the gap in the boards. He stuck out his head. An acre or so of pink tongue promptly washed his face for him. Pushing Patsy Ann aside, he pulled himself through the hole in the barn wall and stood up.

The rain was lighter than he had expected it to be, but felt like it meant to stay for a while. Jeff looked around. Facing him was the steep side of the mountain, bare rock and overhanging slopes where skinny trees climbed upwards into wreaths of low mist. Moisture dripped from stiff green needles and lay like crystal pearls on cushions of emerald moss.

The alley here was really only a footpath leading off in either direction from the small barn where he had spent the night. From beyond the barn, the noises of working machinery and traffic came much more clearly now. As she had before, Patsy Ann set off at a walk, then turned and glanced back at Jeff before going on. This time he followed her without question, pulling the collar of his denim jacket tight against the rain.

Once again, Patsy Ann kept to the fencelines and back alleys, staying away from the busy main streets of Juneau. Several times she stopped, sniffed, then darted for the nearest cover, Jeff close on her heels. From behind a stack of cordwood or a raspberry tangle so dense it made a tent of canes and foliage over a patch of dry earth, Jeff heard other people go by. *They must still be looking for me,* he reasoned.

At length they came back to the waterfront. Across a street, several rows of enormous wooden crates occupied most of the wharf. No one was in sight. Patsy Ann looked both ways, then galloped across the street and into the lane between two rows of crates. Jeff sprinted after her. At the far end of the crates, a long, low mountain of shiny black rocks hid them from sight of the street. *Must be coal*, Jeff figured.

But soon Patsy Ann led him away from the water again, to where a track ran along the back of a row of vegetable gardens, right under the mountain. Beyond the pole beans and cabbages, Jeff could see a line of houses not much bigger than garden sheds. *More like shacks,* he thought. *Yeah, but dry shacks!* The rain had soaked through the denim of his jacket by now, and he was beginning to get cold. He stopped at one especially healthy-looking tomato plant. Its bamboo pole was bent under the weight of heavy red fruit. Jeff could smell ripe tomato, just waiting to be bitten into. His stomach clenched. Ahead of him, Patsy Ann barked sharply.

At the last garden, Patsy Ann turned right and followed a row of onions almost as tall as herself until they were beside a small cabin. It was built from logs and faced out to the harbour across a two-lane, paved road. From a tarpaper lean-to at the back came the sweet smell of rhubarb pie, just out of the oven. Jeff's mouth watered. The rain picked up and a miniature Niagara poured off the shanty's tin roof and down Jeff's neck. He began to shiver.

A car hissed past them in the rain, windshield wipers beating double time. No other traffic was in sight. Patsy Ann tugged at his pantleg. They crossed the two lanes of wet pavement quickly. On the far side, a weedy slope led down to a dirt path running along the edge of the harbour. Through the rain, Jeff could make out tall pilings, rows of docks and boats of every description rocking gently at their moorings.

After about five minutes, the path climbed back up the embankment and rejoined the road by the water. From a gravel parking lot, a wooden gangplank led onto a maze of floating docks. Without pausing, Patsy Ann walked down the steeply tilting ramp. Jeff followed. The docks were like long skinny rafts held in place by pilings. They bobbed and tipped alarmingly as Jeff stepped from one to the next. The rain had made the green wood slippery, and Jeff had to step cautiously to stay on his feet. But Patsy Ann was undeterred, her white tail advancing confidently down one dock after another.

As they picked their way toward the further reaches of the bobbing docks, the boats seemed to become more run-down and neglected. The pilings looming to either side were thickly carpeted in green seaweed and chalky white barnacles. Even the floating docks seemed to sink deeper into the murky harbour waters.

They turned onto the last float. Jeff felt its mossy planks tilt dangerously to one side. From in front of him came a soft gurgle. Looking through the rain, he saw the far end of the dock slip beneath the black water and slowly resurface. As it did, the sea made a sucking sound, as though reluctant to let it go. The vessel tied to the decrepit old dock was in no better shape. The ropes that ran from rusted cleats were furred with moss and smelled of mildew. No sails hung from the two bare masts. Paint peeled in curling sheets from the sides of a long, low cabin. The boat looked deserted. *What the …? Why would she bring me* here? *There's got to be some mistake.*

But there was no mistake. Patsy Ann stepped confidently out along the rocking dock. Reluctantly, Jeff followed her. His heart was tripping over itself again and his mouth felt dry. His eyes fell on the flaking paint at the boat's wide, round stern. So much of it had fallen away from her wooden planking that Jeff could barely make out where the name had once been painted in graceful gold letters. Looking closely, he managed to pick it out: *DogStar.*

Jeff's spirits lifted a little. Looking up, he saw that a thin tendril of blue smoke rose from a tin chimney over the shabby deckhouse. His spirits lifted a little more. Patsy Ann barked loudly. Jeff nearly leapt off the dock. "Jeez, Patsy Ann! Give me some warning next time, eh?" He was still catching his balance on the rocking float when she barked again, louder than before.

The rail of the boat dipped slightly. A door opened in the deckhouse and through it stepped an erect figure in a dark sweater and khaki work pants. The man's lined, tanned face and silvery beard made him look *even older than Grandad.* In the half-light of the overcast day, the man's grey eyes were bright and piercing. It wasn't a particularly friendly face. But it wasn't hostile either. Mostly, it seemed to Jeff, it was watching and making up its mind. Its owner didn't seem surprised to be receiving unexpected visitors. *Should I say something?* Jeff wondered. But he couldn't think of anything useful to say, so he said nothing.

The old man looked evenly at Jeff for a while, then he looked down at Patsy Ann where she stood at Jeff's feet. Rain dripped down Jeff's forehead into his eyes. He clamped his teeth together to keep them from chattering.

Finally the old man coughed, as though he didn't use his voice very often. Then he said, "Well, lad, seeing as you're a guest of Patsy Ann's, ye may as well come in out of the rain." He held out a brown, calloused hand. "Step aboard."

eight

ON BOARD

AS RUN-DOWN and scruffy as the outside of the old boat was, its owner kept it shipshape on the inside. Jeff stepped first into an enclosed wheelhouse that reminded him a little of the bridge he had visited on the cruise ship, only in miniature. He recognized the compass but noticed that there were no electronic screens and gauges.

The old man pointed him to narrow stairs that led steeply down and forward. Jeff found himself in a compact but tidy cabin where an oil lamp burned. Its light flickered warmly on gleaming wood and polished brass. Looking forward, Jeff saw a book on a table, turned face down so as not to lose the reader's place. The title on the cover was *Sailing Alone Around the World.* To one side, a mug and plate were set upside down beside a small sink to drain. A pot sat on a tiny stove, giving off a toothsome smell Jeff couldn't identify.

He realized he was dripping on the cabin floor. The old man looked down at the puddle spreading around Jeff's high-tops, seeming to see something there that puzzled him. But what he said was, "Go on forward, lad, and strip out of those wet clothes. I'll see if I can't find something dry for you to put on."

In a tiny triangular cabin tucked far forward in the boat's bow, Jeff pulled off his sneakers and stripped out of his soaked jeans and T-shirt. As he did, the door opened just far enough for the old man to pass through a dry towel, a pair of heavy wool socks, patched but clean cotton trousers and a blue knitted pullover jersey. Gratefully, Jeff wrapped the towel around himself, rubbing hard to bring some warmth back to his chilled skin. Then he reached for the borrowed clothes. After he rolled up the trouser legs, they fit reasonably well. Pulling on the heavy socks last, Jeff found the dry warmth more than welcome. Quickly, he hung his wet clothes around the small space and stepped back into *DogStar*'s saloon.

The old man directed him to a seat on a cushioned bench facing the table. Like the one on the cruise ship, this table was built into the floor, Jeff noticed. "Now, lad," the old fellow said, settling himself in a heavy armchair facing Jeff, "tell me your tale." He reached down to where Patsy Ann leaned against his knee and scratched her ears. His eyes lingered on the scrape above Jeff's left eye and the second one on his nose. "Looks like ye've been in a fistfight."

"Um, yeah, I mean *no!*" Jeff stalled. "No fight, I just ran into something I didn't expect, that's all." He didn't want to bring the police into it just yet, not if he could avoid it. And as for being from the future ... *I don't think so.*

"Well, I'm from Halifax," he began. "We came ... that is, my parents and I came, to Juneau on a cruise ship called *Passage Princess*." The old man's eyebrows lifted, but he didn't say anything.

"Only somehow I got lost," Jeff continued. "And, uh, now the ship's gone and I think maybe my parents left without me. Anyway, I don't know where they are and Patsy Ann found me and brought me here!" He ended in a rush, hoping it sounded like it made some kind of sense.

"Well, I've been lost a time or two myself," the old man observed with a wry smile. "No great shame in that, lad. But I've a feeling there's more than you've told me." He fixed a sharp eye on Jeff.

"No, sir!" *Well, not really.* What he'd just said was the honest-to-goodness truth. *And what I've left out, the old guy almost certainly won't believe anyway.* "I just got sort of, well, *separated* from my mom and dad, that's all. And I can't seem to get back to them." *That's true enough.*

"And Patsy Ann brought you here to lie up until you figure out what to do," the old man said thoughtfully.

"Uh, yes sir. I guess that's about it."

"Hmm. What's your name, lad?"

"Jeffrey Beacon, sir. Jeff."

"I see. Well, my name's Harper. Used to be *Captain* Harper. But ..." He paused, as though deciding whether to say more, but when he spoke again, he said, "And how old are you?"

"Almost fourteen."

"Thirteen, then. I was thirteen the year I shipped on my first vessel. Out of Massachusetts, that was. And as I recall, I was pretty much always hungry at that age. When did you last have something to eat, lad?"

About sixty-odd years from now, Jeff thought to himself. But what he said was, "I guess it was yesterday morning." *And that's true, too, in a way.*

"Let me see if I can scrape together a little stew," the Captain said, rising and stepping into *DogStar's* postage-stamp kitchen.

"Oh, yes sir, please!" Jeff's stomach grumbled loudly. "I mean, that would be great. Thank you."

When it appeared, the stew was thick, gluey and white, with potatoes and some kind of sweet-flavoured fish. The Captain served it piping hot, with a large dollop of butter melting on top. It was the best food Jeff had ever tasted and he went through two full bowls of it before he was done, saving a big hunk of potato from the second one for Patsy Ann. Before he could give it to her, a deep-throated growl sounded from down around Jeff's feet and grimy white shoulders pushed past his legs. Patsy Ann scrambled up the steep steps to the wheelhouse, growling continuously.

Captain Harper rose and went to a round porthole. He pulled aside the tiny curtain that covered it and looked out.

"You in trouble with the law, boy?" The old man spoke sharply, but he didn't sound angry.

"I ... I'm not sure," Jeff dithered. "I mean, I *know* I didn't do anything wrong. But," *c'mon goof, own up,* "but, for some reason, yeah, the police have been chasing me." *And if they find me, I'm going to have to explain how come I'm not even born yet.*

Captain Harper stepped quickly forward past the end of the table and into the corridor leading further forward in the boat. He bent down. When he stood up, he was holding a piece of the floor. "Quick, get down in here," he said, his voice low.

Eh? Jeff slid along the bench and looked down. The old man had lifted up a hatch in the deck. He was looking down into the very bottom of the boat. A sour, musty smell rose out of the darkness and Jeff saw light reflecting from pools of water in *DogStar*'s bilge. *It's like the black lagoon down there.*

Patsy Ann growled again. Almost at the same moment, Jeff felt the boat tip as someone stepped onto the deck outside. There was a sharp knock on the wheelhouse door and from just beyond it a deep voice rapped out: "Harper! Police. Open up!"

Gulping hard, Jeff slid into the foul-smelling hole. Groping with his feet for something to lie on, he saw that heavy timbers crossed the boat's bottom from side to side. *DogStar's* wooden planks were visible between them. If he rested on those timbers and stuck his legs and bum forward into the darkness under the floor, he could just manage to fit himself into the shallow space.

Another rap came on the door, harder than the first. "Hey, Harper! Shake a leg there! Police."

Jeff was lying flat under the floor now, arms stretched down his sides and his head resting on the hard edge of one of *DogStar*'s ribs. Captain Harper replaced the hatch and Jeff was in total darkness. Sweating in the confined space, he struggled to breathe normally. He wanted to hear what was going on over his head.

The first noise he heard was a soft *swoosh,* just over his head, followed immediately by a *thump* as something heavy hit the hatchway. This was followed by scuffling sounds that suggested Patsy Ann was now lying on top of the hatch. He heard the Captain's footsteps climb the steps to the wheelhouse, then heard him call out, "Coming, coming," his voice muffled. The door opened and two new sets of feet followed the Captain's tread into the saloon cabin.

"It's customary to ask permission before coming aboard a man's vessel." Even through the floorboards, Jeff heard the edge of contained anger in the Captain's voice.

"Blow it out yer ear, Harper," growled a thick, insulting male voice. "It's customary not to lose your vessel in the mist, too." The thick voice seemed to find this very funny. A second, reedier voice joined in the coarse laughter.

"What do you want?"

"Well now, maybe a whiskey would be nice, *skipper.*" The thick voice stretched the last word. More rough laughter. "You'd stand a couple hardworking coppers to whiskey, now wouldn't you, Harper? Or maybe you just drink it when you're at the wheel."

"There's no liquor aboard this boat," the Captain answered. "And there was none on the bridge of any ship under my command." There was quiet for a moment, then the Captain spoke again. "What is it you want with me and my vessel?"

"We're looking for a con man," said the second voice. It was thinner than the first one. *Whiny.* "A young punk who's been passing funny money around town."

"Yeah," the thick voice said. "Kinda sounded like your type, Harper."

"Skinny kid, tall," said Whiner, "fourteen, maybe fifteen. Red hair, cut short. Dressed kinda foreign."

"P'tick'lary his shoes," cut in Thick Voice. "Sid Amory got a real good look at his shoes. Said he'd never seen anything like 'em before."

Jeff curled his toes inside the Captain's thick wool socks and thought about his almost-new Nikes lying with the rest of his damp clothes in *DogStar's* forward cabin.

"Well, I haven't seen him," the Captain was saying with brisk impatience. "So ye'd best go bother someone else."

"Now, now. Don't let's be unfriendly," came the thick, sarcastic voice again. "Or hasty. I think we better look around a little before we go, don't you, Tommy? Just to make sure this *old* crook don't have a *young* crook hidden away somewhere. Whad'ya say?"

"Show me a warrant," the Captain cut in before Tommy could speak.

Thick Voice chuckled. "Aw, c'mon Harper. You're not goin' to get all *legal* on us, are ya? Do that, and we might just have to get all legal about your permit to keep this old scow in our fine harbour." There was no more humour in the menacing voice now. "And then one stormy day we might just have to come back down here and cut them rotten ropes of yours. Get rid of you once and for all."

Jeff heard movement. Feet scuffling, doors opening and closing, drawers being pulled out. *Like I'm going to be hiding in a drawer?* Heavy feet moved forward, closer to where he lay in the dark space between the floor and the bottom of the boat. He held his breath and tried to relax the cramps in his limbs without making any sound. From directly over the hatch, he heard a deep, angry growl.

"Jesus!" It was the whiner, *Tommy.* "Patsy Ann! What're you doing here?"

"Is that worthless mutt here?" Thick Voice said from somewhere farther aft. "It figures: one no-good stray bunking in with another. We oughta put yez both outta yer misery." He was cut off by more growls — deep, bubbling snarls that made Jeff think of snapping teeth and bones cracking.

"Yeah, well, we're not finding nothin' here anyway, Sarge." Tommy's whine was more pronounced now. "I say we let the old souse alone."

"Yeah ... Yeah, awright." Sarge sounded disappointed. Heavy feet stepped away from Jeff toward the door. "But you watch yourself, Harper. That boy turns up, you let us know ... Or I'll want to know why not."

Jeff felt the boat lurch and heard the Captain's step returning alone to the saloon. A moment later, the hatchway was lifted. Yellow light and fresh air poured into the stifling bilge. Stiffly, Jeff climbed back out into the saloon. He sat back down on the bench, eyeing the Captain. *OK, now what? The old guy hasn't turned me in to the cops. At least, not yet. That's good. But what was that talk about losing a ship? And all that about drinking?*

Captain Harper stepped back to the porthole in the door to check that the police had really gone, then returned to his armchair. The old face looked strained, the grey eyes tired. He looked thoughtfully at Jeff.

Jeff looked around. "Where'd she go? Where's Patsy Ann?"

"Oh, she's off on her own business," the old man said. "Left with those two fine examples of the local law."

"But …" For some reason Jeff had expected her to stay with him. *Certainly she shouldn't go off with those two creeps, Whiner and the Sarcastic Sergeant.* "She went with *them*?"

"Patsy Ann's her own dog, lad. No use expecting her to do anything except what *she* wants to do. And I wouldn't be too quick to condemn her taste in company, either," the Captain added sternly. "Not if I were in your shoes." Jeff's toes curled again in Captain Harper's socks.

"I'm not a criminal, Mr. Harper, sir. I mean *Captain* Harper. Really, I'm not." *Oh please, please, PLEASE believe me.* "All I did was try to buy something to eat for me and Patsy Ann. I gave them some money my mom gave me. Now they think I'm some kind of criminal." *You have to believe me, you just have to.* If the old man didn't believe him, it wasn't likely that anyone else in Juneau would.

Please. Jeff was beginning to lose it and he knew it. Too much had happened since yesterday. *Or was it the day after the day after tomorrow … times a few thousand?* He felt lost in space as well as time. And without Patsy Ann beside him, he was beginning to feel scared. Tears burned in the corners of his eyes and he blinked them back. He swallowed hard, waiting.

At length, the Captain coughed and said, "Well now, lad, I don't know anything about 'funny money.' But I do know who I trust. And it's surely not the fools who wear police badges in this port. It wouldn't be the first time this town's hunted the wrong dog. Not by a long shot. Patsy Ann brought you here and she vouched for you. And that's something else again." He paused and seemed to be thinking for a moment, then went on. "Now, I don't know *why* she brought you here to *DogStar*. But I've never known Patsy Ann to do something without a good reason. So I'm guessing there's an explanation somewhere and it will come in its own good time. Meanwhile, it sounds to me like you could use a berth and three squares a day somewhere out of sight."

The Captain eyed Jeff closely. "Now, as it happens, I might just be looking for crew aboard *DogStar* for a spell. Whatever those two had to say," he went on, "I've heard it before. But maybe I should listen to some of it this time. It's pretty clear that Juneau's got no more use for me than I have for it. I think maybe it's time *DogStar* slipped moorings here and found herself a kinder harbour."

He sighed. "It would take near a month to get *DogStar* ready for sea on my own. Working together, we can have her Bristol fashion in half that. So here's my proposition, lad: You sign on as crew and you'll get full rations and a dry berth and fifty cents a day while we're fitting out. And a free passage to Vancouver when we sail. You want to, you can catch a train from there home to Halifax, supposing that's where you're really from." He looked closely at Jeff. "It's the fairest I can offer. What do you say, lad?"

Jeff considered it. *Two weeks! Mom and Dad will go totally ape!*

He thought again about what his parents must be doing right now. *I bet I'm on TV as a missing kid.* He wondered if the cruise ship had left without him and what would happen to Buddy's ashes. He shook himself back into the present. If he was going to be here for a while, he would need a place to stay, that was for sure — and something to eat. And he had to agree that Patsy Ann seemed to think he and the Captain belonged together. Besides, if he was really stuck in the 1930s he'd better get out of Juneau soon, or he'd be behind bars too.

Jeff could feel the Captain's eyes on him and looked away. His gaze came to rest on the oil lamp. It was attached by a brass bracket to the wall near the old man's shoulder. Hanging around the bracket was a worn leather dog-collar.

The Captain caught the direction of Jeff's look and smiled. "That was Maddie's old collar," said the Captain. "Picked her from a litter in Mexico and she sailed with me for fourteen years. I keep her collar out to let her know she's welcome, wherever she may be now."

Jeff thought of Buddy's black nylon collar by his bed back in Halifax. And he just knew. He stood up and extended his hand across the table. "Deal," he said.

nine

DECKHAND

JEFF OPENED his eyes and blinked. *Where is Buddy?* And why was the ceiling so close? It was bent, sort of. *No, more like curved.* A soft lapping sound came from somewhere near his left ear. Then the bed rocked. *Yikes! Where ...*

This morning, the confusion didn't last nearly so long. The low ceiling resolved itself quickly into his berth on *DogStar*. And even the impossible fact that he had somehow slipped through time and was living in 1933 didn't seem quite so strange today. Not nearly as hard to accept as being without Buddy. *I should have brought him with me*, Jeff thought sadly. *If only Rosemary hadn't made me feel like an idiot for carrying him around.*

He brought his wrist up and looked at the time on his watch. *Odd.* Now the digital face read 1:35 p.m. *And it still reads "Tuesday."* His watch had moved forward barely twenty minutes from when he'd looked at it last, yesterday morning in the barn. *Definitely screwed up. Or is it?*

Another thought hit him and he quickly slipped the watch off his wrist. Jeff wasn't sure when digital watches first came out, but he could remember Dad teasing him, saying that *he* had had to learn to tell time from the hands on a *real* clock. Jeff reached under the bunk and put the watch in a drawer. The Captain had told him the drawer could be his for as long as he was on *DogStar*. He rolled back into the middle of his bunk and listened. He could hear ropes slapping in the wind outside and felt *DogStar* rock restlessly on her lines. He heard the Captain moving about the boat, the rattle of pots and pans. *Guess I'd better get up.*

That turned out to be easier said than done. As Jeff's feet touched the floor it rolled sharply away from him and he fell, cracking an elbow on the hard edge of his bunk and landing painfully on his bum. Nursing his lumps, he got back to his feet. He was still wearing the pants and jersey he had borrowed yesterday. His own clothes hung damply from assorted hooks and handles in the cabin. Not bothering with shoes or socks, he made his way aft toward the saloon, holding onto things to keep his balance and feeling a little queasy.

The Captain glanced up from the pot he was stirring and smiled. "You look a little green around the gills, son."

"Where is the bathroom please, sir?" Jeff asked.

"You're afloat now lad, so you can call things by their proper names," the Captain said. "It's the head. And it's right behind you." He pointed to a door at one side of the narrow corridor Jeff had just come through. The door opened to reveal a room like a very small cupboard. Jeff had no problem figuring out the purpose of the white porcelain object that took up most of the cramped space. He ducked inside and closed the door. Settling down to business, he leaned forward and braced himself against the boat's roll by resting his forehead on the inside of the door. *That works.*

At least, it did until he looked for the handle to flush. There didn't seem to be one. *Oh great!* He really didn't want to have the Captain see what he'd been doing in there — *that's why you go to the bathroom by yourself.* But it looked like he might not have a choice.

There was a knock on the door. "Have ye drowned in there, boy? Breakfast's waiting."

"Um." *No way out now.* "I, uh … I'm afraid I don't know how to flush this thing."

To his deep relief, the Captain stayed on the other side of the door. "Look to the right of the head, lad. See a bar sticking out there?" Jeff located it. "Now just pump her steady, up and down, not too fast. But keep at it and it'll work for you." Jeff caught a good-natured chuckle on the far side of the door.

It took several minutes of energetic pumping, but in the end the head did indeed work for him. So did a similar mechanism, only smaller, that sat beside the tiny sink. When Jeff pumped the handle, enough fresh, cold water squirted from the single tap to let him wash his hands and splash his face. Drying them both quickly on his jersey, he stepped out into the cabin.

The Captain was just putting two deep enamel bowls of steaming hot cereal down on the table. Beside them, he placed a thick bowl of brown sugar and a blue-and-white tin of evaporated milk. Then he brought two enamel mugs of coffee to the table and set one in front of Jeff. Even with the slight queasiness that remained in his stomach, Jeff thought that porridge had never tasted quite this good before. The strong bitter coffee tasted much as he remembered it from the odd cup at home in Halifax, but stronger. *Probably has caffeine in it,* he thought.

Licking the last sticky oatmeal from his spoon, he felt very awake. The Captain rose, collected their bowls and placed them in the sink. Then he returned to the table. "Well then, lad, ready to start?"

"Yes, sir," Jeff answered. "I mean, Aye-aye." *Am I allowed to joke? I mean, he's the* Captain! He looked up and met the old man's bright grey eyes. They were smiling.

"Good," Captain Harper said. "Then you can begin in the galley," he nodded in the direction of *DogStar's* compact kitchen, "with those dishes. No room on board a vessel to let dishes pile up on you. While you're doing that, I'll make a list of what we'll need to ship in the way of provisions for an extra hand on board."

Jeff stood and managed to keep his footing as he stepped up to the galley counter. The tap there worked on the same principle as the one in the bathroom ... *The head, I mean.* Looking around for hot water, he spotted a kettle steaming on the stove and splashed some of its contents into the sink.

Behind him, the Captain hummed tunelessly as he went through *DogStar's* lockers with a pencil in one hand and sheet of paper in the other. Every now and then, he muttered to himself and added another item to a growing list.

Jeff opened a cupboard door beneath the sink and found a towel hanging inside it. He pulled it out and began searching drawers for the one where the cutlery lived.

The Captain emerged from the last cupboard holding several tools in his hand. All of them consisted of wooden handles with pieces of metal in various shapes attached to one end.

Jeff put the last spoon away and hung the towel back in its place. As he turned back to the saloon, the Captain thumped one of the tools into his hand.

"Know what that is, lad?" the old man asked.

Is this a trick question? Jeff turned over the tool in his hand. A steel blade was set crossways into the end of the wooden handle, like a small garden hoe. He shook his head.

The Captain chuckled. "That's a scraper, boy. And believe you me, you'll be well acquainted with it shortly."

A FEW HOURS later, Jeff was regretting how true the Captain's words had turned out to be.

The old man had shown him how to use the scraper to remove loose paint from the peeling sides of *DogStar*'s deck-house. When he was done, Harper had said, they would put on the fresh paint that he was going to buy in town.

"But you're going to have to stay out of sight," the Captain had warned him. "If you're spotted, I won't be able to help you. I don't draw much water in this town, as you may have noticed."

"Yes, sir. I mean *no* ... sir!" Jeff had reddened.

"So, if you don't want to get arrested, just work on the port side of the boat. You'll be out of sight of shore there."

"OK."

"Lie low and keep your head down."

Got it. But ... "Um, Captain, which side is the port?"

The Captain's watchful grey eyes had looked speculatively at him for a second or two before he replied. "Facing the front of the boat, port is to your left and starboard to right. Facing astern, port is to right and starboard to left. But in your case," the Captain had added dryly, "it'll be simpler to remember. Just keep the deckhouse between you and the shore."

With that, the old man had left Jeff alone on what was evidently the port side of the boat. He had felt *DogStar* rock as the Captain stepped off. Then he'd set to work scraping paint from the weathered planking.

The work was hard and his mind wandered. Jeff could spend hours chasing a thread on the Internet, but his "stick-to-it-iveness" at other tasks was a sore point in the Beacon family, especially with Dad.

He studied the flakes of paint, which were like grey snow as the breeze caught them and sent them spinning. Looking across the water, he noticed how much wet green seaweed there was on the pilings in the distance. Jeff knew about tides from living in Halifax and from school: how the moon pulls the world's oceans up into a bulge that travels around the earth, making the surface of the sea rise and fall twice every day. *Tide's out*, he thought.

Jeff wanted to do a good job for the Captain. By the time the sun came round the port side of the boat, he was covered in flakes and speckles of hard grey paint from his determined scraping. Gritty dust clung to his hair and skin and got into his eyes, making them water. Even with the diminishing breeze, the sun was hot. Jeff took off the Captain's jersey but sweat still dripped from his forehead and ran down his back. He surveyed his work. *Wow, I've really done a lot,* he thought. Jeff wished Patsy Ann would come back. She reminded him of Buddy. But somehow it made him feel good, not bad. He renewed his efforts, scraping at the paint with a vengeance, as if somehow that would make things happen faster.

A shriek and a splash startled Jeff out of his thoughts. He jumped to his feet.

"Help! Help!" a voice screamed. Then came more splashing. The sounds were coming from somewhere near *DogStar's* bow. Jeff ran to the front of the boat.

Below him, and a few metres away across the water, a dark head was disappearing beneath the oily surface of the harbour. With a splash and another burbling cry for help, a girl's face reappeared, then dipped again below the surface.

Jeff looked around for a life ring, but none was in sight. Nor was there anyone else nearby. Another scream ended abruptly with more splashing. *No time! Just do it!*

Jeff threw himself off *DogStar's* bow, legs wide and arms out, the way they'd taught him at life-saving class. He reached the flailing girl in a half-dozen strokes, but it took frantic seconds longer to subdue her panic enough for Jeff to get his arm around her. When finally he did, he used his free arm to sidestroke to the nearest dock. Jeff placed her hands on the edge of the float, then heaved himself out of the water. Turning quickly, he put a hand on each thin wrist and pulled the drenched figure, fully clothed, up onto the dock.

It was his first close look at the girl he had rescued. She looked like a drowned spaniel, with auburn hair coming loose from her pigtails and plastered wetly to her face. But she was breathing. The girl scrambled to her feet and shook water from her sopping overalls.

"You ought to be more careful," he said.

She looked at him out of wide green eyes but didn't answer.

"What were you doing? How'd you fall in the water?"

The green eyes regarded him in a way that tugged strangely at Jeff's memory. Finally she spoke. "I was just picking mussels from the dock … and … I slipped."

"You should have watched where you were going."

"I did! But I was watching the seals." As if on cue, a sleek grey head popped out of the water a stone's throw from the dock. "See?" She turned around to point, wet pigtails whipping the air. Suddenly the girl's face fell. "Oh no! My pail, it's gone! It's brand new and my momma's gonna kill me!"

"I'm sorry. I … I didn't notice it," *Lame, Jeff. Really lame.*

She was looking him over closely and Jeff tried not to squirm under her scrutiny. *Time to get this back under control.* "What's your name?" he asked, gruffly.

"Rose. What's yours?"

"Uh … Jeff." Too late he thought, *Jeez, maybe I should make up another name.* "Where do you live?"

"Back there," she pointed down the shore in the direction of Juneau. "But my momma's going to kill me twice if I come home soaking wet."

Yeah, Jeff thought, *and the Captain's going to kill* me *if he comes home and finds me standing out here talking to a soaking wet girl.* "Come on," he said, taking Rose's arm. "We need to get you dried out."

He hustled her on board *DogStar* and sent her into the forward cabin to get out of her wet overalls. When she handed her sodden clothes through a crack in the cabin door, Jeff took them to the galley sink and wrung them out. Then he hung them above the galley stove. He turned in time to see Rose come down the corridor wrapped in the heavy wool blanket from his bunk.

"I know where the best blueberries in Juneau are," she said. "I can show you, if you like."

"First I better come up with some way to explain what you're doing here," said Jeff unhappily.

The girl settled herself on the bench, clutching the blanket tightly about her. She regarded Jeff. "I know a secret way into the old mine tunnels, too," she confided.

But Jeff's mind was still on the present. "And I'll have to explain why you don't have any clothes on."

"Oh," she said, appearing to hear him for the first time. She looked at her overalls. "How long do you think they'll take to dry?"

Too long, Jeff thought. He stepped to the door and looked out through the porthole. His heart skipped a beat. Through the forest of masts and rigging, he could see the Captain stepping briskly along the footpath beside the water, parcels in hand.

"Rose," he said urgently, sweeping up her overalls and thrusting them into her hands, "take these and go back into the cabin and don't come out 'til I tell you to. Trust me on this one."

Rose looked surprised, but did as he asked. Jeff watched her go, then turned back to await his fate.

It was clear as soon as the door opened that Captain Harper knew *something* was up. Grey eyes sharp and inquisitive, he asked, "What's all that water doing on the deck?" His gaze fell to the sodden pants that Jeff had not had time to change. "You fall in?"

Before Jeff could answer, the Captain bent down and plucked a small, wet canvas shoe from the deck. "And whose is this?"

"Well, sir, uh Captain, sir. I can explain that. You see ..."

"Can I come out?" Rose's voice carried clearly back to the saloon from the cabin.

Jeff winced. *I knew she went in there too easily.*

"Please do," the Captain said, loudly enough for Rose to hear. His eyes stayed on Jeff.

She was still wrapped in the blanket, only her bare toes peeking out below it. She held out her wet overalls in front of her.

Jeff leapt to explain. "I was scraping the boat, just like you told me to. And all of a sudden, I heard a splash and there she was in the water. No one else was around. I couldn't let her drown!"

The Captain turned to Rose. "And how, pray tell, did fair maiden fall in the well?" He raised one bushy grey eyebrow.

"I was just collecting mussels," Rose said, looking the Captain in the eye. "I was standing on the edge of the dock, picking them off the piling. And," she looked at Jeff, "he saved my life." Now Jeff really did squirm. The Captain regarded the two of them: Jeff in his still-wet borrowed pants, Rose with salt already stiffening her hair. "All right, all right," he said gently. "No one died, did they?" He reached out with a large, lined and leathery hand to pat Rose's smaller one.

"What's your name, lass?"

"Rose Baker. And you're Captain Harper, aren't you?"

"Aye, I am that. You're Sylvia Baker's daughter?"

"Yes, sir. And my momma's gonna kill me for falling in."

"Well now, first things first," said the Captain. "Let's just get you both cleaned up and dry." He rummaged in a drawer for a towel and held it out to Rose.

"You'd best go rinse the salt out of your hair." He nodded toward the head. "Right through there. Then I'll take you on home and we'll explain things to your mother."

Rose took the towel from his hand and walked forward in her blanket. The Captain picked up her wet clothes from the table and hung them above the stove.

When he spoke next, it was to Jeff and his voice was low. "I knew her poppa a little. He died when she was just a baby. Off chasing a gold claim in the mountains in the middle of winter. They found him with his compass still in his hand. Frozen stiff as a board. It was terribly hard on Rose's mother." He shook his head, then asked, "How much does she know?"

"Nothing. We were only back on the boat a minute before you got home." Jeff wondered how much trouble he was in. "I really didn't have any choice but to save her, Captain. Honest."

"I know you didn't, boy. You're not in dutch with me. Heck, you'd be a town hero if you weren't already a fugitive. But that's the problem — we need to ask her not to tell anyone else you're here."

The Captain broke off and looked at Jeff. "You're still soaking wet yourself, boy." He selected one of the parcels he'd brought back with him. "You'll find a work shirt and another pair of denims in there. And some boots." Harper fixed his grey eyes on Jeff. "You might want to put those fancy Halifax shoes of yours somewhere out of sight, don't you think?"

"Uh, good idea." Jeff retreated to the forward cabin to change. When he returned, Rose was back in the saloon and in her own clothes. Her overalls were still damp, but no longer soaked. She sat beside the Captain, who was demonstrating an unexpected competence at putting braids back into her long red-brown hair.

While Jeff had been drying and changing, he had worked out a plan for asking Rose to keep his presence on *DogStar* a secret. Now he launched into it. "Rose," he said, "I saved your life, right?"

"Mmm-hmm," she agreed, holding her head straight for the Captain but managing to keep her spirited eyes on Jeff as he crossed the cabin.

"Well, now I need you to do something for me."

"OK," she agreed readily. "What is it?"

The Captain looked up, brows knitted, and Jeff moved on quickly before he could intervene. "I'm not really from here," he told Rose. *Now that is an understatement.* "I'm not really supposed to *be* here either. And I can't tell you why, but you have to trust me." *I've seen her somewhere before,* Jeff thought again as he searched her face. *But where?* He shook off the thought and continued: "I'll be in a lot of trouble if anybody, and I mean *anybody*, finds out I'm in Juneau."

Rose pondered this for a moment, then looked up. "I won't tell anyone," she said. "I promise. Not a soul."

The Captain spoke. "This is very serious, Rose. If you don't keep that promise ..."

"Then we'll *never* be able to see each other again," Jeff said, staring deeply into the girl's eyes. *Rose won't want that to happen,* he guessed. For a moment, he felt like he was taking advantage of the girl. But if he were ever going to go home again, he had to stay out of jail. Patsy Ann wouldn't be able to take him home if he was behind bars.

Rose's face was serious. With her right index finger she made an "X" over her chest, then held her hand up, palm out. "Cross my heart and hope to die," she declared. "I won't tell anyone. I swear."

Jeff wasn't sure *how* he knew, but somehow he *did* know, that Rose would not let him down.

ten

HAMBONE & HUSKIES

PATSY ANN trotted in the direction of downtown Juneau. The plump rat she'd sniffed out from under the docks an hour ago had proven to be faster on its feet than most of its kind. She'd chased it, sleek, brown and smelling sharply of well-fed rodent, through the garden patches south of town until finally it had scuttled into the safety of a woodpile. Patsy Ann had barked at the obstacle long enough to express her annoyance, then put the insolent creature out of her mind. There were better things to be thinking about at this hour. The lunch crowd would be breaking up at the Gastineau by now and Jerry the cook would be setting aside the tastiest of the leftovers.

Her short legs made a blur under Patsy Ann's thick body and her skimpy white tail trailed out behind her as she moved quickly along. Beady dark eyes roamed the street ahead. Her black nose twitched and wrinkled as it sampled the scents of the warm afternoon.

She passed the soapy smell of O'Doule's Barber Shop, then the thick wave of smoke-and-beer that flowed from the Red Dog Saloon. At the Nugget Shop, she stopped and put her nose down at each of the three totem poles to catch up on the local canine traffic.

"Patsy Ann!" Rose shot away from Captain Harper's side and ran the rest of the block, sliding onto her knees when she got to the dog. She threw her arms around the dog's neck and squeezed until Patsy Ann squirmed free and her long pink tongue began depositing wet kisses on Rose's face. Laughing, Rose pushed the dog's head away and stood up, still scratching the warm fur behind Patsy Ann's neck.

The Captain came up. In one hand he carried a pail. The sun shone off the bright surface of the silvery new metal. "Best of the afternoon to you, girl," he said to Patsy Ann. Her lolling grin showed off Patsy Ann's teeth admirably. Captain Harper pulled a piece of dry biscuit from a pocket and held it out. The large white teeth came down on it with surprising gentleness.

The old man and the girl were heading away from the Gastineau, but Patsy Ann kept them company anyway. As the three of them came around the last of the warehouses and onto the road leading past the cottages that belonged to the gardens, the hair on Patsy Ann's back stood up on end. Her head went down and her ears went back. She growled softly.

Looking ahead, the Captain saw Sergeant Ed Kelly and Officer Tommy McGraw standing at the door of a shipshape little cabin where pink and purple sweet pea vines climbed the white-painted walls. The two police officers were talking to a slender blonde woman wearing a waitress's uniform from the Baranof Hotel. When the woman saw Rose, she pushed past the two men and came flying down the walk.

"Rose Elizabeth Baker! Where have you been?" Sylvia Baker said. Her arms went around Rose's shoulders. She squeezed tightly, then pulled back quickly. "Why ... you're *wet!*"

"I was collecting mussels at the dock and I fell in," Rose ventured.

Captain Harper spoke up. "Had to fetch her out with a boat hook, ma'am. Wet, but serviceable. Fortunately. She was concerned about losing her pail, though. Poor lass. I didn't want to see her getting into any trouble." He held out the shiny new pail.

Sylvia laughed and took the Captain's other hand and shook it. "Oh, Captain Harper, thank you, thank you so much. I don't know what I'd do if I ever lost Rose." She patted her pockets. "Here, let me pay you for that pail."

"Oh, no need for that, ma'am," said the Captain. He looked away from Sylvia Baker's animated blue eyes and saw Kelly and McGraw watching him, stony-faced. The two officers walked slowly out to the road. As they left, Sylvia assured them, "If I see hide or hair of that boy, I'll let you know." The two men walked along to the next cottage and up to the door. There they turned and stood looking back at the little group in front of the Baker home.

Sylvia addressed the Captain again. "At least come in, then, and have some coffee and a piece of pie. Fresh wild strawberry! It's just cooling."

For a moment, it seemed as though the Captain would accept the invitation. But his eye caught the sergeant and

Tommy still watching him and he shook his head regretfully. "I would be delighted, Mrs. Baker. But I'm afraid I can't just at the moment. We, that is *I*, am getting *DogStar* ready for sea and there's a great deal to do. But perhaps another time?"

"Yes, any time. Any time at all."

With a tip of his peaked black cap to Sylvia Baker and a wink to Rose, Captain Harper strode off in the direction of the boat basin. Patsy Ann looked up at Rose's mother. The dog's dark little eyes were bright with interest and her tongue dangled out the side of her open mouth.

"How do you know, you funny old dog?" Sylvia said, laughing. "But you're right, as usual. I've been saving a soup bone for you all week. Why don't you come in and get it?"

Patsy Ann's normal poise was gone. She butted her broad head into Sylvia's legs, then bounced away, her stocky little body spinning in the air. She barked and thrust her warm muzzle impatiently into Sylvia's hand. With Patsy Ann barking and getting happily in their way, Rose and Sylvia went through the tidy cottage to the kitchen at the back.

Opening the door of an upright chest that stood on legs in one corner, Sylvia reached inside and lifted a bundle from beside a big block of ice. It was wrapped in newspaper and tied with string. Patsy Ann's excitement redoubled.

"All right, all right," Sylvia said with a laugh. "Just let me get it unwrapped." With practised hands, she slipped the string off the package and unrolled a thick bone from the newspaper. Redolent shreds of pink and brown meat still clung to it. Patsy Ann dropped her tail to the floor and aimed her nose at the bone, every white hair on her tight little body seeming to quiver.

"Here you go."

With an unladylike little grunt and the sharp *clack* of polished ivory on hard bone, Patsy Ann's jaws closed on the treat. Holding it in her mouth, she scooted under the big white cookstove. Soon there came alarming sounds of gnawing and chewing, and of bone splitting.

Sitting Rose down on one kitchen chair and seating herself in another, Sylvia faced her daughter. She waited to speak until the girl's lively green eyes looked into her own.

"Now, young lady," she began. "What have I told you about going down to the docks by yourself? You can't swim, and that water's cold. And when that tide's running, it can pull you under in a heartbeat!"

She leaned forward and put her arms around Rose and held her for a long time. When she went on, her voice was much softer. "If Captain Harper hadn't been there, honey, I might have lost you, too." Sylvia pulled away but kept one hand on each of Rose's shoulders. She caught her daughter's eye again and held it. "I'm warning you now, if you *dare* wander down there alone again, I won't be able to leave you alone anymore. You'll have to come to work with me until school starts again. I mean it, Rose Elizabeth."

Rose's face held a trace of rebellion, but she managed to say the right thing. "I'm sorry, Momma. And don't worry," she added. "I won't play down there *alone* ever again." She smiled innocently up at her mother.

Patsy Ann picked up her bone and pushed the door to the Bakers' cottage open with her nose. At the back corner of the row of gardens, she found a patch of soft earth where she could hide the bone for more attention later on. Scratching the last pawfuls of black dirt over the cache, she sniffed the air. Too late for the Gastineau now. But Patsy Ann's afternoon program had several other stops besides that one. Her tongue flicked out and ran once around her pink-and-white chops. She set off in the direction of town.

Fifteen minutes later, Jefferson held the side door open for her as Patsy Ann slipped into the Federal Building. Again, she followed the corridors to the stairs and climbed to the second floor. But this time, she carried right on past Judge Burns' door to a much larger office in a far corner of the building.

"Have to go, dear," a woman with short dark hair said into a black telephone. "My company's here!" Laughing, she put the phone back on its cradle, pulled a purse up from the floor and placed it on the desk in front of her.

Patsy Ann went to the desk and fit herself between it and Shirley Wenzel's knees. Her nose rested on the soft knitted lap of Shirley's dress, her sharp eyes following every movement of the woman's hands. A flat white packet appeared out of the purse, and Shirley pulled off paper and foil wrapping. A rich, dark, sweet smell filled the room. Breaking off a piece of the chocolate bar, Shirley fed it to Patsy Ann.

Dr. Nickerson, the vet, claimed that chocolate was bad for dogs. But Shirley had been buying a chocolate bar for Patsy Ann every day for almost as long as Patsy Ann had been in Juneau. And it hadn't seemed to hurt her yet. Maybe Bull Terriers had stronger stomachs than other dogs.

Patsy Ann gulped down the last square of forbidden chocolate and gave Shirley's fingers a wet lick for good measure. Then, with a soft *thump*, she dropped to the floor at the woman's feet, stretched out so that her fat hams stuck out behind her and her black nose rested on her forelegs out in front.

From here, she had a view into the carpeted and paneled inner sanctum that belonged to Mayor J. Samuel Shrite. Sunlight streamed in the tall windows and warmed the lifeless fur of the mountain sheep, lynx and elk whose heads hung on the walls. Shrite himself seemed oblivious to both the golden light and the reproach in the glass eyes as he sat at his desk and pored over the crabbed columns of figures in front of him.

"Shirley," he bellowed, so loudly that his secretary winced. "Get that idiot Beggs on the line. Pronto!"

Shirley busied herself at the telephone.

Shrite's voice echoed from his office just moments after Shirley had connected him. "What do you mean he's vanished?" he bellowed into the phone. "What kind of incompetent department are you running, Beggs?" There was a welcome silence, then more shouting. "I don't care what Burns says. I'll make it simple for you, Beggs. You find that boy, and soon, or the next council meeting's going to be discussing the need for a new police chief in Juneau. Do I make myself clear?" The phone slammed down into its cradle with a bang.

Shirley looked up at the clock on the wall and rose. Stepping just inside the door of Shrite's office, she reminded him, "Mr. Mayor, the ladies are expecting you down at the Temperance Hall at three. It's five to three now."

"Darn it," Shrite cursed. Patting the pockets of his dark suit, he stood and glanced one more time at the papers on his desk, then stormed past Shirley and out of the office.

Patsy Ann rose from her spot under the desk, shook herself and followed him. Just as she reached the door, a loud yelp echoed through the hall. It was followed by a scuffling noise, then the crash of something heavy falling. Patsy Ann ran to the corner where one corridor led into the next and came sliding to a stop, her nails scrabbling to brake on Jefferson's well-waxed hardwood.

In front of her, Mayor J. Samuel Shrite lay wriggling on the floor, legs and arms flailing. They seemed to be entangled in some kind of dirty yellow netting. The mayor's puffy round face was flushed red, glowing with sweat and bad temper. He was making confused, angry noises.

"*Darn it*, Burns," he managed to spit out. "This is a public building! What do you think you're doing?"

Just beyond the flailing mayor, Henry Burns sat cross-legged on the floor, his black judicial robes puddled around him. His long fingers patiently worked saddle soap into the supple leather of a spidery web of well-worn dog harness. From where Patsy Ann stood, not even the spicy smell of the saddle soap could overcome the powerful smell of Husky. "Waiting for a jury to make up its mind," the judge snapped. He picked up a flat glass bottle that had fallen out of Shrite's jacket and skated across the floor. He handed it back to Shrite. "Here, better keep that in your jacket while you're lying to those women about temperance."

Shrite, dusting himself off and straightening his suit, blushed a deep shade of scarlet and thrust the bottle back into an inside pocket.

Without looking up, Henry Burns asked, "What's this I hear about you sending the police around the docks to roust out fishermen?"

"Just the derelicts," Shrite snarled. "Overdue. Get rid of the eyesores like old Harper and put some pride back in the civic image. Be good for the whole city of Juneau."

Henry Burns fixed a cold eye on the mayor. "Shrite, fishermen are the future of this territory, whether you can see it or not." He picked up another leather trace, dabbed soap on it and began to rub it in. "And why this obsession with old Ezra Harper? The man faced high seas and danger for you for years, and paid a mighty high price for his one mistake."

"The man lost a ship. *My* ship. And four million dollars in cash and gold," Shrite spat back. "That's reason enough."

"Tarnation, Shrite. None of that was *your* loss. You didn't go down a penny out of that wreck, and you know it. You could afford him a kinder attitude."

Shrite smirked. "It wasn't my fault no one else had the good sense to insure their cargo." He stepped carefully around the web of harness. "It's the principle of the thing."

"You don't know what the word means," Henry Burns snapped back. Standing, he started to gather up the leather harness. "By the way, I've spoken to a couple of old friends in Treasury. I've asked them to take a look at this counterfeiting problem we've been having. The one our *police* can't seem to get a handle on." He stood at the door to his chambers and glared at the mayor. "They're a little busy in Chicago just now, but they'll be along right smart when things quiet down." He turned into his chambers and shut the door behind him.

Shrite sneered at the closed door, then hurried down the stairs to his date with the Temperance women.

Patsy Ann shook herself from nose to tail and followed him at a more leisurely pace, pausing only briefly to run her nose over the polished floor for further traces of Husky.

IT WAS LATE afternoon by the time Patsy Ann returned to the waterfront and barked at the big double doors of the Longshoremen's Hall. Jake Earness let her in. She trotted over to the corner by the stove, where a soft pile of old sacks stood beside two tin bowls. Sinking her nose into one of them, Patsy Ann drank long and loudly.

Over her head, half a dozen men wearing work clothes and occupying the hall's mismatched collection of hand-me-down chairs and sofas resumed their conversation. Hank

Watson was holding forth on the red-headed kid the police were looking for. "Passing bad bills, Tommy McGraw said. Well, heck," Hank was saying, "if I had a real gold dollar for every bogus sawbuck that's turned up in Juneau the last few years, I'd be a rich man. The kid probably didn't know any different."

"If there even *is* a kid," Snuff Malakov put in.

"If there is, he's long gone," was Jake Earness' view. "Probably in Canada by now."

"And older than he looks, too, I'll bet," offered young Bobby Welsh, who was always trying to look more mature than his baby-faced twenty-one years. "Pull something like that, he'd be more like nineteen than fifteen."

"Speakin' of age," Hank changed the subject, "old Harper was in town this morning. Don't know what he's up to, but he looked ten years younger than I've ever seen 'im."

"That so?" asked Snuff. "That'd place him about 110, I guess." A chuckle ran around the hall.

"Who wouldn't look old, everything he's been through," Hank spoke up again. "He's never stopped blaming himself for losing that ship."

"The town won't *let* him stop," piped in Bobby.

"Hard to blame 'em," sniffed Jake. "A lot of folks lost everything they had on that ship. And him coming back three weeks after the passengers, and never being able to find the wreck again? Well, I ain't sayin' he did it. But it sure looks bad, that's all."

Nods and murmurs indicated general agreement.

"Maybe he's like that fella in the movie they have up at the 20th Century," suggested Snuff, filling his voice with theatrical foreboding. *"Dr. Jekyll and Mr. Hyde."* More laughter, and the conversation turned away from Harper and the fugitive counterfeiter. Curled up on her bed of old sacking, Patsy Ann put her head down on her paws and drifted into sleep.

Hank elbowed Snuff hard in the ribs and nodded over to the corner. "Look who must've had a long day."

eleven

STRAWBERRIES

IT WAS Saturday night. *Saturday! Four whole days already!*

Jeff was in *DogStar*'s tiny head, trying to get the same effect from a basin of lukewarm water and a washcloth as he did from a long, hot, steaming shower back home in Halifax. It wasn't really working.

Jeff's body ached. He had never in his life worked so hard. He had scrapes and cuts on his knees, blisters on his fingers and smears of paint on pretty much all of him. But old *DogStar* was beginning to look like a real boat again. Her deckhouse gleamed a sparkling new white and a fresh coat of green made her look smart down to the waterline. One evening, the Captain had shown Jeff an elegant kind of braid called a "splice," with which they put loops on the ends of several lengths of new brown rope. Now *DogStar* was tied to her dock with spanking new lines.

He'd been too tired at the end of the days to think much.

But once or twice, bone weary and wondering if he was ever going to see Mom or Dad again, or his own bedroom, or Buddy's old collar, he had felt lost and scared. Whether by plan or by accident, Patsy Ann had chosen those moments to visit *DogStar*.

Have I only imagined the promise in Patsy Ann's eyes? What if she were just a dog after all? What if he had made up that look, and Patsy Ann had no more idea how to get him back to his own time than any ordinary mutt? Then he was stuck here. *Stuck someplace where I can't even take a shower! Would Mom ever hate that!* He wished he could talk to Buddy. *Buddy would know what to do.*

He slipped out of the head and stepped forward to his cabin. *Home.* He felt a pang of loneliness. *I wonder what Mom and Dad are doing right now?*

Kneeling on the floor, he pulled out the drawer the Captain had given him as his. Inside was his watch. He picked it up and glanced at it. The time had now crawled all the way along to 2:25 p.m., still on Tuesday. He tossed it back into the drawer in disgust and pulled out his own jeans and T-shirt, the clothes he had worn the day they'd arrived in Juneau. He put them on, all but his Nikes, and felt better.

Jeff walked back through the companionway (that was one of the boat words the Captain was teaching him), and stepped into the saloon. He hardly noticed *DogStar's* rocking anymore and moved around the boat with sure-footed confidence. His spirits lifted some more when the comforting smell of onions frying in butter greeted him from the galley (another one of those boat words). And they nearly soared when a sharp bark came from the harbour side of the boat. He fought down the question he wanted to ask every time Patsy Ann showed up, *Now? Is it time now?* Instead he clambered up the stairs to open the wheelhouse door and let her in.

Patsy Ann followed Jeff back down to the saloon, ducking underneath the table to sit and plant her grimy white side firmly against Jeff's legs. There she stayed, while the Captain added boiled potatoes and spinach from a can to the steaming skillet. *Ohmigosh, it's Popeye!* Jeff bent down to hide his smile and share the joke with Patsy Ann. She had her muzzle up on his knee now. Her eyes met his. His earlier doubts came back to him. Jeff looked into the dark, intelligent brown eyes. *I remember,* he saw there.

There was a sizzle in the galley and the rich aroma of frying halibut filled the deckhouse. Dark had fallen outside the portholes and the yellow light of the oil lamp gleamed on brass fittings and glossy varnish. The wind was up again, and *DogStar* murmured and creaked on her sturdy new lines.

Minutes later, they sat down to a dinner that tasted better than anything Jeff could remember ever being served at the fancy resorts where Mom and Dad took him. *Good thing they can't see this,* he thought, wolfing down a buttery forkful of spinach. *Ruin my image.* He chuckled.

After they were done they sat back, Jeff on the soft cushioned bench and the Captain in his deep armchair, and regarded their empty plates with satisfaction. At Jeff's feet, Patsy Ann licked her forepaws, running her pink tongue with concentration between each pair of toes, in case she had missed a flake of halibut or crumb of potato there.

The rising wind grumbled and shrieked through the boat basin. Out in the darkness, it set loose ropes on other boats whipping against masts in a tiresome tattoo. Indoors, the oil lamp swung in its brass gimbals, sending light and shadow chasing after each other along the cabin walls.

"Halifax," the Captain said thoughtfully. "I was there once or twice."

Jeff tucked his toes further in under Patsy Ann, feeling her warm fur press down and lift up again in a gentle rhythm as she breathed. He looked at the Captain and waited for more.

"First time would have been, let me see, '93, I guess."

Eh? Jeff cocked his head and looked at the old man. *How could he do that? Does* he *time travel too?* Then it came to him. *Jerk! He means 1893.*

"I would have been your age. Thirteen. Just a young squab on *Elissa,* a schooner. My grandfather's ship. Pretty thing, 119 feet on the waterline, deep Yankee blue with gold trim at her beak and transom. Sails like clouds." The grey eyes looked into the distance, remembering.

"That year we were three months on the Grand Banks. Fishing cod every day, gutting and salting every night. Falling dead in our bunks at eight bells and getting up again at first light." The Captain's face cracked in a leathery smile and he shook his head. "Ninety-four days to fill the hold, then we turned and reached for Boston."

A strong gust set *DogStar* shivering and rocking at the dock. The oil flame wavered and flared. "Two hundred miles off Nova Scotia, we caught the tail of a Bahamas hurricane. It blew for six days. We couldn't light the stove. No proper meals, just ship's biscuit and water, when we could keep it down. Swinging on the end of a spar hauling sail in the dark with the gale going by you. Soaked all the time."

One hand rested on the Captain's chest as he spoke. He fingered something Jeff hadn't noticed before. A medallion hung at the base of the leathery neck. It seemed to be made of bone or ivory. There were markings on it Jeff couldn't make out.

"We left the Banks with fourteen ton of cod. By the third day of the hurricane, we were at the pumps watch on, watch off. We began throwing the cod over the side, trying to lighten her. Three more days that storm ran. Took us another week after that to raise Halifax. By the time we made port we were like living ghosts. Our sails in rags and only half a mainmast. And three ton of cod, and that half-spoiled. Barely paid the chandler's bill." The Captain laughed again. *DogStar* shook in the wind and her new lines creaked as they stretched. He shot a look at Jeff. "It was a lucky voyage, lad."

Jeff looked back, letting his disbelief show. *How's that go? Lucky?*

Lamplight glittered in the dark grey eyes. "Eighteen hands shipped out on *Elissa*. And eighteen hands sailed home."

The Captain's eyes held a distant look. The wind whistled and chattered in the night. Patsy Ann turned in her sleep and rolled closer to the boy.

THE NEXT MORNING, Jeff heard the Captain moving around and pulled himself stiffly out of his bunk. He smelled coffee. *Real* *coffee … Dad would hate it.* Jeff's father put caffeine up there with monosodium glutamate and illegal drugs.

Jeff pulled on his jeans and the borrowed jersey and headed aft. The Captain had been right, it had really taken only a day for his stomach to stop flip-flopping. And sleeping on a boat had to be the best in the world.

"'Morning, Captain," he chimed cheerfully, plopping himself down at the galley table.

"Top of the morning to you too," the Captain replied. He seemed to be in an excellent mood, humming as he stirred the porridge. He poured coffee into two mugs.

"Lad, " the Captain said, setting a steaming mug in front of Jeff, "you've worked steady and hard these past days. Another week of the same and we'll be ready to slip our moorings." He placed a bowl of porridge beside the mug. "I'm thinking you're due for a turn of lighter duty this morning."

A break from scraping, hauling and heavy lifting? Awright! "You bet, Captain!"

"With you aboard we've been going through the water double quick," the older man went on. "We're near to dry. After breakfast we'll fill the tank."

The Captain squinted at a sunbeam slanting into the cabin. "And I think I'll lay a course for church. I'm not one for organized praying as a general rule, but I'm feeling more thankful today than I have in years. I think maybe it's time I let the good Lord know I'm grateful."

Church wasn't exactly the kind of break that Jeff had in mind. But the Captain soon relieved his worry. "You can't come, of course. You just stay here out of sight and when the tank's full, turn off the water."

When they had stacked their clean mugs and bowls, the Captain poked the business end of a thick black rubber hose through one of *DogStar*'s portholes. Jeff pulled it the rest of the way into the cabin. Once again the Captain pulled up a patch of the floor, this time revealing the gun-metal grey top of a tank. Unscrewing a fitting the size of a paint-can lid, he thrust the hose nozzle inside and pulled the attached lever a quarter turn. Jeff heard water gush into the darkness below his feet.

"Keep an eye on that now," the Captain said, "or we'll be bailing out our bunks." He chuckled as he shrugged into a black suit jacket that had seen better days. Nodding to Jeff he climbed the stairs to the wheelhouse. *DogStar* rocked gently as he stepped off her onto the dock.

Alone, Jeff checked out the old man's small collection of books. Most were technical volumes about seafaring. Then he found one by somebody called H.G. Wells. It was called *The Time Machine*. Jeff took it with him and stepped out onto the deck. *The port deck*, he reminded himself, out of sight of shore. He settled into a corner out of the wind, where the rising sun warmed the cabin wall, and opened the book.

He had read no more than a page when he heard the familiar bark. Jeff poked his head cautiously around the corner of the cabin and saw Patsy Ann trotting down the docks toward *DogStar*. The day was looking up. Then he saw another figure behind Patsy Ann's, a small one in blue over-alls and checked shirt and pigtails ... *Rose*.

Jeff ducked his head back out of sight. He felt his heart pounding in his chest. *Oh jeez, what now?* He snuck another look past the corner of the cabin. *Hmm. Funny.* Rose was carrying something, holding it carefully in front of her with both hands. And she had something on her head — something like a brown helmet. He watched as the slim figure stepped confidently from float to float, making steadily for *DogStar*.

She was still several docks away when he caught the aroma of fresh pie. He slipped across *DogStar*'s open back deck, ducking to avoid the two heavy poles that hung there waiting for sails. *Gaff and boom*, Captain Harper had called them. By the time he reached the side of the boat facing the dock, *the starboard side*, Rose was standing on the tilted float looking up at him. In front of her she held a pie. A basket was turned upside down on her head; she wore it like a hat.

"Hi," she said.

"Hi," Jeff replied. He was surprised at how glad he was to see her.

"Momma sent the Captain a pie." Rose held it out for him to inspect. "I didn't tell her about you."

"It looks really good," he said. Berry juice had leaked out of a slash in the top, staining the golden crust red and sending up a tart, flavourful smell.

"It's strawberry," Rose said. She met his level grey gaze with her own lively green one. "Can I come on the boat?"

Jeez, where are your manners, goof? "Uh, sure. I mean, 'Permission to board.'" *Maybe I should invite her in and we could have a piece of pie in the galley. No one would see us there.* The girl stepped lightly up over the low rail, Patsy Ann following at her heels.

Rose stepped across the wheelhouse and carefully placed the pie on the broad shelf that ran from side to side beneath the windshield. "I'm supposed to bring this to the Captain, then go pick some more strawberries," she said, turning to Jeff. "Want to come?"

And get off this boat? You know it, but ... "I can't," he said. "I have to stay out of sight, remember?"

"It's not far, and we can get there along the water. No one will see you."

"Really, I can't."

Rose stretched herself up to her full height and looked at him as though measuring him. "Chicken?" she asked.

"No way!" *No girl is gonna call me chicken, especially one wearing a basket on her head.*

"So? What are you afraid of?" Her eyebrows were raised, daring him to wimp out. He looked down at Patsy Ann, but she was no help on this one.

"How far is it?" he asked, playing for time.

"Just over there." Rose pointed toward the footpath that led back to Juneau.

"OK, smartypants. Let's go!" He grabbed the basket off her head.

Off *DogStar* Rose led the way. Jeff followed her and Patsy Ann brought up the rear. The docks were busy on this sunny Sunday morning. Jeff heard the sound of someone hammering. Sails slapped in the breeze. A heavy engine throbbed and sent blue smoke up into the morning from a green fishboat.

Several times they had to step aside to avoid coils of rope or long sausages of bleached fishnet. And several times it was a person they had to step aside for, someone burdened with cans of paint or foul-smelling buckets of bait. One or two stopped for a word with Patsy Ann. But as far as Jeff could tell, no one gave the two kids a second look.

At the top of the gangway that led to shore, they turned left and were soon on the footpath that followed the water. Below them along the shore, green and yellow seaweeds glistened where low tide had left them exposed to the sun. On the other side of the path, bushes hid the foot of a gravelly embankment that sloped up to the main road from Juneau. After so many days of *DogStar*'s gentle but incessant rocking, it felt good to be on land again. Though now, for some reason, he noticed that the solid ground seemed to be moving underneath him almost as much as *DogStar* did.

Rose had been right about how close the berries were. After about five minutes, she took Jeff's hand and pulled him through a break in the bushes on their right. Hidden behind them was a windless slope where a thick carpet of ground-cover grew up the warm gravel of the embankment. The air smelled sweet and almost sticky. Among the clusters of saw-toothed leaves, hundreds of berries glowed.

"See!" said Rose, kneeling on the ground and instantly plucking out a spray of four scarlet berries. She held it up to Jeff.

"Awesome!"

He sat beside her and they began filling the basket with berries. Jeff used what he thought of as the alternate destination plan: *One for the basket, one for me.* Patsy Ann lay stretched out in the sun, idly nibbling berries. A question hit him. "Rose," he asked, "why does everyone in Juneau pick on Captain Harper?"

"They think he sank a ship on purpose."

"On *purpose?*"

"Well, because it was full of money, millions and millions of dollars. People say he wanted to steal it."

"But he doesn't have any money," Jeff objected. "I mean, look at his boat."

"My momma says she won't believe it until it's proved," Rose said, popping berries into her mouth. "'Innocent 'til proven guilty.'" She gave Jeff a long look. "Why can't anyone know you're here?" she asked.

Jeff concentrated on his picking while he thought about how to answer her. *'Cause I'm wanted in twelve states, shweetheart. Like whatsisname … Bogie. 'Cause I'm really from the future, like that other old guy … Buck Rogers.* "It's kind of a long story," he stalled.

Beside him, Patsy Ann pulled herself forward on her round little belly to where a fresh patch of strawberries beckoned. Juice stained her muzzle, legs and stomach.

"Where *are* you from?" Rose asked.

Oh boy. "I'm from Canada. And I got here … well, by mistake." *Now* there *is an understatement.* "I … I mistook Patsy Ann for Buddy. He's my dog and my best friend and … he looks just like Patsy Ann."

Rose nodded.

"So when I saw Patsy Ann, I thought it was Buddy and I followed her and got lost and here I am!" He looked up at Rose and beamed his best *trust me!* smile.

She looked across the basket at him, eyes thoughtful. "If you're here," she asked finally, "who's taking care of Buddy?"

Something seemed to let go inside of him, falling down a bottomless hole forever and leaving that familiar empty feeling. "No one. Buddy's dead." His eyes watered again. *Darn it, I don't want to cry in front of a girl. Maybe she'll think it was the sun.* He looked up at the sun and squinted manfully.

"My poppa's dead, too," said Rose quietly. "I miss him a lot sometimes. I wish I could see him again, just once."

Jeff stole a sideways glance at Rose. Captain Harper had said she had been just a baby when her father died. Was it easier when you couldn't remember someone? Or was it worse? "I know what that feels like," he said. *I'd give anything to wake up just one more time and see Buddy's big toothy grin.*

"Miss Avery says my poppa's waiting for me in heaven and if I'm good I'll be seeing him there."

"Do you believe that?"

"Sometimes. I don't know."

"My father says I have to learn to let go of Buddy."

"Do you believe that?"

"Sometimes. Who's Miss Avery?"

"She's my Sunday School teacher."

A vision of the Captain dressed for "organized praying" formed in Jeff's mind ... only to be chased away by his parting instruction to keep an eye on the hose gushing water into *DogStar*'s tank "or we'll be bailing out our bunks."

Jeff's stomach turned to ice. He leapt to his feet. "Rose! I have to get back! I'm sorrythanksbye," he burbled all in a rush and set off at a run.

He hit the foot of the gangway and tore down the rocking floats, dodging paint cans and nets.

I wonder how long church goes on? Maybe I can beat him back. So far, so good, he thought, as he rounded the last corner and *DogStar* came into sight. Then he froze.

Jeff's heart beat loudly in his ears. Some inside part of him felt as though it were tying itself in a knot around his ice-block of a stomach.

DogStar lolled sluggishly, visibly low in the water. Mooring ropes taut as bowstrings groaned as she rolled. Looking down he could see the fresh paint of her waterline catching the sun's rays several inches below the surface of the sea.

twelve

BUSTED

A GUSH of water from an opening in *DogStar*'s hull broke Jeff's trance. For the first time he noticed the black water hose lying on the dock, the nozzle tightly closed.

Fighting off an urge to turn and bolt back to shore ... *And then where?...* Jeff braced himself and stepped onto the boat. Down below he found the Captain up to the ankles of his Sunday shoes in water, heaving back and forth on a wooden lever. With each heave, Jeff heard a gush as the boat's pump shot a spout of water overboard. Floorboards floated about, banging into each other and the Captain's feet as the boat rocked heavily.

Wordlessly, Jeff stepped to the Captain's side and added his own weight to the effort.

The Captain fell back onto the settee for a moment, breathing heavily. Jeff felt the old man's gaze fixed on him in cold disapproval and anger.

Looking up he saw Patsy Ann. She lay on the wheelhouse floor, her front paws and long nose draped over the edge of the companionway down to the saloon. For the first time, her eyes refused to meet his.

Jeff kept pumping.

After a few minutes the Captain gathered himself and rejoined Jeff at the pump. Silent except for their heavy breathing, the two kept at it, heaving back and forth and listening to the rhythmic gush of water being vomited out into the harbour.

It seemed to take forever but after what felt like hours, even if it was only minutes, Jeff could see that the sloshing tide at their feet was receding. Floorboards came to rest akilter in their frames. At last the pump sucked emptily on air. *DogStar's* movements were once again quick and lively.

Their work was far from done, however. For the next several hours the two laboured in strained silence to pull out drawers and drain the puddles left inside them, wring out sodden clothes and hang them over rails and spars, and finally to wipe dry again the gleaming varnish of the small saloon. Jeff's face burned as he once again hung his soaked Nikes up to dry in his small cabin.

At long last they dropped exhausted into their usual seats. Jeff eyed the Captain warily.

For a long time the grey eyes regarded him coldly in return. "Well, Mr. Beacon?"

"It … Sir … Captain sir … It was Rose." The steely gaze did not waver. "She came with a pie from her mother." Jeff pointed over his head to where the pie sat untasted and forgotten in the wheelhouse. "And she needed me to help her pick more strawberries."

"And where was that?"

"Just past the harbour," he nodded in the general

direction. "On the embankment behind the bushes."

Another long and frigid silence followed.

"My grandfather would have had you whipped," the Captain finally snapped. "Twice. Once for endangering your vessel. And a second time for being behind a bush with a female."

Jeff felt a cold sweat break out on his neck. He'd heard about corporal punishment, stuff like the strap they used to use at school. *But whips?*

"Let me remind you, Mr. Beacon, of a number of facts." Captain Harper's words came out like strokes of a lash. "First, you are a crewman aboard this vessel. That means you follow your orders, when given and as given. Anything less is a danger to yourself, to your shipmates and to your ship. As I hope" the word dripped with sarcasm, "is now clear to you.

"Secondly, you are a fugitive. By giving you a berth aboard *DogStar* I may be falling a'lee of the law myself. I have enough differences of my own with the people of Juneau, Mr. Beacon. I don't need you adding to them.

"And third, there aren't so many places even in Juneau ready to take in a wanted boy. You might wish to think about that before you abandon your post again."

The Captain's expression seemed to warm up a half-degree or so above absolute zero. "Now, I'll not take a whip to you. I didn't believe in the cat then and I don't believe in it now. But I'll not tolerate a crew I cannot trust."

Jeff struggled to put his heart into his voice. "Please,

Captain Harper, I'm sorry. I didn't think. I won't do it again. Please let me stay."

The Captain's fierce gaze fell to where Patsy Ann lay at his feet. "What do you say, girl? You brought this young stray here. *You* tell me. Do we give him what he deserves? Or a second chance?"

Patsy Ann stood and put her muzzle on the Captain's lap. She looked into his face. Then she put one front foot up on his knee and barked.

The Captain regarded Jeff skeptically. At last he sighed and said, "I may be mad. Maybe it's living alone too long. Or living too long with no-one to talk to but a dog. A dog who can't hear me, no less." He scratched Patsy Ann's deaf ears. "But aye, ye can stay."

Before Jeff could get his thanks out, the Captain cut him off. "For now, lad, for now." He stood up and eyed Jeff. "But fail your duty again, Mr. Beacon, and you find another ship."

SUPPER THAT NIGHT was a silent affair. For the first time since he'd come aboard *DogStar,* Jeff thought the Captain's cooking (it was fried pork chops and boiled potatoes) was boring. He found himself wishing he were back in Halifax, with Mom's home cooking. *Yeah, right. "Hy-Ho's by phone for Chinese-deli to the door."* The silly jingle ran annoyingly around in his exhausted brain. Not even thick slices of Mrs. Baker's strawberry pie broke the chill. If anything, Jeff felt a little worse, chewing on the tart reminder of how impulsively he had left the boat on Rose's dare.

There was no colourful sea tale after dinner that night, either. Just a curt "Good night, Mr. Beacon." Nor was there a warm white dog to hug during the night. Patsy Ann had gone off on her own business without sharing their cheerless meal.

MONDAY MORNING was not much better. The weather had turned cold again, and a strong wind from the sea pushed boiling banks of dark cloud ahead of it up the channel. The chill seemed to seep right through *DogStar*'s seams. Jeff yanked on the new pair of jeans the Captain had bought him. For warmth, he put on his denim jacket over the borrowed blue pullover.

The Captain continued the silent treatment through breakfast, which was porridge *again*. While Jeff ate, he let his mind drift to home. *Are Mom and Dad really back in Halifax by now? Or did they stay in Juneau, looking for him? Where is Buddy? Does he think I deserted him?*

"Ready, Mr. Beacon?" the Captain intruded on his thoughts.

No. "Yes." Jeff wished the Captain would knock off the "Mr. Beacon" stuff.

That morning, the Captain said, they were going to "flake the anchor rode." This turned out to mean pulling a rusty chain through a hole in *DogStar*'s foredeck and passing it, hand over hand, down to the dock, where they stretched it out in long, rust-coloured loops over the mossy wood. The chain was heavy and crumbs of orange rust came off it as he passed it through his hands.

When the clouds tore apart to let the strong northern sun shine through, it quickly became hot work. Jeff threw off his jacket. He continued to pass the chain down to where the Captain was laying it out on the dock. By the time they had all of the chain on the dock, the sun was almost directly overhead and the waterlogged old float was half sunk under the weight of iron.

Jeff shook sweat out of his eyes and looked around. He did a double take. He'd been so intent on the work that he hadn't noticed Patsy Ann come aboard. She had settled herself in comfort on the sun-warmed denim of his jacket, where it had fallen at the foot of *DogStar's* wheelhouse.

"Now take this end of the chain and feed it back into the hole," the Captain said.

Jeff stood, swaying a little with weariness and the rock of *DogStar's* deck, and looked down at the Captain. In his hand he held one end of the chain up to Jeff. It was the other end, the one they had first pulled out onto the dock, the one that used to be attached to the anchor. Now, it seemed, he wanted Jeff to put the whole heavy chain back into the same stupid hole from which he had just pulled it, only the other way around from how it came out. *This*, Jeff thought, *must be what Captain Bligh did to bad guys, instead of making them break rocks.*

They had returned half a dozen loops of the chain to its place in *DogStar's* bows when Jeff felt a stinging pain in his right hand. It was wet, too. He stopped to look at it. A blister he'd been working on for days had finally burst. *Man, that hurts*. As he examined it more closely, he caught a sudden movement. Patsy Ann was still lying on his jacket, but her thick white head was up and turning toward the channel. A ray of sun glittered like starlight in her beady black eyes. White ears pointed alertly to the sky and her black nose strained the breeze for news. Then she got up, shook herself briskly and jumped off *DogStar* onto the dock. With purpose in her stride and not a look back, she trotted off down the floats toward shore.

"Hmph," the Captain grunted. "Must be a ship coming in."

A ship! Patsy Ann! It has to be … "Mom! Dad!" Jeff shouted. He looked to the sky, pumped both arms and yelled, *"Yesssss!"* He leapt over *DogStar*'s stubby rail and landed with a splash on the half-submerged dock. He grabbed the Captain's hand and shook it once. "I'm sorry, but I gotta go, Captain. It's my Mom and Dad. I knew they'd come back!"

Captain Harper stood rooted to the dock, mouth open in surprise. Jeff was past him already and beginning to run down the dock, clumping noisily in his new rubber boots.

"Thanks for everything," he yelled back over his shoulder. "See you another time!" *Like maybe in sixty years!* He put his head down and started pumping, trying to catch up with Patsy Ann. She was taking him home, he was sure of it.

Other people were also leaving their chores to follow the stocky white dog. By the time Jeff reached the row of cottages where Rose and her mother lived, Patsy Ann was leading a pack of twenty or thirty men, women and kids, all scurrying to keep up to her. They came to the warehouses at the foot of Franklin Street and skirted the inside of the mountain of coal. *Just a few seconds more and I'll be there*, Jeff thought, and skidded around the last tarpaulin-covered crate.

There was a ship at the dock, all right.

It was even a passenger liner.

But it wasn't the one he'd been hoping for, the one he'd expected to see. It was called the *Victoria*, and it was much smaller and vaguely more old-fashioned than the big, modern cruise ship the Beacons had arrived on. It had just two plain decks of cabins and *no pool, no driving range, no satellite domes*. Jeff was gasping from the run. He felt his heart pounding. *It's not my ship …*

"Well, look who's here," a thick, sarcastic voice said. Jeff felt a heavy hand come down on his shoulder and suddenly he was spinning around on the wooden wharf. He came to rest facing a broad blue-serge chest with two rows of brass buttons marching up it like airport landing lights and a fleshy red face at the top, set in an expression of satisfaction. "We've been looking for you," Sergeant Ed Kelly growled. "You've got some explaining to do, kid."

Jeff's hands were grabbed roughly and pulled behind him. He felt something cold with a hard edge come down around one wrist and then the other, and realized they were hand-cuffs. He heard Tommy McGraw's whine: "Guess we'll be splitting that 200-dollar reward from the chief, huh Sarge?"

"Sixty-forty," said Sergeant Kelly. "I saw him first."

"Think I'll take the wife to the Baranof for dinner," gloated Officer McGraw.

Kelly spun Jeff around again and each officer took one of the boy's arms. Roughly, they pulled and pushed him through the crowd of onlookers gathered to greet the ship.

Oh jeez! Jeff looked wildly around. *They're not here! I got it wrong, that's not the ship. And I really am going to jail. Oh darn, darndarnDARN!* He managed a look back over his shoulder. Patsy Ann was trotting along the edge of the wharf. Passengers were leaning from portholes to toss her treats. Patsy Ann was fielding them. Her tail was wagging and she was grinning hugely. *Even Patsy Ann's given up on me,* Jeff thought. His heart felt like a deflated balloon.

They reached the street curb. Tommy McGraw raised his hand to the driver of a large blue car with a single red globe light on its roof. Jeff heard the engine start. He looked across the roof of the car at the far side of the street and felt the last of his innards collapse into icy emptiness as he saw the Captain rounding the corner.

The Captain's face was flushed with exertion. He stood doubled over, hands on his knees, leaning against a utility pole. His chest shook as he tried to catch his breath. But his grey eyes were steady and hard as they met Jeff's.

The police officers pushed Jeff into the big blue car, climbed in beside him and drove away.

thirteen

TIME

PATSY ANN trotted across the quay to where the Captain sat on a bench. It had been a good ship. The passengers had been generous with their buns and pastries and slices of apple and Patsy Ann's stout tummy felt comfortably stretched. She ran her tongue around her chops and up over her nose anyway, just in case.

The Captain's shoulders drooped. The grey bristles on his weathered cheeks were lined into deep valleys. His grey eyes, usually so sharp and bright, were unfocused, seeming to stare off into mist and nothingness. He was no longer wheezing, but his chest still rose and fell unevenly. His brown hand was unsteady when he reached down to scratch Patsy Ann's ears.

"I don't know why you brought him to me, Patsy Ann. He's been nothing but trouble since he came aboard. I'm better off with him where he is."

Patsy Ann barked, a sharp note of protest.

"Easy for you to say, old girl, easy for you."

The old man gathered his energies and hoisted himself to his feet. Taking a deep breath, he hitched his belt higher on his hips, turned his back on the ship at the wharf, and started walking. He walked slowly back past the covered crates and the coal mountain in the direction of his boat. Patsy Ann walked with him, curtailing her usual brisk gait in order to stay at his side.

When they reached the stretch of road that ran past Sylvia Baker's and the other cottages, the Captain stopped and looked out across Gastineau Channel. On the far side of the sparkling water, the sun was almost touching the summit of Mount Douglas. Soon it would be down and Juneau would slip into the long dusk of a late summer evening. The evenings were already growing shorter and chillier as the summer waned. He looked down at his feet. Below him, the afternoon sun shone on the low groundcover of small green leaves that carpeted the gravel embankment. Hidden among the saw-toothed foliage, sweet-scented fruit glowed like jewels in the golden light. "Strawberries," the Captain said aloud and shook his head. "There's not much I could do, Patsy Ann, even if I had a mind to. I expect they'll turn him down for bail tomorrow."

He sighed and started walking again, Patsy Ann keeping step at his side. "I'll admit this to no-one but you, old girl," he said as they walked. "But I'll miss the boy, too. He made me feel as though I still had voyages to make." They turned down onto the gangway that led to the docks. "I guess he made me feel young again."

Patsy Ann's friend looked anything but young as the two came up to the last dock. *DogStar*'s new paint was brown with rust that had flaked from the anchor chain earlier in the day. The chain itself still dangled untidily from the rail down to the dock, where it lay, half awash, in long rusty loops. It took the Captain much longer, working alone, to haul the rest of the heavy chain up from the dock and feed it back into the little hole that led to the chain locker below the deck. When he finally had the whole length stowed and the free end shackled once again to *DogStar*'s iron anchor, it was dark. The sun had taken away its heat along with its light when it went down, and a cold dew was settling onto the varnished rails and oiled decks. The Captain grunted softly as he straightened his back and shook the cramps out of his shoulders.

Patsy Ann stood too. While the Captain worked, she had once again commandeered the boy's blue denim jacket, lying where he had tossed it during the hot morning so many hours ago. Now, she stretched extravagantly, "fore and aft" as the Captain thought of it, shook herself equally lavishly, and stepped off the soft cotton material onto the wooden deck.

The Captain was ahead of her, making for *DogStar*'s cabin. Patsy Ann barked. He looked back. She stood in place while the old man stepped forward again along the deck and bent down to retrieve the jacket. As Captain Harper straightened, his back gave off a creak. Patsy Ann nosed forward and ran her tongue over his gnarled hand. Then she followed him inside.

A match flared brightly and the old brown fingers held it against the wick of the oil lamp until the flame burned evenly. Yellow light flowed into the cold cabin. Jeff's jacket lay across the bench where Captain Harper had thrown it in the dark.

He stood in the galley, staring uncertainly at the two bowls, two mugs and two spoons that stood beside the tiny sink.

Patsy Ann barked. He turned.

The white Bull Terrier was up on the saloon bench. She was pawing at something. Looking past the edge of the varnished table, the Captain saw it was Jeff's jacket. He stepped closer. "What is it, girl? Something crawl into the pocket? A mouse?"

Patsy Ann's nose was pushing into the jacket. The black tip disappeared inside a pocket and the Captain heard her snap at something. Then her nose came back out of the denim and her muzzle came up. Something shiny and flat and brightly coloured hung from her teeth.

The Captain reached out his hand. Patsy Ann gave the brochure up to him. Then she put her tail down and sat, black eyes bright and watchful in the lamplight. Captain Harper sat beside her and examined the little booklet. His fingers rubbed the glossy paper. He opened the pages and began to read.

He looked at the ad for whale watching, and its picture of people in bright red overalls with matching headgear riding in a fast boat that appeared to be made out of giant rubber donuts. He looked at another one, at a machine like an insect with an oversize propeller on its head that took people skiing on the tops of mountains. And some Scotsman named McDonald claimed to have served "billions" at a Juneau restaurant he had never heard of. As he read, his grey eyebrows knitted slowly into a woolly hedge across his brow. Patsy Ann sidled closer to him, squeezing her hard little flanks tight against his hips and leaning heavily into the Captain's shoulder. Her warm breath and the wet flick of her tongue caressed his dry cheek.

DogStar rocked at her moorings. Ezra Harper sat straight up, eyes alive as he flipped through the pages of Jeffrey Beacon's brochure, at first slowly, then more quickly. In his clear grey eyes, curiosity gave way to confusion, doubt and then to a dawning, astounding certainty.

Suddenly he stopped, the brochure held open before him. His left hand reached up and played absent-mindedly with the silver chain hanging from his neck. He pulled it out from under his shirt and his fingers closed around the medallion at the end. The knuckles enclosing it turned white. In the lamp-light, his pale face looked like dried wood, sun-bleached and lifeless. In his right hand, the shiny pages shook.

A colour photograph showed a sheer rock face where a vein of white minerals formed a natural blaze reaching almost to the brilliant blue water at the bottom of the picture. The photograph faced an outline of the Alaskan coast with thin straight lines laid over it in a simple grid. Beside some of the vertical and horizontal lines were numbers.

For a long time, the Captain seemed not to breathe at all, then he began again. He blinked and shook his head violently. Then he leaned his head against Patsy Ann's and asked, "Who is this boy?"

He leafed through more pages. When he had gone through them all, he looked for a long time at the back cover. Then he went back and found the page with the picture again. "What in God's name is going on?" It was a whisper, almost a prayer.

He stood, and stepped away from the table to a drawer that was built into the opposite wall. His body cast a dark shadow in the flickering yellow light and for a moment he fumbled in the darkness. Then he found what he was looking for and tugged. The drawer opened with effort and he reached in.

When Captain Harper turned back into the light, he was carrying a book in one hand, its blue cover bleached and stained. In the other was a roll of heavy paper the colour of dark ivory.

He sat back down and laid them both on the saloon table.

fourteen

A VISITOR

SERGEANT KELLY and Tommy McGraw sat Jeff down on a wooden stool and stepped back.

He was in a room with no windows. The walls were painted pale olive green. *Sort of pastel snot.* The only other furnishings were a wooden table and two upright metal chairs. Overhead, fluorescent strips made the room artificially bright. A ventilator rattled in one corner.

I just want to hit the "back" button on the browser now ... But this was no computer screen. This was real. And he was in trouble, real trouble. *Oh Buddy, we gotta think fast here. They think my money is counterfeit. I'll just tell them I didn't know that the money was fake and they'll let me go.*

The door opened and two men came in.

One of them was only of medium height but very fat and almost bald. He had piggy blue eyes and a brush of dark moustache. The other one was tall and wore a police officer's uniform with four wide gold stripes at the cuffs.

"OK, boys," said the tall man in uniform, "you can wait in the squad room."

The bald fat man placed one of the chairs behind the table and sat down on it facing Jeff. The police officer came and stood in front of him. "Empty your pockets," he said.

Jeff looked at him helplessly and waggled his arms. They were still handcuffed behind him.

The tall man in uniform flushed scarlet and yanked open the door. "Kelly!" he yelled out into the hall.

"Yes, Chief?" Jeff heard the sergeant's thick voice. *Yikes, this is the Chief of Police.*

"Gimme yer keys," Chief Beggs growled. He grabbed the ring that Kelly produced and turned back into the room, slamming the door closed behind him.

He stepped around behind the boy. Jeff heard a click and the handcuffs released their grip on his wrists.

"Now stand up and empty your pockets," Beggs said again.

Jeff did as the chief had asked. Standing, he patted himself down. He was wearing the Captain's borrowed jersey; it didn't have any pockets. In the new pair of work denims the Captain had bought him, he found three rusty screws and a bent piece of steel he'd used to scrape paint from *DogStar*'s curved rails. He patted his hip. *Oh yeah, and my wallet.* He pulled the thin billfold from his back pocket and put it with the screws and the hunk of brass on the table.

The chief stepped back as the fat man pounced on the wallet, pulling it open and shaking out its contents. Two American twenties fell out and fluttered onto the table. His thick fingers pawed at the little window in Jeff's wallet and soon afterward his "phone home" card joined the bills on the grey metal tabletop.

"Step back and sit down," ordered Chief Beggs.

Eagerly, the other man's pink fingers snatched the two bills and held them up. The moon face beamed. Then he examined each bill closely, using a jeweler's glass to peer at the paper, and holding it up against the bright tubes in the ceiling. "Astonishing, Beggs," he sighed. "Brilliant." He leaned forward and fixed his tiny blue eyes on Jeff. "Where are the plates?" he snapped.

"Pardon me?"

"And the paper? Where are you getting paper?"

Eh? "You're looking for dinnerware and stationery?"

"Watch your mouth, punk," Chief Beggs growled from behind him. *Oops, wrong room for humour.*

The fat man held up the two twenty-dollar bills and dangled them from his fingers. "Forty dollars is a pretty fat roll for a kid to be packing. Too bad these are both as phony as Russian stock certificates." He placed them carefully side by side on the table. "Phony ... but almost perfect." He reached inside his suit jacket and pulled out a third twenty-dollar bill and laid it beside the other two. "Just like this one. Perfect. All three identical in the quality of the work. Products of the same master of the craft."

He leaned forward again. "And all three either found on your person or seized as you tried to pay for lunch with a laughably large note. An obvious ploy to pass the paper and still end up with a useful amount of clean cash."

"I don't know about any counterfeit anything!" Jeff heard his own voice echo off the bare walls. He sounded scared.

Surely they don't put you in jail for an honest mistake, even in Alaska.

"One fake bill might be an accident, punk," Beggs said, coming around to stand beside the table. "Two might even be coincidence. But three can mean only one thing: counterfeit currency. That's a twenty-year rap, punk. Think about it."

"How old are you, kid?" the fat man asked.

About minus fifty-three. "Thirteen, sir. Almost fourteen."

"Well there's nothing here that proves it. Your name Jeffrey Beacon?"

"Yes, sir."

"Then who's this *Kenneth L.* Beacon?"

Eh?

The fat man held up the "Phone Home" card. It was on Jeff's father's account and showed both their names.

"That's my dad."

"And where is he?"

Well, nowhere right now, because he hasn't been born. "Uh ... I'm not sure. He brought me here to Juneau. But then we got ... separated. I'm not sure where he is now."

"You'll have to do better than that," Chief Beggs growled. He picked up the calling card. "What is this thing anyway, some kind of secret society? What do all these numbers mean? That some kind of code? You a spy?"

The fat man cut in. "How long have you been in Juneau? And how did you get here?" His blue eyes narrowed into glittering slits between pink pouches of flesh.

Jeff tried to count off the days. *Too much has happened.* He guessed. "A week," he said. "We came on a ship."

"Of course you came on a ship," snarled the fat man. "There's no other way to *get* to Juneau."

"The *Passage Princess.* It's a cruise ship."

"He's lying," barked Beggs. "There's no such ship."

"Anyway," the fat man reasoned, "the *Victoria* is the first cruise ship we've had in three weeks. You're lying."

"I'm telling the truth!"

The fat man turned to the chief. "Check the passenger list on the *Victoria*. If there's any chance he's telling even part of the truth, I want this 'father' of his found. His accomplice, more likely."

Oh great. Dad's going to be a wanted man before he's even born. And it's all my fault.

"And hear me, kid," the fat face leaned across the table. Jeff could see greasy crumbs in his moustache. "I don't care how old you really are. You keep with the tight lip, you're going down for a stretch, a long stretch, with some bad palookas. You know what sharks like that will do with a fresh little fish like you?"

Not exactly, Jeff thought. *Only that TV heavies always ask that question to scare kids about jail, so it must be pretty bad.* He had some ideas actually, but he didn't like to dwell on them.

"Well, you think about it, kid. Because here's the deal." The fat man licked his thick pink lips. The crumbs stayed on his moustache. "You take me to those plates and this paper, and you sail out of Juneau free as a bird on the next ship. Clam up on me, and you last as long as you last in the Big

House." He looked at the man in the uniform. "How long do you give him, Beggs?"

"In the Big House? Six months, tops. They'll take him out in a box."

"Or maybe …" the fat face leered at Jeff across the table. "Maybe you'll manage to keep that sorry skin alive. And when you come out … your own mother won't recognize you."

I'd have to do sixty years. Is that possible? I'd be old enough to be my mother's father! "Really, mister, I can't help you. I'm telling you the truth and I don't know anything about any plates or paper."

The men kept him sweating in strained silence for a little longer, then Beggs stepped to the door and yelled, "Kelly!"

The sergeant and the other police officer returned and frog-marched him toward the door. Before they got to it, the fat man stopped them. "Kid!" Jeff turned. "Think about it."

They took him out the door, along a corridor and down several flights of broad stairs. At the bottom, they came to a wide green steel door. It shut behind them with a metallic clang that echoed in the bare corridor beyond.

They made him stand up against a wall and took his picture facing forward and then facing the side. *Just like in the movies. Or on the late news.* Suddenly he felt very afraid.

A small man with black hair, wearing a different uniform, opened a door made out of painted steel bars and the two police officers took him through. It led into a corridor with similar doors all along one side. They stopped at one near the end. The little guy turned a key and opened this door too. Strong arms pushed him forward and the door clanged shut behind him. He heard a *snick* as the key turned.

Jeff was alone in a cell just a bit longer than he was himself, and about as wide. Along one side was a bare metal bench. An olive-coloured blanket was folded at one end. The white porcelain thing in the corner looked like it was meant to do double duty as a sink and a john. *Whatever, it's gross.*

He looked up. The ceiling was way up there, much higher than he could reach. A wire grill protected a single bulb. In the corner above the bed was a small window, reinforced with wire and grey with dust. There were bars in front of it.

Jeff took two steps forward, turned, and sat down in the middle of the metal bunk. He was shaking, he realized. His head felt light. *Shock.* The word for these sensations came to him. *We took this in health class.* He swiveled and swung his legs up onto the bench, lay back and let his head fall onto the folded blanket.

Well bozo, he told himself, *this is what you get for running off half-cocked like a jerk.* He looked up at the bare, unpainted cement ceiling. *And boy does it SUCK! What will they do with me? Will they really send me to the Big House ... or was that just to scare me?* Even if they sent him to some kind of junior prison for kids, Jeff was pretty sure it wasn't going to be a barrel of laughs.

The Captain must hate him. *Aw jeez!* Captain Harper was such a good guy. He had given Jeff a second chance. Whatever the town thought, he'd been fair and kind to Jeff. *And I let him down ... again.* He heard noises from down the row of cells, someone cursing the guard. Other prisoners, he thought. *I'm a prisoner. I'm in jail. Now I'll never see home again!*

He wouldn't mind so much being in jail if he could just have Buddy with him. He remembered how his friend always knew his moods and would come to him with a rope or stick when he was feeling down, to make him play until he felt better. Now, he didn't see how he'd ever feel better again.

Even if I get home, Buddy will still be dead. And if I'm in jail ... his throat felt thick. *If I'm in jail, how can Patsy Ann help me?*

JEFF HAD BEEN in the cell about an hour when the little guard with black hair came back. He was carrying a tray with a bowl and a mug on it.

"Stand back from the door, kid," he said, his voice not unfriendly.

Jeff stood at the back of the cell. The guard put the tray down on the end of the metal bed, stepped out of the cell, and closed and locked the door again.

"*Bon appetit,*" he said before disappearing.

"*Merci,*" Jeff answered weakly.

It was wieners and beans, heavy on the beans. The mug contained milk. He ate hungrily, thinking of the Captain's savoury pork chops and potatoes.

When he was done, he was still hungry. *Please, sir ... can I have some more? Yeah, that's me, Oliver Beacon. Nah. Seconds aren't likely to be on the jail menu.*

After a while, the same dark little guy came and made Jeff go through the same back-of-the-cell routine while he took the tray away again. A little later, the overhead lights went out. A bulb somewhere down near the far end of the corridor cast a weak light and long shadows over the wall opposite Jeff's cell. Jeff lay on the metal bed and fought back the tears. It was cold in the dark cell. He had never felt so alone, never so scared.

He heard steps in the corridor. Footsteps, and *something else?*

"You have a visitor, kid," the little guy with the black hair said. There was a soft *chink* and the door to his cell opened just wide enough to let Patsy Ann's broad white shoulders push through. Then it closed again. In the dim light, Jeff thought he caught a wink from the man between the bars.

Patsy Ann climbed stiffly onto the bed beside him and stretched out in the dark. Her wet tongue found his face, licking until he pushed her away. Then she buried her nose in his neck and lay still until they both fell asleep.

fifteen

AT THE COURTHOUSE

THE BLACK-HAIRED jailer let Patsy Ann out when he brought Jeff his breakfast of scrambled eggs and cold toast and coffee. When he came back later to get the tray, he stopped for a moment at the door of the cell and looked at Jeff. The small man's face was thoughtful and, Jeff thought, even a little sympathetic.

"Scared, kid?"

Uh-huh. "No."

"Sure," the little guy stood in the door, tray in his hands. "Let me tell ya something my mother used to tell me, kid. Seems there was these two frogs, fell into a bucket of cream. They both tried to jump out but they couldn't do it. The first frog gave up. Told himself, 'I can't jump out of here, so I might as well drown.' An' that's just what he did."

The guy cocked his head and looked Jeff in the eye. "But it seems the other frog figured it different. 'There's only two things in the world I know how to do,' that frog told hisself. 'Swim and jump. Since jumping don't do me no good, I'll just swim 'til I think of something else.' And ya know what happened, kid? That there frog swam and swam, as hard as he could, kickin' them long back legs out behind him like a regular champion. And it wasn't too long before he began to feel something happening around him. He kicked so hard, that there cream turned into butter! And as soon as it did, froggie got his footing and jumped right out of the bucket."

The steel bars of Jeff's cell clanged shut, and this time the man *definitely* winked through them. "You keep swimming, kid," he said, and whistled his way down the corridor.

Officer McGraw came for Jeff later that morning. Once again, he put the boy in handcuffs. This time though, Jeff was allowed to keep his hands in front of him instead of behind his back.

McGraw led him upstairs and out a side door to a small blue panel truck. *So this is a paddy wagon,* thought Jeff. *It looks like they stuck a packing crate on a Model-T.* Inside, benches ran down both sides of the narrow vehicle. Officer McGraw motioned Jeff to sit on one and plumped himself down facing the boy on the other.

The paddy wagon rocked alarmingly at corners but the drive was short. At the end of it, Jeff was led out of the truck, into another side door and up more stairs. Finally, McGraw escorted him into a large room with a high ceiling, sat him in a chair behind a large empty table and removed the handcuffs.

Facing him was a judge's raised bench and broad desk, with the Stars and Stripes standing behind it on a polished flagstaff. To his right was a desk identical to his own. Chief Beggs sat there, whispering to the fat bald man who had been with him the night before. Looking over his shoulder Jeff recognized a sort of wooden fence separating the working part of the court from rows of wooden benches worn shiny with use.

The room hummed with half-suppressed chatter. In front of the judge's bench, two women sorted stacks of papers and gossiped with someone in a grey uniform like the one the jailor had worn. Scattered thinly around the pew-like benches was a mixture of people in twos and threes, some in dresses or suits and some in work trousers and open shirts.

One man sat thin and upright a little apart from his nearest neighbour. Embarrassment washed over Jeff like a hot, sticky wave at the sight of the grizzled beard and familiar blue jersey. Across the room, the grey eyes looked at him evenly. Jeff tried to read their mood. *Probably came to see me get what I deserve,* he thought glumly.

Then he saw two things he would never have expected. First, by craning his neck just a little, Jeff recognized the patch of white on the Captain's knee; it was Patsy Ann's thick head and pointed ears. Then he caught the Captain's eye ... and the Captain *winked! Holy cow!* Jeff gaped. *Did I really see that? If everybody's winking, I must have a chance!*

His attention was pulled back to the front of the court-room by a large voice announcing: "All rise!"

A tall man in black robes came through a door beside the flag and stepped up onto the bench. He arranged his robes beneath him and sat down. The large voice, which belonged to a man with an equally large belly declared: "U.S. District Court, Southeast Alaska Division, is in session. The Honourable Henry T. Burns presiding."

Judge Burns rapped his gavel once and ran his eyes around the room. Then addressing the women at the tables near his feet, he said, "Clerk, what is the charge?"

A woman in a print dress stood and read out something written on a piece of paper. She read with the speed and intonation of a freight train and Jeff caught only part of it. "That Jeffery Beacon, also known as Kenneth L. Beacon, did ... in Juneau, Alaska ... fraudulently utter or attempt to utter ... counterfeit currency ... in violation of the U.S. Penal Code ..."

Holy doodle. "In violation of the penal code." It sounded way more serious read out like this in a courtroom. *Keep cool, breathe deep,* he told himself. He glanced back at the Captain and Patsy Ann. *Friends, just remember you have friends.*

"Young man," Judge Burns was saying, apparently not for the first time. *"Young man!"*

"Yes, sir. I mean, your honour." Jeff had been to court in Canada to see his Dad at work and had heard him call judges "My Lord." But he figured that was probably a Canadian thing.

"How do you plead?"

"Not guilty, your honour."

"I see. Well then, this court will bind you over for trial ..." he looked expectantly at the woman in the print dress, who stood and whispered something up at him. The judge nodded and continued, "... two weeks from today." The woman smiled and sat back down at her table.

"Now," Judge Burns looked across at Jeff and then at the table where Beggs sat. "In the matter of bail, who speaks for the people?"

Beggs stood. "I do, your honour. Chief of Police Carter Beggs. With me is Mr. J. Samuel Shrite, Mayor of the City of Juneau, president of the Chamber of Commerce and ..."

"I know who he is," the judge cut in. "And who you are, too, Chief. Get on with it." Suppressed laughter rippled over the benches until Judge Burns' glare brought silence. *Holy cow, that's the mayor*, Jeff thought with alarm as his eyes rested on the fat man.

"The people strongly object to granting bail, your honour. This suspect has no known address in Alaska, is possibly an alien, has no documentation and was found with a mitt full of phony twenties." Chief Beggs rocked back on his feet and concluded, "Red-handed, your honour. We got him red-handed."

Judge Burns looked balefully at Beggs. Then he raised his voice and addressed the room. "And does anyone speak for the accused?"

Jeff looked around. *Isn't there something about the right to a lawyer?* But the chair beside him was empty.

Judge Burns opened his mouth to sat something, but then another voice cut him off.

"I'll speak for the lad." Captain Harper stood.

A ripple of comment ran around the court, silenced by a rap of the judge's gavel. "The court recognizes Captain Ezra Harper."

"Your honour," the Captain's voice rang out strongly in the high-ceilinged chamber, "I'll vouch for the boy. He's not from here, it's true. But then, neither are you, your honour."

Burns' face darkened. *Way to go, Captain,* thought Jeff. The brief flash of hope he'd felt when the old man stood up began to fade away. "In fact," the Captain went on, "most of you in this room hail from other places. That's no kind of reason to jail the lad. He tells me he's become separated from his parents and didn't know the money he had was counterfeit. And how was he to know, in a strange country, what the currency was supposed to look like? Surely he committed no crime by trying to spend what he honestly believed to be the local money."

Jeff could barely believe his ears. *This old guy is too much!* Jeff felt as if he had let the old man down at every turn. And now the Captain was standing up for him. *Thank you, Captain, thank you.* The words went around in his head. He just hoped he got the chance to say them out loud.

"Your honour," Mayor Shrite rose to his feet.

"Yes, Mr. Mayor?" Judge Burns got past the words quickly, as though they tasted bad.

"Your honour, as you are well aware, we have for some time now had a significant problem in Juneau with regard to counterfeit currency." Shrite's voice was oily with his desire to persuade. "Well now, here we have a suspect, a strong suspect, a highly *suspect* suspect, if I may say it. Caught *red-handed*, as the Chief says. Your honour," he turned and fixed pouchy blue eyes on Jeff. "We do not want to take a chance on that suspect getting away."

Jeff's heart sank. *This guy's the mayor. He'll carry weight around here ... More than the Captain, that's for sure.*

Judge Henry Burns seemed to be thinking. He drew himself upright behind the desk. "The operative word is 'suspect,' Mr. Mayor. Young Jeffrey Kenneth Beacon here has not been proven guilty of anything, yet."

Jeff shot a glance at the Captain and Patsy Ann. The old man's sharp eyes looked back at him from beneath thick grey brows. *I think he smiled!*

"On the other hand, it's certainly overdue that we saw some break in this rash of counterfeit money. This young man, meanwhile, has few ties to Juneau and every reason in the world to try to abscond." The judge's mouth pursed and his head tipped forward in what appeared to be deep thought.

Jeff heard a scrabbling on hard wood behind him. He turned to see that Patsy Ann had climbed onto the bench beside the Captain. Now she sat with her ears up and her alert gaze turned toward the front of the courtroom.

Jeff turned his head and felt something like a mild, but not altogether unpleasant, electric charge go through him. *The judge is looking at Patsy Ann!*

Judge Burns coughed and turned his eyes away from the dog. He looked quickly around the courtroom, his gaze resting for a moment on Shrite and Beggs, and again on Jeff. Then he spoke. "On the one hand, the law exists to protect innocent people from unreasonable confinement."

Jeff's heart soared.

"On the other, it exists to protect society as a whole against the risk that further crimes will be committed before a jury can assign blame for the first."

Across the room, Shrite and Beggs beamed.

Judge Burns turned to the two men. "You say the territory fears for the boy's appearance, and thereby request him bound over in custody." He looked over at Harper. "You say the boy is of good character and you'll vouch for him."

He looked at Jeff and said: "Bail is granted ..." *thank you, thank you, thank you,* "... in the amount of one thousand dollars cash, gold or property." His gavel cracked down.

A thousand dollars! Jeff's hope collapsed into a cold pit somewhere below his rib cage. *Ohmigosh, I'm going to jail.*

"With the court's permission ..." It was Captain Harper's voice again. The Captain was on his feet again, Patsy Ann standing beside him on the bench, wagging her tail furiously.

"Captain?" the judge said.

"I'll put up *DogStar* as bond for the boy."

Silence descended over the big room.

DogStar? He'll put up DogStar for me? After I nearly sank her? Mayor Shrite leapt to his feet. "Your honour, your honour!" the fat man sputtered in protest. "That old scow of Harper's isn't worth 200 dollars! And he's no better than a crook himself!"

This time, the gavel came down with a sound like a rifle shot. "Worth cannot always be measured in numbers, Mr. Shrite." He glared at the mayor. "And I do not recall that Captain Harper has been convicted of any violation of law ... criminal or marine. But I admit I am a bit surprised myself." Judge Burns' fierce look turned on the old man. When he spoke, his tone was one of genuine puzzlement.

"Captain Harper, with all respect, why would you do this? You barely know this boy."

The Captain straightened his back and looked over at Jeff once before answering. "Because he's innocent, your honour. And he doesn't deserve to be in that man's jail," he nodded at Shrite. "On top of that, he has a right to prove he's innocent, and he won't have that chance if he's behind bars."

Jeff could still hardly believe his own ears. *The Captain believes me. He believes in me.* For the first time, Jeff wondered if maybe, *just maybe*, he could risk telling the *whole* story to Captain Harper. *A guy like him,* he reasoned, *a guy who keeps his dead dog's collar around just so she'll feel welcome, a guy who'd do this for me after I let him down twice. For sure he'd at least* listen.

The judge spoke again: "The court accepts the vessel *DogStar* as surety in kind for the appearance at trial of Jeffrey Kenneth L. Beacon." He leaned forward in his robes. "But with a condition and a warning for you both. Boy," he looked at Jeff, "I am holding Captain Harper responsible for you and your conduct. I want you to think about that before you do anything to dishonour his confidence in you. And you, Captain Harper. Have no doubt: If this boy does not show up in my courtroom to face this charge, I *will* take your boat. Court dismissed!" The gavel came down a final time. Judge Burns looked at Jeff one last time and added, "You're free to go, boy. But I'd stay a day's hike out of trouble if I were you."

The big voice cried "All rise!" again. In a daze, Jeff stood. Feeling a little unsteady on his feet, he stepped away from the big desk where he had been sitting and toward the low fence that enclosed the public benches. Patsy Ann and the Captain met him where a little gate opened in the fence. She pushed her warm muzzle into his hand as the Captain dropped a hearty slap on Jeff's back.

"Thank you," was all Jeff could think of to say. *Oh doodle!* He felt hot tears sting the corners of his eyes and overflow onto his cheeks. "Thank you," he said again, weakly, then stood there opening and closing his mouth, blinking, and trying to get his eyes to stop doing that.

Through the blur of tears, Jeff saw that the Captain was grinning at him. *Like the cat, the one in* Alice. "You and I have a lot to talk about, son," he was saying. "Let's the three of us get out of here."

Jeff looked down. At his knees, Patsy Ann's grin matched the Captain's. Together they made their way out into the sun.

sixteen
THE CAPTAIN'S LOG

THEY WERE BACK at the wharf, sitting on the park bench. *In sixty years, this will be your square,* Jeff thought, hand down near the ground and scratching at Patsy Ann's grimy white ears. He felt a pang as another thought struck him. He wished Patsy Ann could have met Buddy. The Captain, too. Maybe then they'd understand why Jeff had run off the way he had.

Buddy and Patsy Ann. He looked down at the broad white head leaning into his fingers. Pink and black lips pulled back in smile wrinkles around strong canine teeth. Suddenly he wasn't too sure he still wanted to go back, back to a time when Buddy would be dead again and Patsy Ann would be a statue in a square. *Why can't you ever* keep *people?*

The Captain returned from the Gold Dust Cafe. In one hand he held three paper packages and in the other he carried three open bottles of soda. "The one without the peppers is hers," he said, and handed Jeff two of the wrapped sandwiches. Patsy Ann lay stretched out on the patch of grass in front of the bench, fat little hind legs spread out behind her like a wishbone. She waited while Jeff broke her lunch into pieces and laid it out on the paper before her. Then she inched forward and reached out her nose.

Jeff unwrapped his own Klondike. The salty smell of cheese and the yeasty sourdough bread brought back the memory of the sandwiches he had been forced to abandon untasted. *At last, my beauty.* He raised the moist stack to his mouth and bit into it. *Awright! ... Mmm-hmm.*

For a few minutes, only the sounds of eating came from the bench and the little patch of grass. Jeff noticed with amazement that Patsy Ann actually chewed her bites of sandwich. *Piece by piece. Buddy would've had the whole thing down in three gulps.* It was a good sandwich. He took a long drink of Coke and watched as the Captain held Patsy Ann's bottle out for her to drink. A great deal of it got onto her chest instead of into her mouth, but she didn't seem to mind. At last, the sounds of eating turned into sighs of contentment. In front of them, Patsy Ann rolled onto her side, legs sticking out stiffly in front of her on the warm grass, and closed her eyes.

The Captain looked at Jeff from over his handkerchief, which he was using to wipe mustard from his whiskers. His steel grey eyes seemed to hide a twinkle. "Jeff," he began, "when you ran off yesterday ..."

Jeff winced. *Am I gonna get reamed after all?*

The old man reached inside his salt-stained blue coat. "You left your jacket behind, and this." He produced the brochure that Jeff had been handed by a smiling crew member of *Passage Princess ... just over there, sixty-five years from now.* He handed the little booklet to the boy. Jeff looked down. The brochure was folded open to a picture of Patsy Ann Square. He looked back at the Captain. His cheeks felt cold.

"No need to look so scared, lad," the Captain said, patting his knee. He leaned over and whispered, "I'm the one who should be scared, don't ye think? After all, *you're* the one from the future."

Not so loud. Saying it right out like that, in the Captain's voice, made it seem different, more *serious*, somehow.

"You know?" Jeff whispered back. "And you believe it?"

"Aye, I do." The Captain took back the brochure, riffled through the pages and folded it open in a different place. He handed it back to Jeff. The brochure was turned to the back page. At the bottom, some printed words had been circled in pencil. They read, "Copyright 1998, Inside Passage Cruise Lines Ltd."

"Then, of course, there's those Buck Rogers shoes of yours."

Jeff looked up. It took him a moment to realize that the Captain was teasing him. *He really* does *believe me.* Things were definitely improving.

"I won't pretend I have any idea *how* you got here, Jeff," the Captain continued, his voice low and serious. "But I do think I have an idea *why* you're here!"

What? "What? Tell me!" *Knowing why I'm here would be halfway to getting home.*

The Captain laughed heartily. "Why, I'll do better than that Jeff. I'll *show* ye."

JEFF FELT a little ashamed when they arrived back at *DogStar.* The Captain had not only finished putting the heavy anchor chain away by himself, he had also evidently had time to wash the rust flakes from *DogStar*'s flanks. Her fresh green and black paint sparkled in the sun.

He stepped onto *DogStar*'s broad rail and felt the boat dip under his weight. *This feels like coming home.*

Inside *DogStar*'s cabin, the Captain led Jeff to the saloon table. On it, a weather-stained ship's chart lay spread out, cans of Van Camp's Pork & Beans holding down the corners. On top of it was a worn, hard-bound book, its dark blue cover pale with the kind of ghostly white waveprints that are left behind after immersion in salt water.

The Captain picked up the book and opened it. "This is the log of *Cerberus*," he said. "My last command, November, 1916. Seventeen years ago." He opened the book, found a page and passed it to Jeff.

"Read this," he said, indicating a passage. The handwriting was small but clear, what Jeff's mother would have called "copperplate." Jeff read aloud: "1500 hours." He did a quick computation in his head: *3:00 p.m.* "Thick fog. Course 227 True. Heavy fog, visibility 50 yards. Wind southwest 10 to 15 knots. Speed dead slow, horn operating. Lookouts fore and aft.

"1523 hours. Break in fog. Cliff sighted, bearing port 45 degrees, estimated one half mile. Very striking rock, a white stripe runs down it like stone lightning. Do not recognize. Confirm heading 227." Beside the words was a rough drawing, done in pen, of the cliff with its distinctive blaze.

"1525 hours. Fog has closed in again.

"1532 hours. Aground. Holed. Taking water. Wind rising."

The next few lines were blurred, as though the ink had run, and after them the handwriting became shaky and uneven and difficult to read.

"Now look at this," the Captain's voice was hoarse and low. In his hand was Jeff's brochure again. It was open to an outline map of the Alaska coast and a brightly coloured picture of a cliff. *Ohmigosh! It's got the same white streak!*

Jeff held the brochure beside the sketch in the logbook. "This is the same place!"

"Aye, that's what I think." The Captain gently took the logbook back from Jeff and laid it on the chart. "You're welcome to read what you like of that log, lad, if you've a wish. And make what you will of it, too. God knows they did at the hearing. And I don't doubt you've heard some things about me, too. But the brief and true account of what happened next is this: I really had no idea where I was. On the course I'd thought I was keeping, there were no rocks to strike. There were four in the crew and six passengers, one of them your friend Mayor Shrite. 'Course, he wasn't the mayor then. Old *Cerberus* was taking water badly and the glass was dropping. It was November and if it came to blow, I'd no doubts she would break up on whatever rock it was we had struck. If she did, all aboard her would be swept into the sea with whatever bit was the last of her to break up.

"We'd seen a shoreline less than a mile to port not much earlier. I put the passengers and the rest of the crew into two of the boats and sent them away. I figured they'd get ashore before the surf rose too high." He chuckled. "As it turned out, they went the wrong way, missed land altogether and got picked up by a Canadian mail boat a day and a half later."

Jeff was watching him closely. He winked. "No lad, I didn't plan to 'Go down wi' the ship.' I had a third boat run out and ready to let go if I needed it. And I did. It got dark and the wind came up. The tide was making. Whether it was the one or the other I don't know, but around midnight *Cerberus* groaned and shrieked like all the lost dogs of hell and lifted off that rock. She was already half full of water, of course. Engine room flooded and no power. She was just adrift, wallowing, letting in the sea, dying." He was no longer chuckling. His face looked strained and his hand slipped inside his shirt and grasped the medallion hanging there.

"I did what I could with the one hand pump. But it was a child's toy, really, against the seas that were coming in. For about forty-five minutes, we drifted and *Cerberus* sank deeper into the sea. The wind got stronger. She was taking green water over the waist. Then she struck rocks again and I could hear surf in the darkness to either side. That's when I cut the last boat loose." The old man seemed to drag his vision back from the past and refocus it on Jeff.

"The Coast Guard found me, but not for twenty days. I'm told I wasn't making a great deal of sense when they picked me out of the boat. There was a hearing. There always is after a vessel sinks. The passengers got together and hired lawyers who made a great deal out of two facts. One was the amount of time between their rescue and mine. And another," he took a slow, uneven breath, "another is that when they sent a vessel to salvage *Cerberus* where I said she'd be, where that book says she is," he pointed at the log, "they found no trace of her."

"But she was wrecked!" Jeff protested. "What good is a wrecked ship?"

"Aye, she was wrecked, lad. But there was four million dollars in her strongbox ... most of it in cash and gold specie."

A tingle ran up and down Jeff's spine and his eyes got large. *Four million dollars! Holy cow! That's* still *a lot of money.* No wonder some people were kind of mad at the Captain. "Wow," he said aloud.

"As you say," the old man glanced at him sideways, "wow!" He was silent a moment, fingering the chain around his neck. "Shrite claimed that I'd been drunk on the bridge. It wasn't true but it ruined me as a sea officer. And he collected two million dollars from his insurers for his share of the cargo."

Captain Harper shook himself and went on. "But that's all in the past. Here's the more interesting part." He leaned out over the chart. "According to my best reckoning at the time, and according to that log, when *Cerberus* foundered she was about *there*." His long finger pointed to a faded penciled "X" on the chart.

The chart reminded Jeff a little of the maps in some of his computer games. The Captain's "X" was right at the edge of a big area of blue that Jeff took to represent water, up against an area of faded grey that must be land. The shoreline looked straight where the "X" was, and as far as Jeff could see, no reefs or rocks or even other islands interrupted the blue area of sea. He nodded and looked up at the Captain. "OK …"

"But look here." The Captain held up the brochure. "According to this wee chart of yours, this cliff in the picture, the one I saw just before we went aground, isn't down there at all, it's *here!*" His finger stabbed down on a new spot on the chart, half a metre away from the first.

Another "X," sharp and dark on the stained paper, had been newly penciled in. It was nearly lost among stars and circles and printed notices that warned of "rocks" and "drying reefs." A little distance away, a ragged stretch of grey indicated a torn and rugged shoreline.

"They're more than forty-five miles apart," the Captain snorted. "No one ever looked for her that far north."

"But how could that happen?" Jeff asked.

The Captain brooded on the question for a moment, then shook his head. "I don't honestly know how it could, Jeff," he said at last. "And I've been giving it some thought, as you can imagine. It was foggy, a tide was running, I could have been out a little in my dead reckoning. I said as much at the hearing. But forty-five miles? No, I can't imagine being that far off. That defies explanation. Then again," the twinkle seemed to have reignited in his eyes, "a lot of things seem to be defying explanation these days."

He looked at Patsy Ann and then the boy, his old grey eyes searching deeply in Jeff's young ones. "I think she brought you here to show me this, to help me find that ship."

It made sense, it made a LOT of sense. His mind raced. "So, shouldn't we take this map and go show Mayor Shrite? We can show them they were wrong about you, show them where the wreck really is!" *This is great.*

The Captain smiled ruefully. "That's a fine idea, lad. But what do you think Mr. Shrite will make of our tale?"

Oh. He thought about it for a second. *Magic dog, kid from the future, map upsetting all norms of navigation. No, maybe not.* "I guess I see your point."

"Shrite would have the two of us in the mental home. They say it's worse than prison."

"Then ..." Jeff looked at the Captain and thought about what he was about to suggest. The more he thought about it, the stronger was his feeling that it was the right idea ... *at the right time! YES! This was what he was* here *for!* "Then we'll go and get it without them," Jeff said.

Now it was the Captain's turn to hesitate. He looked uncertainly at Jeff. "What if it's not there?" he asked.

"Then we keep on going! We can be *Thelma and Louise* on *The African Queen!*"

"Who? On what vessel?"

"Sorry, Captain, I guess that was a little time travel humour. What I mean is, we could just keep going ... to Hawaii!"

The Captain continued to look skeptical and started to shake his head. "I've made an obligation to the court," he began, but Jeff cut him off.

"You have an obligation to the town, too — to get their money back! Besides, just like you said, this has to be why

I'm here! The reason Patsy Ann brought me here ... back to the 1930s ... to *DogStar*. It has to be."

The Captain looked at Jeff with renewed doubts for a moment, then he glanced up at Maddie's collar around the gimbaled wall lamp. His face cleared. "Well," he said, "why not?" His face crinkled into a smile. He and Jeff shook hands across *DogStar's* saloon.

seventeen

RIGHT PLACE, WRONG TIME

WHEN JEFF woke up the next morning, the blood was pumping in his veins and he knew exactly where he was. A circle of reflected sunlight rippled over the white-painted planking above his head, the underside of *DogStar*'s foredeck. *I'm on a treasure hunt with a* real *treasure!* Even the Net was going to seem a little dull after this. Now that they knew why they had been brought together, the Captain and Jeff had talked late into the night, working out the details of salvaging *Cerberus'* safe. Another few days of hard work and they would be ready to cast off. And the work would go much more quickly now that Jeff no longer had to hide from view.

Then he thought about Buddy. *This is going to be exactly the kind of day that Buddy liked.* He would have been spinning around at Jeff's feet by now, doing circles and going *boing* like Hobbes the tiger, bouncing off things in his eagerness to fill the day with adventure. *"Are things happening? Are we doing stuff?" That was Buddy.* Yeah, and probably breaking things too. When Buddy's enthusiasm got the better of him, his cement-like body had regularly knocked stuff off low-lying tables. A few times he'd even knocked over low-standing people too. *Then he terrified them even more by licking their faces!* Jeff remembered, smiling to himself.

He thought about the brass canister back on *Passage Princess*, and felt a twinge of guilt. "I'll be back," he promised, whispering it aloud to himself to be sure. *I'll be back soon. I promise.*

He rolled over in his bunk and reached his arm down the outside of the berth. He pulled open his drawer and rummaged in it until he found his watch. He rolled back and held the watch up to look at it. It read 3:34 p.m. now, but it still said Tuesday, the day he had "left," as he'd started to think of it. *If I were still there, I'd still have just under two and half hours to make it back to the square*, he thought idly.

The mild electric shock feeling went through him again. *Hang on, maybe the watch wasn't broken after all. Maybe Mom and Dad haven't missed me at all,* he thought. *Maybe they don't even know I'm gone yet!* Could that be possible?

Anything's possible. *Call me living proof. Real time pretty much stood still while Marty skateboarded through the 1950s in* Back to the Future, he recalled. He frowned at the watch. It had read a few minutes past one when he had "arrived" in 1933. That meant it had moved forward two and a half hours in the time he had already been here. A chill went over him. *Ohmigosh! It's past halftime already,* Jeff thought wildly, *and I only just figured out the play! No time at all to waste — I'd better get up.* He put the watch back in the drawer and twisted off the bunk and onto his feet. Water slapped the outside of the hull by his ear and *DogStar* rolled. Jeff rocked lightly, hardly noticing the motion while he tugged his blue jersey over his head.

Jeff stepped aft and into the head. He emerged five minutes later and walked the few steps to the galley, swaying comfortably with *DogStar*'s motion. He was feeling quite seaworthy. "Mornin', Captain," he piped. Then he inhaled deeply ... *It's not porridge!* But it was an aroma he knew, all right. "Are we having pancakes this morning?" he asked.

"Flapjacks," the Captain corrected with a smile, setting a golden plateful in front of Jeff. "It's the beginning of a new day, lad." He moved a square tin can from the galley counter onto the saloon table. A printed paper label, emblazoned with maple leaves and a picture of a guy in a toque in the woods in winter, identified the contents as maple syrup from Quebec. Jeff poured it generously over his panca ... *flapjacks!*

The Captain brought two mugs of steaming coffee to the table. When he returned with his own plate and finally pulled his chair up to the saloon table, he was frowning. "Only one thing bothers me still," he said. "I can't figure out what took me so far off my course. Tide, the fog ... I stayed up 'til past midnight working it over in my mind." He shook his head. "Still can't explain it."

Jeff squared his shoulders. "That's the past, Captain. We're here now, and we're going to find that ship. That's what counts." *Jeez, I'm starting to sound like my father.*

The Captain considered this for a moment, then nodded briskly. "You're right, lad." A smile broke across his craggy face. "And we've got *pancakes* for breakfast," he teased, raising his coffee mug in a toast.

After they were through, the Captain leaned back and looked at Jeff. "We're going to need more supplies," he said. "Especially if we plan to be away from the dock for a while. But we don't want to arouse suspicion by buying too much of anything at one time. So I have an idea."

Jeff nodded.

"One way and another," the old man winked, "you've been cooped up long enough for a lad your age. How about you run into Juneau this morning instead of me?"

"Awright! Cool!"

"Cool?" the Captain repeated, a question mark in his eyes.

"That means good," Jeff explained.

"Ah, I see," the Captain nodded. "Wow."

Jeff's laughter erupted through a mouthful of coffee, spraying it across the table. Wiping his chin with his sleeve and still laughing, he managed to ask, "Where do you want me to go?"

"Amory's, Benson's Hardware and the Empire Ship Chandlery," the Captain answered. "They're all handy to the wharf. I have a list for you."

"What's a chandlery?"

The Captain looked over at him darkly: "It's a place where scoundrels stamp the word 'marine' on a nickel box of brass nails and charge a dollar for it! But it's the only place to buy some things for a boat, like those shackles on the list there."

The idea of a visit to town on his own, without having to worry about being arrested, elated Jeff. *Maybe I could go blue-*

berry picking with Rose one day, too, he thought with excitement. *I'm a free man. Almost.* "Sure thing," he said to the Captain.

Taking the list and two well-worn five-dollar bills from the Captain, Jeff stepped onto the float and made his way to shore. He was getting used to this obstacle course now, and he dodged nimbly among the piles of rope and stacked oars and engine parts laid out on the docks. When he reached the stretch where the road ran past the garden cottages, he saw Rose ahead of him. She was just leaving her door carrying some sort of contraption in front of her. Patsy Ann was worrying at her ankles.

As Jeff approached, he could see that Rose's burden was a wire basket affair made to hold two pies, keeping them secure and safely apart. It was the pies, not Rose, that Patsy Ann was dancing around.

"Hi," he called out.

"Hi," Rose called back. *Does she seem different? Shy somehow?*

"What's with the pies?"

"I'm taking them to the Alaska Hotel for Momma. She bakes them every Wednesday and they pay her thirty-five cents for each one," Rose explained. "Where are you going?"

"Errands for the Captain." It sounded agreeably official. "You want me to carry that?"

"No thanks, I'm OK."

He wondered if she was mad at him. "Guess you heard about me, eh?"

"Yeah."

"What do you think?" *Might as well get this over with.*

"As my momma says, 'Innocent 'til proven guilty.' Just like Captain Harper." She squinted up at him. "Hey, do you want to go to a baseball game with me on Saturday?"

OK, so maybe she's not mad at me, he thought. "Saturday?" *Jeez ... What day is Saturday?* He struggled for a moment.

"It'll be at Diamond Park. There'll be hot dogs and popcorn," Rose continued. "Juneau's playing the Sitka Whalers. They're coming by boat on Friday." With each new attraction, she seemed more determined to persuade Jeff. "Everyone'll be there."

"Well, it sounds like fun," Jeff conceded. "I'll have to check with the Captain."

Rose beamed at him and skipped a few steps, carefully, so as not to jounce the fresh pies.

"But if he says it's OK, then sure! That would be fun." *Gee, I've just been asked out on my first date!* He chuckled secretly. *And Mom can't even say no!*

"What's so funny?"

Eh? Had he laughed aloud without knowing it? Jeff gave the girl a perplexed look. "What do you mean, 'funny'?"

"You were smiling inside yourself," Rose said, her green eyes bright. "I could see you, that's all!"

"I ... was just looking forward to Saturday. It's been a long time since I saw a baseball game live!"

She looked at him curiously. "You watch dead baseball games?"

"No! I mean ..." *on TSN ... unh-unh ... Try ...* "I listen to them ... on the radio." Then he remembered the 300-dollar price tag in the shop window. *Jeez, she probably thinks I'm rich!*

But she nodded her head, apparently satisfied.

They had come to Amory's. "I have to stop here," Jeff said.

"OK," said Rose. "I have to take these to the Alaska and collect the money. Maybe I'll come down to the harbour tomorrow and see if it's OK for you to go to the ball game."

"OK ... see you."

"Bye."

Patsy Ann stayed with him. "Geez, girl," he said, rubbing her head, "I'm flattered. You chose me over pie."

Patsy Ann dropped her thick white self down in a patch of sunlight and stretched out. Jeff smiled at her and entered the store. He heard the sudden, expectant silence that comes when a crowd of people all stop talking at once. Four or five men and women stood looking at him from where they had been gossiping near the counter. He felt hostility and suspicion wash over him like a hot wave. Colour rose in his cheeks.

"Isn't that the counterfeit kid?" observed a sharp-nosed little man with wire glasses and a white shirt done up tight to the collar.

"I'd sure check his money real careful," offered the tall woman beside him in a shrill, scolding voice.

Jeff felt his ears burning as he pulled out the Captain's list and started down Amory's single aisle of groceries.

"I wouldn't serve him at all if I were you, Sid," another disapproving voice said behind him. "You'll just get stiffed, mark my words."

What do you know, you old busybody, Jeff fumed. The unfair criticisms made him seethe, but he bit down on the smart-aleck comebacks that leapt to mind. *Cool it, guy,* he told himself, *you're in enough trouble in Juneau already.* Instead of flaming back, Jeff set his jaw and picked what he needed from the shelves. *Wait 'til we come back with that treasure,* he comforted himself. *You'll be singing a different tune then.*

But when he brought his purchases — flour, salt, potatoes and some tins of peas, pears and evaporated milk — to the counter, he was still unprepared for the attitude that met him there. "I'll take the little punk's money." Sid was the same burly man who had told Jeff that he couldn't telephone Halifax from Juneau. *Or from 1933,* Jeff thought now. He looked Jeff in the eye as he spoke, the intentional insult perfectly plain. "But I'll sure check it out real good. You're right about one thing, Jed — I expect he's trying something on me."

They've already made up their minds, Jeff seethed. *I'm guilty. What a bunch of narrow-minded, stupid people.*

The storekeeper punched in Jeff's purchases on the ornate silver cash register, adding each to a paper sack as he did so. They came to $3.65. Jeff held out one of the Captain's five-dollar bills to the scowling storekeeper. Sid made a show of examining the old, time-softened bill minutely, tugging the paper at each end for strength and taking it over to the window to peer through it at the sun. Finally and reluctantly, he said, "Well, I cain't see anything *obvious* wrong with it."

"OK, kid," he said, making a decision. "There's your grub.

And here's how far your money goes in this town." He punched "sale" on the cash register and it went *ka-ching*. The cash drawer came out. Sid put the five-dollar bill in and removed some coins. He tossed them on the counter.

Jeff watched the quarter and the dime spin to a stop on the counter. He noticed that the little group beside him had stopped talking and was staring at him again. *Wait just a second.* $3.65. Math had never been his strong point, but $3.65 from five still left ... *That's a dollar short!* He looked up at the big storekeeper in amazement.

Sid looked back at him, smirking. He leaned back on the counter behind him and crossed his arms. "Call it a premium, kid. For doing business with a high-risk customer." A spray of laughter told Jeff that the peanut gallery thought this was a good one.

"That ... that's not fair!" Even to himself, Jeff's voice sounded young and unsure.

"I think it's most proper indeed," snorted the tall woman in her nasal voice.

"You want to argue about it, kid, how about we ask Sergeant Kelly to referee." Sid looked over Jeff's shoulder at the street. "I think I see him over there now."

Ohmigosh. Stay away from trouble, Judge Burns said. And here he was, about to have the police called on him the very next day. *Darn, darn, DARN!*

He scooped up the coins in one hand, threw his arm around the paper sack, and made for the door. As he pushed it open, he heard laughter break out behind him and loud approval of how expertly Sid had handled "the young thug." He felt his face burning.

Stupid people! Jeff's shame and anger were compounded now with a feeling of remorse at having cost the Captain a dollar. He didn't even have any of his own money left to offer the Captain to make up for it. *I can give you a twenty, but first you have to get it back from the police, then you have to wait sixty years to use it. Great.* He hated feeling like a common criminal. The worst part was not being able to defend himself. *That's what a trial's for,* he could almost hear his dad's voice. Anger pounded in his temples. *I hate this town, and I hate these people!*

Patsy Ann's head came up. Jeff ignored her, storming away from the store and heading fast along the sidewalk. She climbed to her feet, shook herself all over, then followed him at a fast trot. The red-faced boy wasn't paying much attention to where he was going, too lost in furious thought to notice. As a result, when Jeff finally found himself standing in front of a plate-glass window, a display of books inside it and a green canvas awning holding back the late-morning sun, he wasn't entirely sure how he'd gotten there.

But wait a second! To Jeff's left beyond a patch of bricks was a little storefront office. It had an awning, too, a red one that matched the green one over the store. *Hang on ... this is where I came in!* It was indeed the alley through which he had arrived in the past. But it was still blocked by solid brick.

Jeff looked back along the boardwalk the way he'd come. Patsy Ann stood watching him. He let the sack of groceries fall to the ground and ran to her. He dropped to his knees and wrapped his arms around her neck, burying his face in her fur. For a long time he held her tightly. When finally he released her, he sat dejectedly on the boardwalk and searched her beady little eyes.

"Why are people like that, Patsy Ann?" he asked. "Why won't they give me a chance?"

She stared back at him. *The Captain gave you a chance.*

"But why me? Why does it have to be *me* that helps the Captain, Patsy Ann? Why can't I just go home now?"

Patsy Ann gazed back at him as though she might answer him. But then Jeff's anger rose again. *Get real*, he told himself. *She's just a stupid dog. And you're just a dumb kid who's gonna end up in jail in this stupid town.*

Then the dark eyes moved. Not Patsy Ann's whole thick head, just her little pink-rimmed eyes, the short white fur over them furrowing as she looked up over Jeff's shoulder.

Jeff turned and his gaze followed hers. "Holy doodle!" he gasped aloud. *No. No, no ... this can't be.*

It was. Now the green awning was over on the left, the red one was on the right, and the brick wall was gone altogether! *Ohmigosh! It's open! The alley's open. I can go home!* Jeff scrambled to his feet and moved toward the alley mouth. *Quick, before it closes again!* Then he stopped.

He looked down at the paper sack at his feet, seeing the supplies it contained. *The Captain's waiting for these. Do I want to let him down a third time?* He turned. Patsy Ann was sitting now, as still and silent as a white statue, a living dog made of ivory, dark eyes fixed on him.

Jeff met her gaze. *How did you do that? Who are you? What are you?* He stepped closer to her and dropped to his knees. In the shade of the awning, her dark eyes were ebony pools where tiny stars twinkled. He leaned forward, nose to nose with her long pink muzzle. He felt her warm breath on his face. He saw himself in her eyes.

Then, beyond his own reflection, he saw the Captain busy at *DogStar's* bows, a spring in his step. He saw Judge Burns leaning down from his bench and read on his stern lips, "I *will* take your boat." Then he saw Buddy's brass canister on the dresser in the cruise ship. He swallowed hard and closed his eyes.

I will come back for you, boy, I promise. Jeff squeezed his eyes tight to hold back the moisture. *But I just can't do it right now.* When he opened his eyes, Patsy Ann was on her feet again, waiting for him. *You're too spooky*, Jeff thought and took a deep breath.

"OK then, let's go," he said, collecting the sack. He settled it in one arm and looked at the dog. "Well, this is your town, Patsy Ann, take me to the hardware store." Patsy Ann barked joyfully and set off. Jeff fell in behind her, his eyes on the departing white flag of her tail. He didn't look back.

At the end of the block, Patsy Ann glanced over her shoulder at the boy. Only she saw that the alley was once again a brick wall. But being as colour-blind as any other dog, she couldn't tell that the awnings were also back to their old places — red on the left, green on the right.

eighteen

BATTER UP!

SATURDAY MORNING dawned blustery and cool. But neither Jeff's excitement nor his confidence were in the least cast down. Quite the opposite. He was feeling more up than ever about the task he and the Captain had set themselves. *Sure feels way different from before.*

The five days since his arrest and four days since his release had flashed by. After the strange reappearance of the alley, the people at the hardware store and ships' chandlery had been cool toward Jeff, but had treated him with none of the taunting he'd experienced at Amory's. Alone or with the Captain, he had made several more trips to town since then. Now *DogStar*'s lockers groaned with tins and packages of food, enough to last for a lengthy voyage if need be.

They had worked far into each evening to complete the repairs and preparations needed before putting to sea. Most of these involved *DogStar*'s rigging: the ropes that held up her masts or controlled her sails, and the fittings of wood or brass they attached to. There seemed to be hundreds of these, and they all needed to be checked and cleaned and sometimes repaired or replaced. Finally the sails themselves had to be retrieved from lockers, pulled from their heavy canvas bags and lashed in place on their booms, ready to be raised.

At last, by late Friday night, the Captain had declared the old boat "Ready for sea, lad."

This morning they would cast off. Not for the *real* voyage. Not yet. "This'll be a shakedown trip across the harbour," the Captain had said. "We'll take her across the channel to the float where they sell fuel, and fill up her tank." Jeff felt a surge of excitement when *DogStar*'s engine grumbled into life.

A few minutes later, the Captain took up position at one of the boat's two steering wheels. One was inside the wheelhouse, for steering in bad weather. The other was outside, mounted on the back of the wheelhouse beside the smaller of *DogStar*'s two masts. From there, the Captain could both steer and reach the many ropes that controlled *DogStar*'s sails.

Jeff stood on the dock, waiting for the word to untie the line holding the boat's stern. When the Captain called out "Cast off astern," his skin tingled.

"Cast off forward."

Jeff scrambled to the forward rope and untied it. On *DogStar*'s deck, the Captain quickly hauled it in.

"All aboard, lad," the old man laughed, reaching out one wiry hand to heave Jeff over the rail as it slid away from the dock. Jeff grinned as he found his footing and looked around. *DogStar* felt different away from the dock. Even in the placid and protected water of the harbour, the deck lifted and fell gently under his feet. *She feels alive!* he thought, as the slow *thump, thump* beat of her big engine came up through the deck into his feet.

As Captain Harper had warned him, it was a short maiden voyage. Soon after leaving her own sinking slip, *DogStar* was tied alongside a rugged wharf of new tarred timber. The Captain directed a heavy nozzle at the end of a thick red hose into a hole on her deck. A foul smell that made Jeff's stomach clench enveloped them.

"You plannin' a trip, Skipper?" the man who ran the fueling dock asked. He ran close-set dark eyes curiously over Jeff.

"No," the Captain answered, casually. "Just replenishing while I have a hand on board."

"Good thinkin'," the fuel man said, brown teeth bared in a wide grin. "The way I understand it, yer crew might not be around for long."

After that, the Captain had paid for the fuel and they had returned *DogStar* to her own slip in thoughtful silence. There was plenty to think about. After consulting his charts and considering the tides, the Captain had decided that they would leave at half past midnight that night. Sunday morning, properly speaking. "At zero-zero-thirty hours," the Captain had said, a fierce light in his eyes.

If all went well, they should be at the site of the wreck by late Sunday evening. According to Jeff's brochure, the cliff with the blaze was on an out-of-the-way bit of shoreline hidden behind reefs and rocky islands. It was still partly uncharted, the Captain said, but it was only about 160 miles from Juneau by water. They never spoke about the unthinkable: what would happen if they *didn't* find the ship. *That's cuz we're going to find it,* Jeff told himself whenever the thought came into his mind.

Jeff finished washing his hands and came out to *DogStar*'s saloon. At his place on the polished table were a plate with a thick ham and cheese sandwich on it and a mug of milk. Beside them were two rumpled dollar bills and seven quarters. "What's this?" he asked.

"That's your pay," the Captain replied, sitting down to his own sandwich. "I didn't pay you for the day you went to jail, or the half day we spent getting you out. But for the rest, you've worked hard, lad, and you earned it."

The old man's grey stubble cracked into a grin. "I thought ye might like to have some money for that baseball game." The Captain had willingly given Jeff permission to go with Rose to the game "so long as *DogStar* is ready to sail on her tide first." When Rose had come by the boat to confirm the date and had found reasons to keep coming by each day since, the Captain had teased Jeff about the crush he seemed to have inspired in "yon maiden fair." *Now I'll be able to treat Rose to something,* thought Jeff.

But ... *I can't take all this. I owe* him! Jeff carefully separated four quarters from the coins and slid them across the table towards the Captain. "I owe you a dollar, sir. For Amory's."

The Captain shot him an appraising glance, then smiled. "Well son, that's very square of ye and I commend it. But I have a hand in that, too. I knew what I was doing when I hired on a lad accused of forgery. Let's call it even between us." He lifted the top two quarters and slid them back toward Jeff.

Jeff nodded. "Thank you, sir." Then, that thank-you somehow not enough, he added, "In fact, thanks for everything." He gathered up the money. There was still more than he'd need to splurge a little at the ballpark. A bottle of Hires R-J root beer was only five cents … "When a nickel goes a long way." He'd seen that on a poster in Amory's.

"No need to thank me," the Captain replied, "you worked for it, fair and square."

Jeff did up the dishes and was waiting at the cabin door when Rose arrived. She had a ball cap on, backwards. Backwards, Jeff pondered. Backwards. How long has that trend been around, anyway?

"What's your ball cap say?" he called out to her across the dock. Rose turned it around on her head. It was a New York Yankees cap, dark blue with the white embroidered "N" and "Y" overlapping on the front. Jeff recognized it right away. Yankees caps are cool. "Where'd ya get it?"

She smiled at him. "This was my poppa's cap." She twisted the bill once more around to the back of her neck. In her overalls and red and black lumberjack shirt, backwards ball cap and sneakers, she wouldn't have looked out of place at Halifax Junior High, Jeff thought. Wait a minute, sneakers?

"Where'd you get the shoes?" Jeff asked. D'uh, nice going dweeb, dumb first-date question number 17.

"Oh these?" she answered with a toss of her braids. "They're my new Keds. Momma sent to Seattle for them with her pie money." She turned to the Captain. "Are you coming to the game, Captain Harper?"

"No, lass," said the Captain, who had been observing their exchange with a reserved humour that did not escape Jeff. "I've got some work to do. Work never ends on a boat, you know." He sighed theatrically. Then he fixed an eye on Jeff and lowered his voice conspiratorially. "We'll meet up afterward, lad, and have us a last meal ashore." He smiled and winked heavily.

Jeff glanced at Rose just in time to catch her eyebrows on their way back down. *Yikes,* he thought, *she caught that.*

"You two better run along, though," the Captain dismissed them. "You've got a fair hike ahead of you."

IT TURNED OUT to be a hike all right, all the way past downtown and out to the flats north of the city. But they had fun on the way. When they passed a patch of blueberries climbing the first rocky slopes of the mountain at the side of the road, Jeff insisted that they stop and sample them.

"We don't want to be late," Rose cautioned.

"But what," he asked, "if we never walk this way again?"

"I walk by here almost every day," she protested. But after a little persuasion Rose had agreed, and together they scrambled up the slope and sat side by side, raking fistfuls of fat berries into their mouths.

When they got to Diamond Park, Jeff was impressed. It wasn't exactly Toronto's SkyDome, where Grandad had taken him last summer. *Or whenever.* But it had dugouts and bullpens for each team, bleacher seats and a big black scoreboard behind centre field. There was even a guy over a PA system announcing each team's batting lineup. Jeff was reaching into his pocket to pay for their tickets when he discovered something he found even more surprising. *Free admission?*

"Sure," Rose told him. When the Juneau Nuggets went up against the Sitka Whalers, she explained, it was a town event open to all. Including Patsy Ann. They spotted her as they settled onto weathered wooden bleachers up behind the third-base line. The thick white dog was sitting below them, at the outfield end of the Nuggets' dugout.

"Hey," said Jeff, "she doesn't look like Big Bird."

Rose looked at him with puzzlement.

"Never mind." He'd better watch himself. *I can't get too cocky, can't forget where I am,* he thought. *I mean, when I am.* He looked around. Most of the men wore open shirts and a few women wore pants with blouses. But many women were in dresses, and quite a few men were beading up with sweat in suits and ties. He didn't see anyone in shorts and a T-shirt and a goofy baseball cap. *They probably don't do the wave here, either.* But there was an excited hum and the hometown crowd stood and stomped and cheered as the Juneau team took to the field in their red and grey uniforms.

The Sitka side came onto the field in black and tan, lining up along the first-base line at their dugout. They got a round of cheers from their supporters who had traveled to the game by boat — *celebrating the whole way, by the sound of them,* Jeff thought — and good-natured booing from everyone else.

The hubbub subsided to a loud murmur and the players on both teams pulled off their caps and placed them over their hearts. Jeff stood up along with everyone else in the stands. A band sitting behind first base struck up the chords of the American anthem. *But these guys aren't even a state yet.* It didn't seem to matter. Every voice in the crowd rang out with the stirring opening line, "Oh, say can you see, by the dawn's early light ..." Jeff found himself wishing there were a little more of the same spirit back home in Canada. The anthem ended, the crowd cheered lustily and a tall older man stepped onto the field to throw out the first ball. Jeff recognized the erect figure: *Judge Burns!*

Judge Burns' opening pitch was no mere formal toss. The wiry judge glared across the plate, then wound up and delivered a smoking fastball that landed in the catcher's mitt with a stinging *thwack.* Then he dusted off his brown leathery hands and stalked away from the mound, smiling every bit as grimly as a happy hangman.

Then Juneau's pitcher put his hands behind his back, bent down at the waist until his upper body was a horizontal line over the mound, and went to work. Jeff snuck a sideways glance at Rose. She was flushed with excitement, her eyes darting around to follow the action in the field. *She must really like baseball,* Jeff thought. He hadn't met too many girls who liked *anything* he liked. *Then again, I guess I haven't met too many girls, period.* Not the way he'd met Rose, that was for sure!

"I wish I could see a real Yankees game one day," she said wistfully.

"Don't you have …" Jeff caught himself in time. He'd almost said, "Don't you have cable?" *Jeez, no TV. Remember that.* Rose turned to him, waiting for the rest.

"… any relatives in New York?" he finished lamely.

She looked up at him through her bangs, her face scrunched up in confusion. "No."

Oh great, Jeff thought, *now she thinks I'm from another planet.* He searched his data banks of baseball trivia for anything at all from the 1930s. He liked to remember everything he could about the sport, hoping one day to stump Dad. *But Jeez, a lot has happened since 1933.* An idea came to him. "Who's your favourite Yankee?" She'd probably pick the Babe. If Jeff remembered right, George Herman Ruth was still a Yankee in 1933.

"Lou Gehrig," she tossed back without any hesitation. "My momma says he's a lot like my poppa was. Everyone likes Babe Ruth. But he's so loud and he's always boasting." Jeff looked at her in surprise. *Boy, she really does know baseball.* "I bet if Lou Gehrig ever stops playing, no Yankee will ever wear Number Four again."

Jeff felt that weird shiver again, little electric feet tap-dancing over his skin from his scalp to his feet. "Bet you're right," he agreed evenly. *In fact, Rose, I know you're right. I even know when: 1939.* Gehrig would have to quit baseball, Jeff remembered, because of a nerve disease that he would eventually give his name to. And it would be the first time any team ever retired a jersey. *Now how did she know that?*

By the seventh-inning stretch, the score was tied 3–3 and the crowd was buzzing. The band struck up "Take Me

Out to the Ball Game." Rose knew *all* the words and Jeff was surprised to find he knew most of them too. *This is too cool. It's like being in a Hollywood movie* — A League of Their Own, *maybe.* Except you could smell the grass baking in the sun, and feel the wind that caught the high flies and held them up against the clear blue sky for precious seconds while red and grey legs pumped around the bases.

Rose's plaid shoulder rocked companionably against the arm of his own blue jersey, moving back and forth in time as they sang along with the crowd. "Buy me some peanuts and Cracker Jack, I don't care if I never go back ..." Jeff looked over at her rapt face, bright green eyes drinking in the action around her.

The song wound down at last. "I'm going to go get us something to eat," said Jeff. "Be right back." He jingled his coins in his pocket, standing up. *I guess you only have your first date once,* he thought, flashing her a smile as he left. *Of course it's normal to wait until after you're born to do it!* That thought kept him amused while he waited to make his way to the front of the press of warm, thirsty people around the refreshment stand. Jeff was tickled to discover that the stand offered "Canada Dry Pale Gingerale ... It's Gingervating!" *I'll get us that,* he decided, *and some Cracker Jacks!*

"That'll be twenty cents," the counterman said, pushing two opened green bottles of soda and two narrow red-white-and-blue paper boxes across to Jeff. He paid with a quarter and carefully put his nickel change back in his pocket.

By the time he got back to the bleachers, the game had

gone on to the top of the eighth without him. The Sitka Whalers had a man at second and a tall, stringy guy at bat. The noisy crowd was giving him rude and unhelpful advice. Rose's face lit up when she saw the boxes of Cracker Jack. "These are my favourite!" she proclaimed. "There's a prize in every box!"

Rose went right after hers. First she tipped the box into her lap until it was half empty. That made enough room in the box for her hand to fit in and pull out the prize. She then proceeded to funnel the Cracker Jacks back into the box, without losing a single golden caramel-peanut-popcorn nugget. *She's done this before*, thought Jeff with admiration.

She shook a few clinging Cracker Jacks off the small cellophane package and opened it, revealing a miniature tin compass on a cardboard strap. "Is this ever neat!" she exclaimed. "So ... what'd you get?"

When he didn't answer, she reached over, playfully trying to grab his box. Jeff laughed and moved it out of her reach. "Oh no, you don't," he said. "We're not allowed to look at the prize until all the Cracker Jacks are gone."

"Is that some kind of silly Canadian rule?" Rose looked at him slantwise. He watched as she strapped the toy compass to her wrist. Its tiny silver fleck of a needle bounced and sparkled in the bright afternoon sun.

The Sitka drive fizzled out and by the middle of the eighth, it was still 3–3. A short, broad guy with flaming red hair came to the plate for Juneau. The hometown bleachers erupted in cheers, whistles and admonitions to "Show 'em, Sparky."

Sparky sailed the ball over the head of the Sitka shortstop and neatly split the distance between the left and centre fielders.

"Hey, look!" Rose nudged him and pointed out to deep left field. *Patsy Ann!* She'd moved from her spot by the dugout and was lying low where the deep grass of Diamond Park merged with the cattails of Gastineau Channel.

By the time the ball found its way back to the infield, Sparky was on second base. A bunt moved him to third. When Juneau's grey-haired pitcher took the plate, with Sparky on third and two out, the crowd was on its feet. When he drove a low, hard grounder into right field and Sparky tore for home, the cheering turned into a frenzy of whistling and yelling and jumping. The weathered grey bleachers shook and trembled under their stamping feet. Rose and Jeff jumped and shouted with the rest of them as the Nuggets pulled ahead 4–3.

All the jumping had spilled about half of Jeff's Cracker Jacks out of the box. Rose laughed and proclaimed: "Good! Now you're closer to your prize!"

The Nuggets took the field for the top half of the ninth inning. By now, Jeff's own curiosity had the better of him. He put his hand into the Cracker Jacks box and dug around in the remnants of his candy. In a moment, his hand came back out. In his fingers was a small metal horseshoe with most of its loop painted red, just the two tips of the metal left silver and bare.

"What's that?" Rose asked.

"Haven't you ever seen a magnet?" he asked.

"Yeah," she replied, "but not in the shape of a *horseshoe*."

"Here, look," Jeff reached over and took Rose's wrist in his hand. The sun reflected off the face of the little compass and Jeff waited until the tiny needle inside had settled down and was pointing more or less steadily out beyond right field.

"That's North, right?" he asked.

Rose nodded.

"Well, watch," he said, and held the magnet over the compass. Suddenly, the needle started to spin wildly.

Just then, a loud "Ooohhh!" escaped from the crowd around them. Jeff and Rose both looked over at the board and then down at the field. The science lesson ended abruptly as all their attention returned to the game.

They were in the top of the ninth and the Whalers were at bat. Juneau's lead from the last inning stood. One more out and they'd take the game. But the Whalers had a man on second. And a lean, wiry batter in black and tan was stepping up to the right side of the plate. Jeff remembered him: he'd driven home two of the Whalers' runs in the sixth inning. The crowd's yelling and hollering rose to a full-throated cry. All eyes were on Juneau's grey-haired pitcher, winding up on the mound.

He released the ball. It streaked across the plate, whacked into the catcher's mitt and the umpire cried: "Steeerike!" The catcher threw back the ball. The pitcher caught it, held it close to his chest and stole a glance behind him. He faked a throw to second and the Whalers' runner sidestepped back to the bag. Neither the runner nor the pitcher, nor the catcher or the batter, not Rose nor Jeff, nor anyone else cheering and stomping in the stands that day, paid any attention to the little white dog pulling herself into a long, low crouch way out in the tall grass in deep left field.

Juneau's pitcher glanced around the bases and the wind-up resumed. The pitcher's arm fanned, the ball flew ... The bat cracked! It was a high fly that looked like it might sail right on out of the park. The batter was already on the way to first base when out of the corner of his eye, Jeff caught the flash of white moving fast. Turning, he saw Patsy Ann peeling at full gallop across the field. She was heading for the exact same spot that Juneau's fielder was running for, his glove out and his eyes turned up to track the descending ball.

Several things happened at once. First, Patsy Ann launched her fat little body airborne on stiff white legs, directly into the path of the oncoming fielder. The impact of Bull Terrier and ball player sent the fielder spinning head over heels onto the grass but it didn't deflect the dog any at all. Patsy Ann was still aloft when her mouth came down on the ball with a *chunk* that folks later claimed to have heard as far away as first base. And *then,* Patsy Ann's four white feet hit the ground, the umpire cried, "Yer Out!" and the stands went *really* nuts!

And Patsy Ann just kept on running, right out of Diamond Park, with the ball gripped tightly between her teeth.

nineteen

THE RED DOG

PATSY ANN ran like the wind, as fast as her little pig legs would carry her, the ball lodged firmly in her mouth. Galloping hard, she crossed the bridge over Gold Creek. Still rolling at full speed, she swung away from the main road and into the first of Juneau's backstreets. She wasn't much used to this flat-out middle-distance running, and her barrel chest heaved the way the Babe's did when he rounded third base. Then again, it had been ages since she'd had a baseball to gnaw on.

At last, the pungent odour of the pigs told her that she was nearly there. She made a hard left past the soapy-smelling corner door of O'Doule's Barber Shop, almost knocking a brand new shave-and-a-haircut into the dust. Then she darted into the last alley. A jog to the right, past the chicken coop and then a fast deke to the left. She threw herself flat and disappeared under the gap in the boards like a runner sliding headfirst into home plate.

For a moment, Patsy Ann rested in the half-light of her secret den. Her pink tongue hung out and her round chest heaved as she panted, catching her breath. Her thick white body lay stretched out to its full length on the straw.

The ball lay wedged between her two grubby front paws.

Now that she had it to herself, she examined it at leisure. She eyed the scuffed white horsehide with its loops of perfect twine stitching. She ran her nose over the surface, cataloguing the many different hands that had left scents behind. She licked it, carefully at first then more generously, tasting salt and the sharpness of new mown grass. But there was only so much satisfaction to be taken from the surface of the thing. Soon she turned her head sideways and brought her molars to bear on the tough horsehide ball. For a while, the small, dusty space was filled with a steady gnawing as her Bull Terrier jaws set about demolishing the delightful, man-tasty toy. By the time she grew tired of it, the league-regulation hardball looked like it had been through a threshing machine. Its tattered skin hung loosely, the grey guts of its inner windings exposed and beginning to unravel. Patsy Ann nosed it toward a corner and under the straw.

She stood and shook, then turned and put her head down to the opening in the wall. Pushing through, she peered to both sides and sniffed deeply. The cool, windy morning had turned warm and close as the day wore on and the late-afternoon air carried tantalizing hints of what was going to be on the menu at Juneau's better hotels that evening. There seemed to be baron of beef somewhere in the wind. Patsy Ann set out for the Baranof.

She found the back door propped open in the late-day heat and peered in. The manager was nowhere in sight. She stepped inside and trotted quickly past the white cotton legs doing their nonstop step dance in the working area of the busy kitchen, to where her bowls stood.

She buried her muzzle in the one that held water and batted her nose at a little yellow curl of lemon rind that floated there. Then she drank, lapping steadily and noisily. After a while, she stopped to examine the bottom of her food tureen, but it was empty. She turned back to the water and lapped some more until her thirst was sated. Then she lay down out of harm's way along the wall, her nose conveniently close to the bowls.

Patsy Ann eyed the wide arc of dining room visible from beneath the swinging half-doors. Her nose twitched and her little dark eyes moved from table to table, watching to see which diners were leaving the most promisingly intact platters of prime rib or grilled salmon.

"Hiya, girl," said Chef Angelo, breaking off a piece of orange and tossing it to her. Patsy Ann turned her head and snapped it out of the air. "Never saw a dog eat oranges before," he commented to no-one in particular.

"There aren't too many get the opportunity around here, either," answered Sylvia, coming through the doors from the dining room. "Not the price they cost."

She paused long enough to scrape the remnants from a plate into Patsy Ann's bowl. "Here girl, you'll have to make do with a chewed-over sparerib."

It was dealt with in far less time than the baseball: a few resonant crunches and it was gone. Patsy Ann stretched her jaws wide, licked her lips and looked out into the dining room. It was busy tonight, and busboys and wait staff scooted around clearing and setting down dishes, delivering and removing food, checking the levels of wine glasses and generally fussing over people at every table.

At every table but one, that was. Off in one corner, a party of two, Mayor J. Samuel Shrite and Chief of Police Carter Beggs, hunched together over the middle of their table. Shrite was in full spate, his puffy cheeks the same colour as the roast beef on his plate. "Fuel? They went to get *fuel?*" Shrite's voice squeaked as he struggled to contain his anger while not being overheard. "He's up to something, I tell you. And even if he isn't, that boy is. I don't like the smell of this one, Beggs. I want them followed like hawks."

"But Mr. Mayor!" Beggs spread his arms and pleaded for some understanding. "You know what Judge Burns said. He wants to see these counterfeiters put away before the next election. He wants no screw-ups before the trial. No harassment, no stepping outside the bounds of the law, nothing that could endanger the case."

Shrite stared at the chief with a look of deep disappointment. "Beggs, Beggs, Beggs," he said, and swung his heavy-lidded gaze around the dining room before bringing it back to the police chief in front of him. Shrite leaned across the table, one plump hand keeping his silk tie out of his Yorkshire pudding. Beggs leaned over to meet him, cocking one ear closer to the fleshy pink lips. Those lips hardly moved when Shrite spoke: "Just don't use your own men, you fool. Hire it out. Discreetly."

Beggs' square jowls darkened, but he nodded. "OK," he said. After a moment's thought, he added, "I've got just the pair to do it, too." He straightened in his chair.

Shrite lowered his face to his plate and cut a large forkful of roast beef. He stuck it in his mouth and chewed. After a moment, he looked up and saw Beggs still sitting across from him. With apparent effort, Shrite swallowed. But his words still emerged garbled around half-chewed roast beef. "Well, what are you waiting for?" he sprayed. "They could be slipping away even as we speak."

Beggs stood up and put his police cap back on. Then he leaned forward again toward Shrite. When he spoke, his voice was low and nervous. "What do you think about these Treasury boys Burns says are comin' up for the trial?"

Shrite looked at the chief and the pouchy folds of his face pulled sideways into a wide and sinister smile. "I think," he replied, "that we had better make sure they get to see someone put away for the crime!" His tiny eyes twinkled with malice. "You just keep an eye on the Captain and the kid and make sure they don't screw it up for us."

Beggs nodded again and turned to leave.

Halfway across the dining room, the police chief detoured smoothly toward the swinging half-doors. Patsy Ann slunk back, concealing more of herself under the counter.

"Mrs. Baker?" the chief called over the doors.

"Oh, Chief Beggs!" Sylvia turned away from a counter in the kitchen to face him, wiping her hands on a dishtowel. "What can I do for you?"

Beggs nodded Sylvia over to one side of the busy kitchen. He leaned down to address her in a low, confidential voice. "With respect, ma'am, I just thought I should let you know that I saw your little Rose out at the ball game today ... and she was looking pretty, well, *familiar*, with that counterfeit kid. The one who's livin' with old Harper down at the docks." He gave Sylvia an ingratiating smile. "I just thought you should know, ma'am."

Sylvia's face fell, then she appeared to recover. "Thank you, Chief," she said evenly. "I'll deal with it. But now, if you don't mind, I need to get back to work. We've a busier night than usual, what with the crowd in from Sitka. And two of our people are out sick."

Chief Beggs tipped his cap and walked back through the dining room to the door. Sylvia watched him go, drying her already dry hands on the dishtowel again and again. She looked tired.

Almost as though she had heard her name mentioned, Rose came through the back door and across to her mother's side. "Are you going to be ready to leave soon, Momma?"

Sylvia started and looked down at her daughter. "Not tonight, Hon," she said. "Martha and Jimmy are both down with the flu. I have to work another shift."

She took Rose's shoulder and guided her to a straight-backed chair that stood beside the kitchen's big new electric refrigerators. "But why don't you sit here for a minute and talk to me?"

"Sure," said Rose, plumping herself down on the chair.

"Did you go to the ball game like you planned?" Sylvia asked, picking up a fresh potato and peeling it deftly.

"Uh-huh," Rose replied. "Here's what I got in my Cracker Jacks." She held up the compass.

"Who'd you go with?" Sylvia asked, slicing the potato crisply in two.

Rose looked startled. "Myself."

"Where'd you get the money for the Cracker Jacks?" *Chunk* went Sylvia's knife through the potato again.

Rose looked caught. Sylvia carried on.

"Have you been down to the docks today, Rose Elizabeth?" *Chunk* went the knife through the hard white potato.

"No, Momma," Rose answered vehemently.

"Who is the boy living with Captain Harper?"

"Jeff." Rose spoke too quickly to take back the name. She bit her lip.

Chunk, chunk, chunk. Sylvia pushed the chopped potatoes aside with the blade of the knife, set the utensil down and turned to her daughter. She crossed her arms and fixed the girl with a serious look. "Rose Elizabeth, have you told me a lie?"

Rose looked down at the floor. Two spots of red appeared in her cheeks.

"Young lady, you march yourself home right now. Go directly to your room. Do not leave your room unless the house catches on fire." Sylvia used her best drill-sergeant voice. "The dining room closes at 11:30 and I'll be home shortly after midnight. If you're awake we'll see to this then. If not, we'll talk in the morning before church."

Rose nodded, shame competing with rebellion for control of her expression.

"Now, off you go."

As Rose raced out into the last pink light of the gathering evening, Sylvia slammed things around for a little while, banging her knife with more feeling than usual into carrots and cabbages. Patsy Ann sighed heavily, waited for a clear moment, then vamoosed out the side door.

IT WASN'T OFTEN the Red Dog was calmer than the Baranof, but this looked to be one of those nights. Patsy Ann went in on the unsteady heels of the Sitka Whalers' pitcher. He weaved his way over to the saloon's bar.

Patsy Ann stayed with him just long enough to let Pete the barman pull a link of pickled sausage from the huge jar on the counter with a pair of silver tongs and offer it to her. Then she headed further into the saloon. Near the back she found the spot she was looking for, a quiet corner away from the pool tables and the jukebox. It was near the table where the cooks and waiters took their coffee breaks. They seldom showed up empty-handed when Patsy Ann was in the Red Dog.

A sheet of newspaper appeared, piled high with golden fried potatoes. Patsy Ann lapped a hand in polite appreciation and tucked in. She was just licking the last evidence of fried potato from the greasy paper when something at the front door caught her attention. Her ears went up and her beady eyes were wide with interest as she peered through the smoky room.

It was Chief Beggs. He was out of uniform, wearing a grey knitted cardigan over a shirt and tie and baggy trousers. The effect fooled nobody. He only managed to look like ... well, like Chief Beggs, but without the right clothes. He looked especially out of place in the Red Dog. Pete the bartender liked to say that "coppers don't spend enough time in the Red Dog to lower the social tone."

Beggs' big square head moved back and forth as he cast around in the smoky dark for something. He seemed to find what he was looking for and crossed over to a table by the Wurlitzer. Two men were already there when he sat down. A blond man with a recent scar across his heavy brows and a thin dark fellow with bad teeth and unshaven cheeks. The three of them talked for a while. Patsy Ann saw Beggs hand something to each of the men. Then he got up and left the saloon.

Patsy Ann put her white head back down on her paws and looked around the room. She checked out the line of people over by the bar, than ran beady eyes over the tables on the floor closer by. The place was lively with debate about the legality of that last "out." Views were predictably divided between adherents of the Sitka and the Juneau causes. It looked like the debate might get warmer as the night wore on, too. There was plenty of drinking going on but no one was eating much.

Time to call on the reserves.

IT WAS NOW dark outside the Red Dog. Patsy Ann turned into the breeze and trotted along the waterfront and past the mountain of coal. At the far end, she took the path she had shown the boy after he'd arrived, the path that led under the eaves of the forest to the row of gardens.

Before she got there, she could smell it, ripening nicely. A few minutes of digging and she had it in her mouth, shaking it back and forth. Hoisting the big ham joint in her jaws and holding it ahead of her like a warrior's plunder, she trotted along the side of the first cottage in the row. She came out on the road that led from town to the boat harbour. In the deep shade cast by a bank of rhubarb leaves gone to seed, Patsy Ann stood and considered.

Her thoughts were interrupted by the approach of the same two men Beggs had spoken to at the Red Dog. Even under the fog of beer and tobacco that hung around the two, Patsy Ann recognized their rancid smell. Getting a more work-doglike grip on her bone, she set out after the men, keeping to the shadows and well behind them. Unheard snippets of conversation flew by her on the light night breeze.

"Don't know what the difference would'a bin 'tween tonight and tomorrow," the dark one said irritably.

"C'mon, what's he to know?" the blond one replied, yawning. "It's a night's pay for sleepin' in the bushes."

They came to the edge of the boat basin. Here, the road followed the high ground around to the parking lot and the gangway down to the floats. The spot offered a clear view of the quiet harbour and the rows of boats rocking restlessly on their ropes. Suddenly the shorter man stopped in his tracks and grabbed the taller one by the arm. "Look!" he pointed down at the floats.

Patsy Ann trotted forward to look where the man was pointing. A boat was moving, pulling slowly but unmistakably away from her mooring in the dark. Even in the dim light, there was no doubt that it was *DogStar*.

"Don't just stand there!" the short one took over. "I'll go tell the boss. You get the boat ready and I'll meet you there. And hurry!" They both looked down once more to where *DogStar* was steadily putting dark water between herself and land. Then they each ran off in a different direction.

Patsy Ann sighed heavily around the bone in her mouth and walked to the edge of the embankment overlooking the harbour. There, she flipped the bone onto the grass and stretched out beside it.

She gazed down. The harbour was calm and smooth and the moon drew a liquid silver line on the channel beyond. *DogStar* was churning up a snowy wake that marked her passage through the black water. It followed her as she passed between the harbour lights and turned away from Juneau.

Patsy Ann gave her attention back to her bone.

twenty

THE PURSUIT

DAWN CAME in stages.

First the glittering carpet of stars overhead faded and became less brilliant over the eastern horizon. Then the mountains in that direction, whose snowy peaks had glowed all night long with eerie brightness under the almost-full moon, flattened into black cut-outs against the sky. *Wow, what a sky.* Above them, icy midnight blue melted into silver that blushed to a soft pink. That finally gave way to a brief blaze of lemony yellow just before the sun rose. It came up between the distant mountain peaks like the head of some ancient fire god awakening.

Jeff sat behind the Captain and watched the steep, green shoreline of an island go by them on the side away from the dawn. As he watched, the rising sun pushed the shadow of the eastern mountains down the wall of forest to the sea. A few minutes later, he felt warmth on the back of his neck, as the first rays of sunlight struck *DogStar*.

Beneath his feet, Jeff could feel the steady grumble of the boat's big engine. The ship's clock rang four times. *Four bells.* He thought for a moment. *Yeah, OK ... six o'clock.* Jeff still hadn't quite gotten a handle on this bell stuff, but he was getting there. The deal was to count off the half-hours from midnight forward in eights, so that 12:30 a.m. was one bell and 1:00 a.m. was two bells, until you came to eight bells at 4:00 a.m. Then you went back to one bell at 4:30 in the morning and so on through the day. It seemed like a pretty complicated way to tell time, but it sure sounded impressively nautical. *I wonder if they use* digital *bells now?* Jeff wondered. *I mean,* then ... *in the twenty-first century.*

The Captain broke the companionable silence. "The weather is with us," he said. "It can kick up squally in this reach. If we keep this up, we'll be where your map shows *Cerberus* lying before sunset. We'll find a spot to anchor and get a good night's sleep. Won't hurt to rest the engine for a little while either." His voice was calm, but his eyes glittered in the morning sun.

After the first few minutes of tension as they had untied ropes and *DogStar* had chuffed stealthily away from the boat basin, their getaway had settled down to an uneventful steam through the half-dark of the moonlit night. Black islands had rolled by on either side. Now and again, Captain Harper had murmured something to Jeff as they passed a blinking lighthouse. After an hour or two, Jeff had drifted off, curled into a cushioned corner of *DogStar's* wheelhouse. But he had woken up again long before dawn, and now he couldn't imagine sleeping. He was wound up tight. *We're going to find it* today! he thought. *I know we are!* Then another happy idea entered his mind. *Wait'll Rose hears about* this.

"How far have we got to go?" he asked.

"Another twelve hours at least," the Captain replied. He shot a glance over at Jeff and added, "Say, lad, would you care to take the wheel for a spell? I could use some relief at the helm if we've that much steaming ahead."

"Could I?" Jeff inquired. *WAY cool!*

"Come on over here," the Captain said. He motioned Jeff to stand in front of him and take the big spoked indoor wheel in his hands.

The boy could see well enough over the high cabin top of *DogStar*'s saloon ahead of him. But he wasn't quite tall enough to read the compass that sat under its big glass dome in front of the wheel. "Just keep her pointed in the general direction," the Captain instructed him. "I'll find something ye can stand on for height." He turned to the cushioned bench Jeff had just vacated. It ran along the back of the wheelhouse, making a settee. The Captain took the outer edge of the seat in his hands. "There's a toolbox under here that should do the trick." He pulled up on the front of the seat. It lifted like a lid.

"Great Neptune!" the Captain swore. Out of the locker rose an auburn head with long braids and a flash of red flannel shirt.

In the sudden light, Rose blinked and rubbed her eyes. She looked at the Captain, thought better of it and shifted her gaze to Jeff at the wheel.

Holy doodle!

"I forgot ..." she yawned and stretched her red plaid arms, "where I was ..."

Captain Harper looked accusingly at Jeff. Jeff took his hands off *DogStar*'s wheel just long enough to throw them up in the air, shaking his head as he did. *Don't look at me, Cap'n, this is a surprise to me, too.*

The Captain appeared to accept this and turned back to Rose. "What are you doing here?" he demanded to know of the girl lodged among the locker's tools, tins of oil, tubes of grease and collection of old rags. She had smears of grease in her auburn hair and on her freckled cheek.

"I ran away from home," declared Rose matter-of-factly, pulling up her back until it was ramrod straight and crossing her arms over her chest.

"Oh, gawd," Jeff groaned. *"Counterfeit Kid Kidnaps Widow's Daughter: The only thing she had left is gone."* Jeff could picture the *Alaska Daily Empire*'s headline already. *And isn't kidnapping even worse than counterfeiting? We're really in trouble now.* He looked at the Captain for help. *What do we do now?*

Captain Harper shook his head in dismay and reached down one hand to help Rose step out of the locker. "Your mother'll be frantic right about now, young lady," he said coldly. "How could you do a thing like that to anyone as kind as your mother?"

What with his surprise, and turning frequently to look at Rose and the Captain, Jeff was having a hard time keeping on course. *DogStar*'s formerly ruler-straight wake now wriggled behind her like a white snake. The Captain noticed. "I'll take the wheel, lad," he said, placing a hand on Jeff's shoulders. "Take our stowaway below and clean some of that grease off her. Then maybe you'd boil us a pot of coffee."

His back to Rose, Jeff mouthed "What are we going to do?" in the Captain's direction. But the old man just shook his head. "I need to think for a while," he said.

He looks a little shell-shocked, Jeff thought. He half-pushed Rose down the steps to the galley. She looked around the familiar little room as though it were entirely new. The beat of *DogStar*'s engine was stronger down here, and you could hear the water rushing past her sides. Circles of sunlight danced across the starboard walls and cabintop. Jeff pumped some water into a pot and lit the stove. He found a dark yellow oblong of soap and pumped some more water into a basin. He set it in front of Rose and rummaged for a clean dishcloth, finding one at last. He put it beside the soap and the bowl and said, "Wash."

Easing up a bit, he added, "I'll make it hot in a second, as soon as this boils."

Rose nodded.

"You know, we could really get into a *lot* of trouble. A lot more than we're in already."

Rose picked up the cloth and dropped it into the basin, watching intently as it soaked up water and slowly sank. "I didn't mean to get you in trouble," she said. "But I had to do something! I would have had to spend the rest of the summer at work with Momma."

"Rose! They're gonna think we took you with us! Now they're going to think we're kidnappers as well as counterfeiters. This is America! They'll probably shoot us on sight!" Jeff's blood was pounding again. *Thank goodness they don't have*

SWAT teams and Blackhawk helicopters yet. I don't think they even have radar.

Rose stuck a finger into the basin and stirred the cloth into a circle that threatened to splash water out onto the countertop.

We had our backup plan, an out, an escape hatch if we didn't find the ship. Just sail to Hawaii. But now what can we do? Take her with us? Then it really would be kidnapping. "We're going to wind up like Bonnie and Clyde," Jeff said gloomily.

"What about Bonnie and Clyde?"

Eh? Does she know about them? "They died in a shoot-out. The cops ambushed 'em."

Rose gave him a disbelieving look again and laughed. "That's silly. They're those bank robbers in Texas. The cops haven't ambushed them, they're *baffled* by them. It said so in the paper. 'Police Baffled.'"

The pot began to bubble. Jeff splashed some steaming water into Rose's basin and returned the rest to the stove. Into it he measured three large spoonfuls of coffee grounds. That was how the Captain made coffee. *Got to learn how to use the automatic drip when I get back,* he thought with a secret smile. *If I get back.* He couldn't ignore the chill in his chest.

By the time the coffee was ready, Rose had finished scrubbing off the worst of her grease stains. Patches of her hair and clothing were wet, but most of her exposed surface was reasonably clean. Jeff had sliced and buttered bread while the coffee was brewing. Now he dolloped generous spoonfuls of rhubarb jam on top of each slice. He put the bread on a wide tin plate and gave it to Rose, along with a mug of coffee. He took two more mugs of coffee and they climbed back up to the wheelhouse.

Jeff gave the Captain his coffee and took a slice of bread from the plate. Then he braced himself in a corner of the wheelhouse against *DogStar*'s gentle roll and raised his mug to his lips. Rose stepped up to the Captain and held the plate for him to take a slice of buttered bread and jam. "Captain Harper?" she said.

"Aye, lass?"

"You're not kidnapping me."

The Captain stopped in the act of bringing a slice of bread and jam to his open mouth. "Say again?" he said.

"Jeff says people might think you're kidnapping me. But you're not, you know. I'm here because I want to be." She looked at him closely. "I want to have adventures too, like Jeff and ... like you."

The Captain's troubled grey eyes looked down at Rose's pale, intense face. "Aye lass, *we* know that. But what we know and how it seems to the world may be two different things. We'll be putting you on the first ship we pass heading north. It's right back to Juneau for you, young lady."

"Oh! No! I'm not going back there!"

The Captain's face grew cold and his eyes pierced Rose's. "Oh yes, you are. Your mother should not be put through this. I'd take you back myself, but ..." He paused, then continued, "But we're bound to see a ship soon. I'm still the Captain of *DogStar* and while you're on my boat, you are under my command. Is that understood?"

Rose looked like she was going to protest again, but in the end she just nodded. The Captain turned back to the compass, worried eyes probing the horizon ahead.

They ate in awkward silence.

Suddenly, Rose said, "That little boat shouldn't be out here. Maybe they're following us."

Eh? Now what was she talking about?

Rose was up on her knees on the bench, looking back through the narrow pilothouse window at *DogStar's* wake. Craning, Jeff followed her gaze. Far down the wide channel, he could see a speck that might, or might not, be something afloat.

"Rose," he said, "I think there could be another boat on the ocean without it being connected to us."

"Nope," she replied with assurance. "Not that one. It's way too little." She paused. "Maybe they're in trouble."

"Take the wheel, lad," said the Captain.

Jeff stepped onto the toolbox. *Perfect.* He had a clear view ahead and down at the compass. "Just keep going straight down the channel," the Captain instructed him. "Due sou'west on the compass."

From the wall behind the chart table, the Captain took a pair of large black binoculars and stepped out the wheelhouse door. Standing on the starboard deck, he leaned one elbow on the cabin top for support and trained the binoculars on the boat behind them. "She's right lad, that's naught but a harbour skiff," the Captain called in through the open door. "Aye, and what's more, I believe I make out her crew." He fiddled with the little wheel that focused the glasses and looked for a while longer. When he put the binoculars down, his face was thoughtful.

"I don't like it," he said, rubbing his right hand over his whiskers. "That looks for all the world like Nat Bradley's little skiff. And Nat in it. Which probably makes the other fella Jonesy Calder. That pair'll do pretty much anything for cash ... except honest work." The Captain stepped behind Jeff. He glanced at the compass and out over the water ahead. His hand came down on Jeff's shoulder. "You're doing well, lad. Steady as she goes."

Steady as she goes! Sooo cool. "Aye, aye Captain."

The Captain turned again and looked at the boat following them. "It's strange though," he said. "Now, if that had been the police boat, it would be more sensible. The police out after the kidnapped girl ..." He shot Rose a look.

"But these two ... Why, they're no more than common thugs. And the folks they work for generally aren't much better." For the next few minutes, the Captain was silent. He bent in thought over the spread-out chart, looking up occasionally to lean out the door and peer aft at their shadow.

The wheelhouse clock struck three bells and the Captain looked up at it. A thought seemed to strike him and he reached for a thin paper-bound book on the shelf behind the chart table. After consulting the columns of dates and numbers printed inside, he pulled a scrap of paper to him and worked something out on it with a pencil. At his back,

Jeff concentrated on keeping *DogStar* on course. Rose was still kneeling on the settee, now with the binoculars resting on its upholstered back and trained through the window on the boat following them. "Yup, that's Nat and Jonesy all right," she confirmed after a while. "And it looks like Jonesy's got his rifle!"

The Captain looked up. "I think I know a way to lose them," he said. "If we're very lucky, and *DogStar* doesn't let us down."

"She won't," Jeff and Rose said together.

"We're here," he said. The Captain's hand went to the chart, pointing to a wide channel between islands. "Now, we could carry on as we're going, down here ..." He drew his finger further along the channel toward the open sea. "Or, we could go this way." His finger left the channel and traced a course that led through a wide bay. On the chart, the bulging sides of two grey islands squeezed the bottom of the bay into the merest sliver of blue water. Beyond it, another channel opened up that also led to the sea. "That's Stoney Narrows. And in a little over two hours' time, it will be impassable."

"But what good is it if we can't get through?" Jeff protested. "That's what 'impassable' means, doesn't it?"

"Aye, lad," the Captain's grey eyes glittered. "And that is exactly what it is at this very moment, and what it will be again in two and a half hours from now. But for about fifteen minutes after 1:20 this afternoon, Stoney Narrows will be as still and peaceful as a millpond. Low slack, y'see lad, when the low tide's fallen as far as it can go and it pauses for a moment before coming back up. It's fifteen minutes of calm water. That's our chance to leave those two on this side of the Narrows. We want to slip through on the very last of the slack water before the tide turns. For the moment it does, that water will change into hell's own front door, with rips and overfalls and whirlpools big enough to take down a bigger vessel than *DogStar*."

Jeff felt the hair on his neck rise. He shot a look at the clock. It was 11:24 a.m. He did some fast math. "So we've only got an hour and fifty-five minutes to get there?"

"Aye, lad, that's right."

"And how far is it?"

"About two and half hours steaming ..."

Jeff felt his heart sink.

"... at this speed." The Captain reached past him and pushed a lever forward as far as it would go. *DogStar*'s engine note climbed and she seemed to lift in the water as she moved more quickly.

"At full speed," the Captain said, standing back. "Well ... I guess we'll see."

twenty-one

THE RAPIDS

TIME INCHED BY. Beneath their feet, *DogStar*'s engine throbbed, yet they seemed to be making no better than a snail's pace across the water. The only good thing was that their pursuers, whether on purpose or because their skiff could go no faster, did not appear to be gaining on them.

From time to time, the Captain raised an instrument like a compass on a handle and took what he called "bearings" on prominent landmarks. He translated these into little penciled "X's" on the chart, showing *DogStar*'s approximate position. Each time he marked an "X," he looked up at the clock and his face became more serious. Even on the chart, the little line of "X's" seemed to be making awfully slow progress toward the Narrows.

Jeff stayed at the helm. The thrill he had felt on first taking *DogStar*'s wheel in his hands had settled down into a mild buzz of heightened awareness. How easily *DogStar* shouldered aside the small waves that were building on the morning breeze. How intensely blue the sky and sea were. How surprisingly good he felt with Rose's eyes on him, considering all the trouble they were in.

With twenty minutes to go, the Captain took over the wheel again. They could see clearly ahead to where the mountains came together, but the Narrows themselves remained hidden from view around a bend. Rose, who was keeping her eye on the boat following them, sang out, "They're getting closer."

They were. Now even Jeff could clearly see the two figures sitting in the little open boat. The shorter one had yellow hair. The taller one appeared to have dark hair. "The one with the black hair is Jonesy," Rose told him. "It's his rifle."

They fell silent. No need for "X's" on the chart anymore. They all seemed to hold their breath and Jeff barely resisted the urge to lean forward, as if that would bring them closer to the Narrows. The Captain eyed the water ahead. It seemed smooth enough to Jeff, almost smoother than the light chop *DogStar* had been slicing through out in the channel. But as he looked more closely, he could see curious veins and ripples in the black water where none should be.

He looked at the clock. *Ohmigosh, we're outta time!* They were not even in the Narrows yet and already it was almost 1:30. Most of the brief window of time when the water would be quiet was already gone. Jeff looked back and saw that the other boat was closer now; there were no more than a few hundred metres separating them. He thought he saw Jonesy shoulder his rifle, but no shot came. *Or maybe I just didn't hear it,* Jeff thought wildly. *Holy doodle, this is crazy!*

"Hold tight, you two," the Captain barked. "We're going to give this a try." His jaw was set and the tendons of his hands knotted as he gripped *DogStar*'s wheel.

Jeff spread his feet and leaned into the corner of the wheelhouse. He clenched his left fist tightly around a handhold bolted near the port wheelhouse door. The other was wrapped tight around Rose's warm hand. He looked at her. She flashed him a grin in return. Her eyes were dancing with excitement.

"Hold on!" the Captain warned again. "Here we go."

Jeff gasped. All his summers spent riding the Tilt-a-Whirl and the Zipper hadn't prepared him for the fury in Stoney Narrows. Ahead of them, waves churned and rolled and tumbled over each other, seeming to swallow their neighbours and disappear before rising again with dripping jaws. *DogStar* suddenly slewed to the left and her bow plunged downward. Her engine roared and her nose lifted slowly out of a pile of froth and moved forward again. The boat spun and bucked. Charts and papers flew around the wheelhouse and a series of crashing sounds came from the galley below. Jeff felt like he was inside a can of paint at the hardware store when they put it in the vise, flip the switch and mix it up.

As quickly as it had formed, the forest of waves subsided. But now a new menace appeared off to the left. *To port,* Jeff corrected himself. There, just ahead of them, the green-black water of the Narrows was smooth and glistening and running fast ... *in the wrong direction. No, it isn't going in the wrong direction at all.* In fact, the sea there was spinning in a vast, malevolent, counter-clockwise circle. At its centre, the rippling water appeared to fold over on itself and vanish obscenely into the depths. As Jeff watched, the evil-looking little fold became a tuck, then a depression and then, before his eyes, a hole drilling itself into the surface of the sea. Jeff's mouth went dry. "A whi ... whi ... whirlpool to port!" he finally managed to blurt out.

A whirlpool to port. Ohmigosh, I'm gonna die out here in the ocean. My parents will cry hysterically when my body washes up on shore seventy years from now. They will identify me with dental records.

"Aye, I see it lad," came the Captain's calm voice. *DogStar* shuddered and shook and her engine roared. All around them, the tortured waters of the Narrows roared and rushed. For a long moment, *DogStar* seemed to hang motionless, straining to escape the dreadful suction. No one breathed. Then, almost too slowly to really notice it at first, she began to pull away. Under their feet, the engine still roared and whined, but beyond the wheelhouse windows the rocky shore of the Narrows was moving past them once again. The hideous mouth of the whirlpool was falling further and further astern.

"They're not going to try it," Rose yelled from her post on the bench looking aft. "They're giving up! Quitters!"

For the first time since they had entered the Narrows, the Captain and Jeff looked back. The skiff that had been following them was on the far side of the tortured water, circling in frustration as the waves and whirlpools grew more violent by the moment. Its two occupants shook their fists and opened and closed their mouths in curses that were lost in the roar of the water.

Suddenly, Jeff was laughing wildly. The Captain eased *DogStar's* throttle back and she seemed to settle onto her own course. Even the Captain was smiling beneath his whiskers. Jeff's whoops died down at last and he gulped great lungfuls of air. *Please exit from the rear of the platform. If you'd like to ride again … No thanks!*

"ARE WE almost there yet?" Rose asked.

After the wild ride through the Narrows, it had seemed only fair to confide to her the real reason for their sudden departure from Juneau. "We'll know in a few hours whether we're right or not," the Captain had concluded. "Once we know that, we can decide what to do about Miss Rose." Miss Rose herself didn't act as if there was any decision to be made. As far as she was concerned, she'd joined the expedition.

After the excitement at the Narrows, the rest of the day was uneventful. *DogStar* followed a winding course through islands and fiords where mountain cliffs on either side of them plunged down into blue water of unimaginable depth beneath the boat's keel.

Finally, they came out to where the islands ended and only the wide Pacific lay ahead — mile upon mile of restless blue water stretching all the way to Japan. They were fortunate in the weather: the ocean was calm, lifting and falling gently in a long, slow swell. The sun was now sliding toward the horizon. When they were past the last island and its rocky outriders, they turned south. *DogStar* made its steady way through the water just a few hundred metres from where the rays of the setting sun cast a golden haze over cliffs and forested mountainside.

They had forsaken the pilothouse for the warm sunlight and fresh air on deck. The Captain steered *DogStar* from the little outside wheel behind the pilothouse. Jeff and Rose sat on the forward edge of the pilothouse roof, legs dangling and eyes eagerly looking forward. "Keep a sharp lookout to port," the Captain advised. "Watch for shallows and sing out when you see bottom."

A high point of land passed them on the left. Beyond it, the shore fell away and the water opened up into a broad bay dotted with dozens of small, rocky islands. *DogStar* turned her bow to port and followed the shoreline around. The Captain cut back the throttle until *DogStar* was barely drifting forward. In the slanting rays of the sun, light green and pale yellow patches amid the darker blue revealed a myriad of shoals and reefs. Jeff and Rose took up positions on either side of the bow, singing out "Rock to port!" or "Reef dead ahead!" whenever a shoal reached up out of the depths towards *DogStar*'s keel. At the helm, the Captain spun the wheel to starboard, then to port, as the little vessel threaded its way through the treacherous shallows.

Glancing back at the Captain, Jeff was startled to see the grim expression he wore. *He's thinking about sailing* Cerberus *through all these rocks in the fog.* Jeff turned back just as *DogStar*'s bow cleared a stony bluff at one end of an island where immense cedar trees hung heavy green eaves out over the water. Beyond, the view opened up across a clear reach of turquoise water. Jeff's jaw dropped. *Ohmigod!*

Less than a mile away, a sheer rock face soared upward. Its black summit was misted with cloud. And down the centre of it, unbelievably white in the setting sun, shot a great jagged streak of snowy crystal, like a bolt of lightning trapped in the black granite of the mountain. *Just like in the log*, thought Jeff. *And just like in the picture.* Except that neither one of them did justice to the majesty of the real thing. All three of *DogStar's* crew stood and gaped in awe-struck silence.

The Captain was the first to break the spell. His voice shook. "That's it. I tell ye, that's the same cliff I saw seventeen years ago! They all thought I was lying. But there it is, that white blaze and all!"

"And that means your old ship has to be close by!" Excitement danced in Rose's voice.

"Maybe lass, maybe," the Captain answered. "But she could also have broken up and gone down without a trace. Seventeen years is a long time."

They carried on, silent again, all eyes on the great curtain of rock cliff beyond *DogStar's* port rail. Waves had sculpted the lower levels of the rock wall into fantastic shapes, scooping out caves and overhangs. As they passed, seals lying on ledges at the cliff's foot flopped heavily into the sea, becoming instantly graceful as they hit the water and swooshed smoothly into the dim depths. Overhead, a bald eagle made lazy figure eights in the golden light. The only sounds were the soft chug of *DogStar*'s engine and the chuckle of water along her sides. The warm air of the evening seemed to be holding its breath.

The muffled dinging of the cabin clock sounding two bells brought Jeff back to the present, and reminded him of the passing time. *How long after they saw the cliff did* Cerberus *hit the rocks?* Jeff tried to remember the Captain's logbook. *Ten minutes?* If they didn't come across the wreck soon, that would mean it really had vanished under the surface. And their escape from Juneau and the terrifying trip through the rapids would be in vain. The tension tightened in his chest.

"There! Over there!" It was Rose whose sharp green eyes first spotted the narrow break in the cliff. She pointed, and the others followed her extended finger.

Yes! Still a quarter of a mile ahead of them, a great shoulder of black rock broke away from the cliff, reaching out to enclose a small, almost circular cove.

The bottom edge of the sun touched the lip of the horizon, spilling liquid fire into the distant sea, as *DogStar*'s bow slipped between great bastions of granite into the hidden harbour. On either side, vast columns of rock rose high above her stubby masts. The still air smelled of iodine and salt and cedar bark. "There!" This time it was Jeff who spotted the first sign of a human hand in this wild place. "At the back of the cove to the right! I mean, to starboard!"

There, already in shadow, the long rusty curve of a ship's rail pushed above the water. Behind it, unmistakable even in the gathering dusk, the square profile of a ship's bridge stuck up at a shallow angle.

"Aye," said the Captain's hoarse voice from behind them. "Aye." It sounded almost like a prayer. "Aye, that's her. That's *Cerberus* all right."

DogStar made a slow lazy circle in the calm water, as all three gazed at the wreck in the fading light.

Then the Captain seemed to shake off his memories and return to the present. "Jeff, lad," he said, his voice resuming its usual businesslike tone. "Make ready to drop the anchor."

twenty-two

MEATLOAF & CASSEROLE

MONDAY WAS meatloaf day at the Gold Dust. Danny had two end slices from the morning's baking already set aside on a plate, waiting for Patsy Ann. But when he finally spotted her late in the afternoon, she looked as though she had other plans. The familiar stocky white figure was headed south on Franklin at a purposeful trot.

Danny tore a big corner from one of the meatloaf ends and ran to the door, waving it in the air and calling "Patsy Ann!" He finally caught her eye and she paused just long enough to take the savoury slice from his hand, but declined to come in for more. Rewarding Danny with a quick lick, Patsy Ann continued on her business. "Wonder if there's a ship comin' in," Danny remarked, wiping his hands on his apron and heading back to the kitchen.

"Na'a," said a man in an open-necked shirt sitting at the window booth. He craned his neck to follow Patsy Ann's progress through the glass. "She turned on south. She's not goin' to the docks." He settled back into his seat. "Fool dog doesn't know what she's passin' up," he said to himself as he tucked into the meatloaf special.

Patsy Ann knew how good Danny's meatloaf was, all right. But there was something she needed to check out, and it was at the docks — although not the ones where the big ships tied up. She trotted briskly past the coal pile and onto the road that led south to the boat basin. There, she descended the gangway and walked quickly out to the end of Dock Three. No one was there, just an empty slip. Untroubled, Patsy Ann dropped into a patch of late-afternoon sunlight and settled down to wait.

She hadn't been there long when the float beneath her vibrated with heavy feet moving on the double. Chief Beggs came hurrying along the wooden dock, square jowls flushed and damp above the tight collar of his uniform. He was shading his eyes as he came down the floats, watching for something coming up the channel.

Patsy Ann turned her head and looked to the harbour mouth. Just as Beggs came to a wheezing halt a few steps away from where she lay, a small wooden skiff pulled around the breakwater. In it were two men. One was short and blond, the other tall and dark. Both of them were angry. Patsy Ann could smell that almost as far away as Danny's meatloaf. Her nose twitched and her ears went back, but her little pink-rimmed eyes turned to watch Chief Beggs. The burly police officer stood at the side of the float, fidgeting impatiently as the skiff approached. When it was still a dozen metres away, he called over the water to its crew, "Saw you coming up the harbour from my office. What happened? Where's the kid?"

Nat Bradley was bringing his skiff in too fast. The dark-haired one, Jonesy, threw a ragged rope to Beggs. The big man caught it and bent down to fashion a very unseaworthy knot around a cleat. Before he could finish it, the skiff rammed hard into the wooden side of the float, nearly throwing the chief of police into the water. Patsy Ann winced.

"Do you know how far those sons of bitches have gone?" Jones fumed. "We almost ran out of fuel on the way back!"

"Where are they?" Beggs demanded. "Did they have a girl with them? There's a girl missing from town. We think they took her. Her mother's goin' half-mad with worry."

The tall man leaned over the side of the boat with another rope in his hand and tied it to the dock, shooting looks of dark dislike in Beggs' direction. "A girl? Could of been, looked to me like there was three of 'em on board. But we were stayin' pretty far back," said Nat Bradley.

"Just like you said, Chief," said Jonesy. His voice was surly and rude. "You said, 'Shadow 'em. See where they're goin'. But don't let 'em know you're there.' And that's what we done." He glowered at the man in uniform.

"Leastways, that's what we tried to do," corrected Nat, speaking into the sudden silence after he shut down the skiff's motor.

"What happened?" Beggs' voice was low but urgent.

"Harper nipped through Stoney Narrows right at the turn from low slack. No way we could follow them in this li'l boat," Nat explained.

"Old fool barely made it hisself," growled Jones. He leaned down into the skiff and stood back up with his rifle held loosely in his hand.

"But he could be anywhere by now!" Beggs choked. "If he made it through Stoney Narrows, he's got a clear run anywhere within a couple hundred miles."

"Uh, yeah. That's so, Chief," Nat admitted, nodding apologetically as he stepped out of the skiff.

"Darn it, Bradley," Beggs was beside himself. "They could be in Canada by now. An old man and a kid, and you let them get away!"

"Now you hold on a minute, Beggs." Jones stepped out of the boat and stood facing the chief. He was skinnier than the police officer but just as tall, and he still had his rifle in his hand. "We was hired to do a watchin' job. Tail 'em and report back and keep our mouths shut. That was the deal and that's what we done. Now, trackin' kidnappers is police business. We weren't hired on as coppers."

Beggs sputtered, "And how am I going to explain that we had the old fool under our nose and we let him get away?"

"I dunno, Chief," said the dark man, the insolence in his voice getting sharper. "But I'll bet it's easier than explainin' to the voters why you're hirin' me and Nat to do coppers' work!" The dark, narrow face split in a coarse laugh.

"Go easy, Jonesy." Nat Bradley took the other man by the arm and started down the dock. With his free hand, he tipped his battered cap to Beggs. "Pleasure doin' business, Chief," he called over his shoulder, pushing Jonesy ahead of him. "Anytime. I'll talk to ya later about the gas. We'll be goin' now. Be seein' ya ..." He tipped his cap again for good measure as he steered Jonesy onto another dock and out of sight.

Beggs stood staring after them, mouth open and face the colour of stewed beef.

Patsy Ann lifted her head and watched the two men retreat. Then she stood up, shook herself and walked down the dock, leaving Beggs alone beside the empty skiff.

AT THE TOP of the gangway, she swung left, trotting quickly, her little white legs a blur under her barrel-like body. She followed the main road leading to town, but turned aside when it passed the row of cottages.

When she came to the one where fragrant sweet peas covered the fence and bloomed up on either side of the door, she turned in. The front door was not quite closed, and Patsy Ann nosed it open enough to go inside.

The floor of the tiny cottage seemed to be all legs. Patsy Ann looked up. A half-dozen people crowded the small sitting room, most of them standing and all of them focused on the distraught woman sitting in one of two easy chairs. Sylvia's face was drawn and white except for her eyes, which were red from crying.

A portly man stepped out of the kitchen. "Casserole's warm out there," announced Angelo, the Baranof's chef. "Everyone help themselves." He bent towards Sylvia and said with concern, "You can't worry on an empty stomach, you know. Eat something! Have some casserole."

Sylvia smiled wanly up at him but waved his suggestion away. "Oh, Angelo, thank you, but I couldn't eat. I just keep thinking about Rose and wishing I could do something."

"I blame myself," said a slim young woman with pale hair and a bright red nose who sat in the other armchair. "If I hadn't been such a weakling and stayed home for a silly cold, none of this would have happened!" She looked like she was going to start crying, but sneezed first. "Oh Sylvia, I'm so sorry!"

"Now Martha, don't be foolish," Sylvia patted her hand.

"Do the police have any ideas at all?" Martha asked.

"Oh, I don't think there's much doubt," Sylvia shook her head unhappily. "She's been mooning over this young stranger, this Jeff, ever since he arrived in Juneau. I'm sure that's where she went." She rubbed her nose with a handkerchief. "The police agree."

"But I hear the boy and that Captain Harper slipped away Saturday night?"

"Well yes, that's just the trouble," Sylvia said. "But Chief Beggs says he has a team following them and that it's only a matter of time 'til they catch up to them. Says there's nothing more to do but wait ..."

"You think she's been kidnapped?" Martha asked.

"Oh, I don't know about that," Sylvia said doubtfully. "Not the way I know my Rose. Or Captain Harper either. I don't think he'd involve himself in a kidnapping. No, this is something Rose has landed herself in the middle of."

Patsy Ann's white and pink nose wedged itself into Sylvia's lap, dark eyes fixed on the worried woman. "Oh Patsy Ann!"

cried Sylvia, surprise in her voice. "Have you come to make me feel better, too?" She rubbed Patsy Ann's ears and leaned forward, bringing her face closer to the dog's. "We sure do have a world of trouble, don't we, old girl," she whispered.

The hum of conversation carried on around the two of them. Sylvia's worried blue eyes searched Patsy Ann's steady brown ones. The little dog stood still, just her whip of a tail fanning the air behind her. Her moist black nose lifted and touched the tip of Sylvia's nose.

Sylvia smiled and straightened up just in time to see Chief Beggs coming up her walkway. Her smile disappeared as she jumped up and ran to the door to meet him. "Is there any news?" she asked, her voice tight with worry.

"I'm sorry, Mrs. Baker." The big man pulled his hat off and rolled it between his hands, looking first at the ground in front of him and then over Sylvia's shoulder at the crowded room. The hubbub of conversation had ended abruptly with his arrival; all eyes were turned expectantly to the chief. Beggs shuffled his feet and rumbled, "Harper and the boy made it through Stoney Narrows just ahead of the tide. They had Rose with them, but our boys couldn't catch 'em."

"Stoney Narrows?" Sylvia gaped. "Where in God's name is that? And how could your men let them get away? You're telling me the police had my daughter in their sights and ... and they just let her sail away?" Her voice was rising with controlled anger.

"Now ma'am, just calm down," Beggs soothed.

Sharply, Sylvia cut him off. "I am not uncalm, Chief Beggs, considering the situation. And yes, I know Rose is probably as much to blame as that boy or Captain Harper for being on that boat. But she's only twelve! She's my only daughter! I want her back home where she belongs! And I want to know what you're going to do about it!"

"I'd like to know the answer to that, too," said Angelo, stepping forward from the kitchen door.

"Me too!" said Martha, standing up and fixing her sharp eyes on Beggs over her shiny red nose.

The heavy face flushed over the chief's tight uniform collar. "Now, everyone," Beggs held his hands up in the air to quieten them down, "we're doing everything we can. We've sent wires to Ketchikan and Sitka. We've put a call into the Coast Guard and they're sending a cutter. It'll be here tomorrow ..."

"Tomorrow!" Sylvia protested. "But you've been following them since yesterday!"

"I know ma'am, but the Narrows — they're the worst on the coast for rips and undertows anytime but slack water. It's more than I could ask of Na ... I mean of an officer," Beggs' flush deepened, "to take a boat through there on a tide. It'd be his life, ma'am."

Sylvia's face went pale with a horrible thought. "And you say Captain Harper took Rose into the Narrows?"

"And got through, too," Beggs answered darkly, as though this were not an entirely welcome thought. "Nat ... That's to say, my men, saw Harper's old scow pull clear on the far side."

Sylvia let out a deep breath. "Thank God she's safe."

"Well, Mrs. Baker, in a manner of speaking she is," Beggs leaned back on his heels. "In a manner of speaking. But I'm afraid your Rose *is* at loose on the high seas with a fugitive in what the law regards as a stolen boat. And now they've made it through the Narrows." He shook his heavy head. "Why, they're free to go anywhere up or down a hundred miles of coastline. That's why we need that cutter. Coast Guard's the only folks for a job like this."

"There must be something more I can do," Sylvia frowned. "It's driving me crazy just sitting here and waiting for word!"

"Really ma'am, you can't get there any faster than the Coast Guard. There's nothing you or anybody else in Juneau can do but wait."

Sylvia searched his face for a moment. Then she looked past the burly figure standing in the cottage doorway. Her blue eyes narrowed as she tried to penetrate the haze where Juneau Harbour melted into the distant Gastineau Channel. Her eyes closed and her lips moved for a second, then she opened them again and took a deep breath.

"Alright, Chief," she said with an effort. "I'll try not to worry. But I'll be counting the hours until you hear from that cutter!"

"You'll know as soon as I do, Mrs. Baker, I promise," Beggs assured her. With a few more polite noises, he put his cap back on and turned away down the walk. Sylvia closed the door behind the departing police chief and stood against it for a moment. Around her, the conversation resumed. Across the room, she caught Angelo's eye.

The round chef smiled. Sylvia smiled weakly back at him. "I'll try not to worry," she said again. "And maybe you're right, Angelo. I think I should try a little of your casserole."

"And a side order for your friend." Angelo winked and turned into the kitchen, Patsy Ann at his heels.

twenty-three

THE WRECK

THEY WERE still alone in the cove the next morning when Jeff awoke and knelt on his bunk to peer out *DogStar*'s forward portholes. His ears buzzed with excitement and he was bursting with eagerness to start the day. *How can those guys sleep?* he wondered about his crewmates.

A metallic crash from the direction of the galley told him that someone else was up and about before him. Jeff pulled on his clothes and headed aft.

He found Rose and the Captain already up. Rose was setting out plates and the Captain cooking pancakes. *Flapjacks.*

They ate quickly, not talking much. There was too much suppressed excitement about what the rest of the day might bring to allow for small talk. The sooner they finished breakfast, the sooner they could get on to finding *Cerberus*' strongbox!

"Tide's falling," the Captain said once, between bites. "We'll leave as soon as we're ready. That should give us at least six hours on her before the water comes back up." Jeff and Rose had merely nodded sagely around mouthfuls of maple syrup and flapjack.

Once they had done eating, Jeff and the Captain left Rose to tidy up the galley while they got the dinghy ready. They dropped the little boat down into the sea from its usual place at *DogStar*'s stern. When it bobbed alongside, they put in several items they might need once they were aboard the wreck: the Captain's largest toolbox, two large flashlights, an ax, several lengths of rope and an affair the Captain called "a block and tackle," but which looked to Jeff like more rope wrapped around a couple of pulleys.

By the time they were done, Rose was hovering around them. In her hands she held a paper sack. "I made some sandwiches," she said. "And there's apples in there, too."

"Thanks, Rose," said Jeff. "We'll take them with us."

"You mean *we'll* take them," Rose replied stoutly. "I'm going too!"

Jeff looked at the Captain, eyebrows raised. *Your call, skipper.*

The Captain looked troubled. "It'll be mighty unpleasant over there for a young lass," he warned. "There's no knowing how safe those old decks will be after seventeen years in the sea. They'll be covered in weed and slime."

"I *like* slime!" Rose declared.

The Captain looked unconvinced. "It's bad enough you've run off from home," he said. "I don't want you coming to harm before we get you back."

"I won't, I promise," she said eagerly.

The Captain looked at her and sighed heavily. "Alright," he said at last. "Alright. But you follow orders and do as you're told, you hear?"

"Oh yes, sir!" Rose agreed happily.

The Captain sent Jeff into the dinghy first. He climbed down a short rope ladder that hung from *DogStar's* rail and settled himself onto the dinghy's stern. Then he held the small boat steady while Rose followed him and took her place in the bow. The Captain came last.

The small boat bobbed and rocked while he settled himself in the centre seat and took the oars. Then they were pulling smoothly across the glassy surface of the cove. It was very quiet. Only the sound of the oars dipping gently into the water, lifting and dipping again, broke the silence.

This is it, Jeff thought with a lump in his throat. He could hear the Captain breathing, *in-out, in-out*, as he rowed. Jeff felt sure his own heart was pounding loud enough for the others to hear.

Twisting in his seat, Jeff looked over the dinghy's stern and down into the clear water. Far below, he saw lighter greens and flashes of white where rocks raised barnacled heads above the sea floor, closer to the sun. Five-pointed splashes of purple and red gave away the presence of starfish. Long fronds of kelp waved languidly up at him from the depths.

He looked ahead again. *Cerberus* lay on her port side, only her bridge and part of her deckhouse above the water. Most of her bow seemed to have vanished. The ruined hull ended in a ragged stump that broke the surface of the cove just forward of the bridge. Bright green algae, black clumps of mussels and the white volcano-shaped shells of barnacles blurred the edges of her rusty orange steel plates.

As they approached the wreck, the Captain let the dinghy drift slowly along the stained and broken plating. He brought one oar close to their little boat, and they drifted silently up to the rust-caked iron. He leaned out and ran one brown leathery hand over the foundered vessel. His expression was distant, his eyes seemed to see things far away. *Or long ago*, thought Jeff, watching him.

The old man turned to look at the boy. "Y'know, young Jeffrey," he said softly, "just finding her again means an awful lot to me, more maybe than the money."

"It'll be there," Jeff answered with confidence.

The Captain smiled at him and leaned into his oars again. This time he pulled the little boat all the way around the broken bow of the wreck. The entire hull seemed to have snapped in two, creating a cutaway effect, and Jeff could see directly down through the clear water into the broken ship. The weedy green tunnel of a passageway ran back and away into deep gloom inside the wreck. Where the forward part of the ship had vanished, small waves lapped at the ruined remains of bunks and shattered lockers. The salt and iodine smells of sea life exposed to the sun wafted heavily towards them across the still air.

Around the far side of the wreck, they found a place where the deck shelved down into the water like a slippery green ramp. The Captain nosed the dinghy closer to the makeshift landing spot.

Before the old man could give the word, Rose seized the dinghy's painter rope in one hand and leapt from her place in the bow onto the tilted deck. She landed lightly on her feet but slipped at once to her knees on the slick seaweed. In a flash, she wrapped her other hand around a corroded chunk of iron and held tight. When she turned back to look at them, she was laughing.

The Captain followed more slowly and carefully, took the rope from Rose's hand and tied it securely to a rusted stanchion.

The last to step onto *Cerberus* was Jeff. In his hand, he carried one of the flashlights.

But the Captain did not descend immediately into the dark depths of the wrecked ship. Instead, he climbed cautiously up towards the bridge, the youngsters at his heels.

As they climbed, working their way up the dangerously tilted steps of what had once been an outdoor stairway, the ruined old ship creaked and shifted. The noises and movement brought them briefly to a halt. But then, cautiously, they carried on.

The bridge itself looked a little like *DogStar*'s wheelhouse, only on a larger scale and very much the worse for wear after seventeen years of battering by waves and weather. Most of the exposed metal was orange and pitted with rust, the wood bleached and cracked by the salt sea air. Shards of thick glass poked out of the empty frames of wide, forward-facing windows. The big wheel tilted at a crazy angle.

The Captain stepped to the wheel and bent forward to examine the big compass that stood on a waist-high pedestal in front of it. With a corner of his sleeve, he rubbed the heavy grey scum of algae from the globe of thick glass and peered inside. His head lifted and he looked around them, craning his neck to glance through the broken windows at the sun. Then he looked again at *Cerberus'* compass and his brows furrowed.

"I don't understand it," he said, shaking his head. "It's still showing the wrong direction."

Jeff was not interested. *What's done is done*, he thought. *Who cares about why the ship got lost. The important thing is, we've found it now.*

"It probably got broken when the ship hit the rocks, Captain," he suggested. "But c'mon, let's find the money! That's what we're here for." He was having trouble containing his impatience.

"Aye, lad," the Captain agreed reluctantly. "That's what we're here for."

From the bridge, the Captain led them to a steeply tilted interior passage that ran down and back toward the ship's sunken stern. It was dark in here, and they moved slowly on the slippery deck plates, following the dancing beam of the flashlight in Jeff's hand. The wet steel walls were furred with seaweed and mussels. Jeff saw a small crab retreat into a rusty recess. Doorways, some open and others sealed tightly shut, lined the corridor on both sides. All around them, the wreck murmured and creaked and the sound of dripping water echoed in the dark.

"I hope she's not slipped too far under," the Captain said.

At last, they came to an oval steel door on the left side of the passage. *Just in time, too,* Jeff thought. Ahead of them, water filled the corridor.

"This was the Captain's cabin," the old man said. "My cabin. It's where the strongbox was."

He put both leathery hands on the rusted metal wheel that served as an oversized knob on the heavy steel door, and gave it a wrench. It turned perhaps a couple of centimetres, then stopped.

Bracing himself against the slippery angle of the deck, the Captain tried again. The wheel did not budge.

"Well now," he said, standing back. "It looks like *Cerberus* isn't ready to give up her secrets just yet." He considered for a moment. "But we have more ways than one to skin a cat. Jeff, will ye fetch the tool box, lad?"

Jeff hurried back the way they had come. When he reached the dinghy, he found that it now lay almost entirely out of the water, its round bottom tipped to one side on the seaweed-covered deck. *The tide must still be falling.*

He lifted the heavy tool box from the little boat and started back. As he was about to enter the gloomy inside passageway, he met the Captain and Rose coming back up it.

"We've got an idea," said Rose. In her hand she held the flashlight.

Quelling a pang of jealousy, Jeff put the toolbox down and followed them.

This time, the Captain led them through several more slanting passageways and open doorways to the outside of

Cerberus' deckhouse. Jeff recognized it as the starboard side, the one furthest from the water.

Again, they made their way aft. But now they followed a narrow outside deck running the length of the ship's battered deckhouse. A row of large portholes on their right, Jeff suddenly realized, must once have given light to the cabins on the same level as the Captain's.

As they slipped and scrambled down the sloping deck towards the water, Captain Harper seemed to be counting something. With just a few metres of deck left before the steel disappeared beneath the surface of the cove, he stopped. Beside him, the last porthole was a round empty mouth in the rusted cabin wall. "Aye," he said in a low voice, as if speaking to himself, and peered inside.

"Give me that light," the Captain said, and Rose handed it to him. He switched it on and pointed its beam through the porthole, then looked inside once more. "Aye," he said again.

"It's my old cabin, all right," he said. "And it doesn't look like anyone's been in it since I abandoned ship."

"That's great!" Jeff burst out. "It means the money's still there."

"Aye, well it may do that," said the Captain, his voice serious. "But getting to it will be another thing. Look for yourself."

The Captain moved aside to let Jeff look. *It looks like a Mixmaster's hit it!* The far wall of the cabin, the one with the door, looked like an old junk pile. Bits of wood, chunks of rusted metal and shards of broken glass lay in an untidy drift against the door. Seaweed and barnacles had grown over some of it. It smelled like the mudbanks at Juneau Harbour when the tide went out.

"Something in that pile of debris is blocking the door," the Captain said. "And without getting in there to move it out of the way, we'd need a cutting torch to open it up." He shook his head grimly. "I'm afraid we may be out of luck."

No! There has to be a way. Jeff mentally measured himself against the size of the porthole. *But that's not it,* he reluctantly had to admit. He wondered if they could break a way through the weakened steel plates.

"I'd fit!" piped up Rose, as though she had read Jeff's thought.

Man and boy looked with surprise at the slim figure in overalls and pigtails. *Jeez,* thought Jeff, *she might, too.*

"But could ye shift the rubbish in there?" asked the Captain, doubtfully.

"I don't know. Is it heavy?" she asked him.

The Captain and Jeff both leaned back to the porthole. In fact, none of what was jumbled against the far wall looked particularly large or heavy. Jeff recognized a wooden chair, what looked like a set of drawers that had pulled out of a dresser and a lot of lumpy muck that might once have been clothes or papers. "It looks more messy and yucky than heavy," he observed.

"What if you can't move it all out of the way, girl?" worried the Captain.

"Then I can always come back out the way I came in," Rose answered.

The Captain looked unhappy. But there really did not seem to be any other way. Reluctantly, he lifted the girl up the angled wall to the porthole.

For a moment, Rose sat perched on the rusted steel of the cabin's outside wall, legs dangling through the porthole. Then, holding on tightly to the Captain's strong brown hand, she wriggled closer to the edge of the hole.

Her legs were in all the way to the waist now. Her arms were raised over her head as she dangled from the Captain's hand and slipped inch by inch into the reeking darkness. As Rose's face slid below the rim of the porthole, one mischievous green eye winked at Jeff.

"OK, I'm ..." Rose's words ended in a yelp and a slithering noise followed by a muffled scrunching sound.

As one, Jeff and the Captain craned their heads to see into the darkened cabin. "It's OK, I'm all right," Rose called up to them. "But get your big heads out of the light!"

The Captain and Jeff pulled sheepishly away from the porthole and glanced at each other.

"You stay here and keep an eye on her," the Captain said. "I'll go back 'round to the other side of the door."

Jeff heard things moving in the cabin, soft thumps and thuds, the sucking sound of something coming away from wet mud or sand. A crash louder than the rest brought his head back to the porthole. Inside, he could see Rose standing with one foot on the slanting deck, the other against the door. She was wiping her hands on her grimy overalls. The boxlike frame of the bookshelf now lay to the right of the door.

Where it had been, he could see a rusted wheel that matched the one on the other side of the door. As Jeff watched, the wheel turned, stopped, then turned again.

Suddenly the door dropped away from the wall into the corridor below. Rose yelled and jumped to one side just in time to avoid falling through the newly opened hole where the door had been. Jeff could hear muffled imprecations floating up from the corridor beyond the cabin.

Abandoning his post, he rushed back along the catwalk, through the passageways they had followed earlier and down to the corridor they had first ventured along. When he got to the open door, the corridor was empty.

He pulled himself up through the now-open hatchway and into the Captain's ruined cabin. Rose grinned hugely at him from a face smeared with greenish-brown gunk. *She looks like a commando.*

"Thanks," he said shortly, surprised at the surge of resentment he felt rising in his throat. *I'm supposed to be the hero.*

The Captain was standing at her side, apparently deep in thought. Jeff followed his gaze. He was looking at the rear wall of the cabin. It met the floor and the corridor wall at a doorway leading back to a second room behind the first. But the way that *Cerberus* lay on her rocky deathbed made that corner the lowest point in the cabin. And black water filled the far room and lapped over the sill of the door.

twenty-four

DIVING FOR GOLD

THE CAPTAIN'S shoulders sagged as he looked over at Jeff. "Well, lad," he said, resignation in his voice, "Wee Rose did well to get us this far. But the sea may beat us yet." He nodded into the dark well of water. "That's where our treasure lies, down there.

"That used to be my office on board ship," the Captain explained. "The strongbox was along the back wall. It's probably fallen to the lowest corner now. There must be two fathoms of water over it."

"Fathoms?" Jeff asked.

"Six feet to a fathom. Call it twelve feet to the back wall." *Twelve feet … make it three metres.*

"I can dive that!" said Jeff. *See if Rose can match that!*

The Captain's eyebrows shot up in surprise. He looked skeptically at Jeff.

"Not a problem!" the boy insisted. "I can hold my breath a real long time. I swim two lengths underwater at school. Just tell me what I'm looking for."

The Captain was shaking his head, looking down into the water as he spoke, "It'll be mighty dark down there, son, you won't be able to see a thing."

"You said yourself the safe's probably fallen into the corner," Jeff insisted. "I'll just follow the corner of the floor and the wall down to the bottom."

"There may be creatures down there," the old man cautioned. Beside him Rose made a face and shivered.

Creatures? "What kind of creatures?" Jeff asked, feeling his first doubt. Rose's wide green eyes were on him now.

The Captain gave him a level look. "Urchins and starfish on the bottom. Eels probably, octopus. Maybe a bigger fish or two. You never really know what's under the surface of the sea."

Jeff eyed the oily black water in the doorway uneasily. *Spooky, no question.* But he knew Rose couldn't swim and he didn't think the Captain could make it down to the bottom either. That only left him.

And I can swim. It's one of the few things I do well. Like that jailer's frog. Besides, Rose's green eyes were on him.

"I can handle it, Captain," Jeff asserted. His voice sounded more confident than he felt.

AT THE CAPTAIN'S suggestion, they spent the next hour preparing for Jeff's attempt to dive down to the strongbox. First, they made their way back to the dinghy, where they ate the sandwiches Rose had prepared in companionable silence. Then they headed back into the interior of the wreck. The Captain shouldered the ax and block and tackle, Jeff hoisted the coils of rope and Rose brought the remaining flashlight.

Back at the flooded cabin, they shifted debris around until they had made a small, more or less level, platform between the doorway to the corridor and the one that led down into the dark water. The water's surface was a little lower now, but the Captain told them that the tide would not fall much further. If Jeff was going to try to reach the box, he would have to do it in the next few minutes before the tide began to rise again, making the task impossible. Jeff felt his stomach knot up, and he forced himself to breath evenly as he counted slowly to ten.

Jeff slipped out of his boots and socks, but left his other clothes on. Partly, he thought they might keep him a little warmer once he was in the water. Partly, he didn't want Rose to see him in his underwear.

"The strongbox will be about two foot tall and the same wide, a bit less than that deep," the Captain was saying. "It's got short legs on the bottom of it, and a dial and a wee handle on the front. With luck, it'll be lying on top of anything else that's down there." He looped one end of a length of rope around Jeff's waist and tied it. "Good luck, lad," he said.

Then the old man and Rose stood back, each with a flashlight in hand, their beams directed down into the flooded cabin.

As Rose had done earlier at the porthole, Jeff slipped his legs into the dark water first. *Yow!* It was cold. *Really cold.* He took a deep breath. *Don't think about it, just DO IT!*

He pushed himself off the rusted steel sill and all the way in. *Ohmigosh, Ohmigosh, OHMIGOSH!* With all of him in it, the water was even colder than he had first thought. *Too late now, just get it over with.*

He took another deep breath and held it. Then he ducked his head beneath the surface and kicked his feet out of the water behind him, forcing his body down into the icy blackness.

He opened his eyes. Everything was blurry. He could make out the lime-green shafts of light from the flashlights but not much else. With one hand, he reached out and felt for the corner between the side wall of the cabin and the floor. He kicked hard with his legs, scissoring them fast to push himself further into the depths. *Don't think about eels,* he told himself. His lungs were beginning to burn.

He was at the bottom!

He could feel hard, irregular surfaces under his hands. As *Cerberus* had settled, junk had piled up into the corner of this office just as it had against the door in the cabin over his head. His eyes were wide open, but his movements brought murky sediment swirling up from below him into the clear water, filling the flashlight's weak beams with dancing motes.

Suddenly he felt something different ... rectangular. His chest felt like it was going to explode. Desperately he ran his fingers over the boxlike shape. *There ... it had to be.* In the darkness, Jeff's fingers traced a round lump. *The knob!* Then, the length of something hard beside it. *The handle!*

But then there was no fighting it any longer, *I have to get to the top, have to breathe.* He turned for the surface, put his feet against the pile of debris and pushed upward. His lungs were going to split apart.

"Pfwaaahhh!" Jeff burst up into the *lovely, fresh, wonderful* air and threw his head back to clear the water from his eyes. "I found it! I found it! I'm sure of it!" he yelled, too excited to even try to speak normally. "It's there! We can get it!" He gripped the sill of the doorway and pulled himself up onto it.

Rose and the Captain were cheering, clapping him on the back. "Well done," the Captain said.

But they hadn't got it yet. When Jeff described how he thought the strongbox was lying, the Captain took one of the ropes and, with a few deft turns and knots, fashioned it into a crude sort of cradle with two loops. This he handed to Jeff, instructing him to slip one loop under each side of the strongbox. The other end the Captain kept in his own grip.

Again Jeff slipped into the water. *It's not so bad once you get used to it,* he thought. *No. That's a lie. But who cares.* He wasn't sure whether he was shaking from the chill or from excitement, but he didn't care about that either.

This time, he found the box quickly and managed to get one loop underneath it before the fire in his lungs sent him back to the surface again.

On the return trip, he used the rope to pull himself down to the strongbox. He opened his eyes but saw nothing. *Way too much muck in the water ... all this messing around.* He groped, found the free loop, groped some more and found the other corner of the box. He slipped the rope loop under and headed again for the surface.

"Got it!" he announced even before he'd swept the water from his eyes. He pulled himself back onto the platform and shook all over like a dog, trying to rid his clothes of as much sea water as possible.

The Captain was already at work. Swiftly, he attached one of the two pulleys that made up the block and tackle to a rusty flange of metal sticking out from the bulkhead wall furthest from the flooded cabin. Then he tugged the other pulley down until it was almost at the surface of the water.

The Captain pulled up on the rope Jeff had secured to the strongbox until it was tight, then he tied it to the lower pulley. Moving to the rope that joined the pulleys together, he tugged on it until it too was tight. Then he waved Jeff and Rose to his side.

When all three of them were braced, each with a portion of the rope leading from the block and tackle in their hands, the Captain said, "Right mates. On the count of three, haul lively now."

"One ..." he said. "Two ... Three!"

They pulled. The rope around the pulleys became tight and began to vibrate. "Heave," the Captain said, and they did.

At first, nothing seemed to happen. "Heave!" the Captain sang out again. And then, slowly, ever so slowly, the lower pulley began to move. As they pulled again on the rope, it inched upward, steadily closer to where its mate was attached to the far wall. And as the lower of the two pulleys came up, so did the other rope, the one that led down into the murky depths.

"Heave," the Captain said. "And heave again ... and again ..."

Rusted steel plates vibrated under their feet as the heavy safe slid across the submerged cabin floor. Suddenly, with a soft little *whoosh* sound, it broke the surface.

Two more heaves and it stood dripping before them on the makeshift platform.

"Yes!" yelled Jeff, as soon as he got his breath back. "Yessss! We did it!"

Rose beamed beneath the grime on her face and even the Captain grinned. Jeff held out his palms to "high five" them. But when they looked at him blankly he settled for shaking each one by the hand and pumping hard. "We did it," he repeated, satisfaction bubbling over. "We got it!"

"That we did, lad," smiled the Captain. "That we did."

For a moment, all three of them regarded the strongbox in triumphant silence. It was covered in greyish muck and water dripped from green fronds of seaweed. A great many barnacles and muscles had made their homes on its square surface and as they watched, a small blue crab stepped sideways out from underneath the thing and waved stalk-like eyes at them in annoyance before scuttling away.

Then the Captain spoke, his voice serious again. "But now we'd best move fast. We need to get this piece of iron across to *DogStar* before the tide comes up and it's back underwater again."

IT TOOK another hour or more to manoeuvre the heavy strongbox out onto *Cerberus'* slanting deck. By then it was clear that the tide was coming back up. Indeed, it was already licking at the stern of *DogStar*'s tidy dinghy.

And something else was also clear, at least to the Captain: the little boat could not possibly carry all three of them, plus their tools and the salvaged strongbox, safely back to *DogStar*. "She'll never hold that much weight," the Captain told Jeff and Rose. "She'll founder and then we'll all be in the water."

"We'll have to make two trips," he decided. "Jeff, you row Rose and the tools across first, then come back. Meanwhile, I'll rig the tackle ready to swing the safe into the dinghy when ye return."

"Aye, aye," said Jeff, pleased to be given this new responsibility.

He slung their spare rope into the little boat and followed it with the tool box. Rose tossed in the flashlights and, with the Captain's help, they slid the dinghy down the sloping deck and into the water.

Rose climbed in first and stepped lightly to the stern seat. Jeff followed her and settled on the middle one, facing Rose. He heard a soft *thump* as the Captain tossed the mooring line into the bow, and he leaned into the oars.

TWENTY MINUTES later, Jeff felt another soft *thump* as the dinghy again made contact with *Cerberus*' weed-covered deck. He looked over his shoulder.

What he saw startled him.

The safe was there, all right, slung in a new and more secure cradle. The Captain had managed to swing one of

Cerberus' rusted old derricks out over the water. The block and tackle was rigged to the end of it, so that all they needed to do was heave on the rope and the heavy safe would be suspended above the dinghy.

It was the Captain's pale, drawn face that was all wrong. *He looks like he's seen a ghost,* thought Jeff. *But I thought no one died in the wreck.* "What's the matter?" he asked.

The Captain looked at him for a moment as though deciding whether or not to speak. Then he withdrew one hand from his trouser pocket and held it out. In his palm was a rust-stained cube of metal, about three centimetres long and two wide, and a centimetre thick.

"What's that?" Jeff asked.

"A magnet."

"Where'd you find it?"

The Captain seemed to have trouble finding the words. "On the bridge. In the binnacle."

This was no help to Jeff. "Say what?"

"The compass, lad. It was in the compass."

Jeff felt a chill that went deeper than his wet clothes. *Holy cow. No wonder he looks like that. The magnet threw his compass off course. None of his readings were even close!* Suddenly an inspiration came to him. "Hey! But that's great, Captain!"

The old man stared at him, disbelief on his face.

"No, really," Jeff explained. "It's great! It means the wreck wasn't your fault! You didn't lose the *Cerberus* after all. She was sabotaged!"

The Captain's expression remained unchanged. "Aye lad,

Perhaps I didn't drive *Cerberus* onto the rocks." He paused. "But *someone* did."

"Oh c'mon, Captain. That was seventeen years ago. Whoever did it is long gone by now," Jeff argued. "The important thing is we've found her. And now we can take the money back to Juneau and prove it wasn't your fault!"

"Aye," the Captain said again, doubtfully.

They set to work shifting the heavy strongbox into the dinghy and let the matter of the magnet rest. But Captain Harper's face remained troubled.

With the safe, a man and a boy all in her, *DogStar*'s dinghy sat dangerously deep in the water. The Captain rowed slowly and carefully. Even so, one or two small wavelets washing into the cove from the deeper water beyond lapped over the side, splashing cupfuls of water into the dinghy's round bottom. Moving carefully, Jeff scooped it back out with a bailing bucket. And eventually they bobbed gently alongside *DogStar*'s comforting bulk.

There was more heaving to get the strongbox aboard the larger boat. But at last it was lashed securely in the middle of the wheelhouse floor.

"Aren't you going to open it?" Jeff asked, surprised. He'd been looking forward to that part.

The Captain shook his head. "Shrite Shipping Lines gave me my cargo sealed," he said with a stubborn edge to his voice. "And sealed is how I'll be taking it back."

Jeff's disappointment was only momentary. With *DogStar*'s deck once again pulsing to the deep beat of her engine, his mind was too full of their triumphant return to Juneau to admit any worries.

We're on our way home. We've got the treasure back. We'll be town heroes! Jeff's grin spread from ear to ear as he put his back into the task of weighing *DogStar*'s anchor.

twenty-five

THE DOG STAR

SUPPER THAT evening was a festive event. While Jeff steered *DogStar* north on her return course to Juneau, the Captain displayed a knack for turning a canned chicken into hearty, if not precisely *haute*, cuisine. They ate in the wheelhouse, the comforting throb of *DogStar*'s diesel steady under their feet.

From somewhere, Captain Harper produced three bottles of soda. And as the sun sank toward the high peaks of the islands to the west, they toasted their success. They toasted Rose's scramble through the window and Jeff's dive into the flooded cabin, and the reception they would surely get back in Juneau.

The evening was calm and warm, the sky pale blue, then yellow and finally a fierce fiery orange as the hot ball of the sun sank beneath the western horizon.

They had talked out every thrilling replay of the adventure aboard *Cerberus* and finally lapsed into a contented silence. Rose, after declaring that she was far too excited ever to sleep again, lay curled on the wheelhouse settee, sleeping soundly.

The Captain had declared Jeff "off watch," and taken over the wheel. He stood now, feet widely placed on the deck, rocking automatically to *DogStar*'s steady, rolling progress.

This time, they would not need to risk the hazardous passage through Stoney Narrows; their course would follow the safer main channel through Frederick Sound.

The Captain had said they should take turns at the helm so the one who was off watch could get some sleep. But Jeff didn't feel like sleeping yet. *There's just way too much energy on this boat to sleep*, he thought. He sat in the open wheelhouse door, back resting against the cabin wall, looking up at the sky.

It looks so different, Jeff was thinking with something akin to wonder. He had to remind himself that he had looked at the same mountains from the deck of the *Passage Princess*. It seemed a lifetime ago. *But it isn't. It isn't really even "ago."* Then, the endless splendour of the Alaskan coast had bored him. Now it felt magical. As the dusk deepened, a carpet of glittering gems unrolled slowly across the dome of the sky.

"I've never seen this many stars in Halifax," he said, gazing upward.

"Ah, the stars," the Captain said, his voice wistful. After a moment's thought, he reached beneath the chart table, pulled out a drawer and removed a length of cord. One eye on the compass and their course ahead, the Captain used the cord to lash the ship's wheel in place. It took several adjustments, but eventually he seemed satisfied that the arrangement would keep *DogStar* true to her course.

He returned to the drawer under the chart table. When he straightened back up this time, there was a wooden box in his hands, its polished surfaces gleaming faintly in the darkened wheelhouse. The Captain slid it under his arm and turned to Jeff. "Let's go sit under the stars," he said.

Jeff moved his legs to let the Captain through the door, then got to his feet and followed him aft.

They settled themselves on the low, curved rooftop of the Captain's small cabin in *DogStar*'s stern. Overhead, Jeff was dimly aware of the creak and sway of the heavy boom that carried *DogStar*'s back sail, furled and held up out of the way with a rope.

Wow, he thought, that sense of magic flooding through him again. *It's night, but it's not dark at all.* Behind them, a fine receding line of glowing phosphorescence marked their passage, where *DogStar*'s heavy propeller had churned up the ocean's algae. High to the southeast, the full white moon cast its restless reflection of silver and ivory onto the glassy sea. And then there were the stars.

The Captain set the wooden box on the cabin roof and slipped open its brass latch. Inside, small padded posts supported a curious instrument. Two dark legs made the shape of an "A." Moonlight glimmered on the polished brass arc that joined the legs. Jeff looked with curiosity, but didn't have a clue what it was.

Carefully, the Captain lifted the object from its box. On one side, it had a handle, and the old man held it so that the top of the "A" pointed up. For a moment, he peered through a tube and fiddled with several small discs that seemed to fan out from a common pivot point. *Like a Swiss Army knife,* Jeff thought.

"What is it?" Jeff asked.

"This is a sextant, lad," the Captain said softly, continuing to fiddle.

"Sex *what*?" Jeff choked.

The Captain leaned back and chuckled. "A sextant is how a sailor finds his way across the open ocean, lad, following the sun and the stars," he began. "You see, Jeff, a compass is a poor, man-made sort of creature. It can make mistakes. But the stars now, the stars never lie." He looked up into the glittering sky. "They are God's chart. And with a sextant, even we mortals can learn to read it."

He held the instrument up and showed Jeff how to use the little tube like a telescope to sight on a star, how to move small mirrors so that the star's image seemed to come down to meet the horizon, and how to read from the brass arc the place of the star in the sky.

"Give me a sextant, an able ship and the stars," the old man said, "and I'll take you safe from the Gulf Stream to the South China Sea."

"Can you use any star?" Jeff asked.

"Not just any. Fewer than a dozen altogether, including the sun. Only the brightest."

Jeff had his hands braced against the rooftop behind him now, leaning back to gaze straight up into the emptiness of space. *Except that it's not empty at all.* In the clean air, the moon seemed to hang just beyond his fingertips, it looked so close against the distant curtain of stars. *But it's not a curtain either, it's … deep.*

In the blue-black void around them, some stars seemed to hang closer than others. Between the bright ones in the foreground were others further away, so many that in places they became nothing more than a glowing mist of distant worlds. *Very 3-D. It's like you can actually see space*, he marvelled.

Jeff felt suddenly as though he were no longer looking *up* from the solid safety of the boat's deck. Instead, he was looking *down* into the emptiness between the stars, sticking to the boat the way a balloon sticks to the ceiling. *Static cling keeps boy from falling into space.* He smiled in the pale light of the moon.

"But the brightest star of all," the warm voice beside him was saying, "is the Dog Star. Sirius, the Romans named it." He pointed to a spot just above the southern horizon.

Jeff followed the Captain's eye to a pulsating pinpoint in the sky. "That *really* bright one? Is that what you named your boat after?" he asked.

"Aye, son, it is. The Dog Star may not be the biggest of the stars, but 'tis by far the brightest light in our sky. That's why sailors have loved her so well for so many centuries."

The Captain removed the silver chain he wore on his neck and held it out to Jeff. On the end was an ivory-coloured disc. "Have a look at this."

Jeff took the object in his hand. It was made out of some kind of bone. He held it up to the moonlight. On one side was a faintly drawn profile of a dog. The artist had placed many-rayed stars at the collar, nose, feet and tail.

"My great-great-grandfather made that, on the Greenland whaling grounds. It's scrimshaw work, etched on whalebone.

My father gave it to me the day I shipped on *Elissa* for the first time. He gave it to me so I would learn to know the constellation *Canis Major,* the Great Dog," he gestured toward the cluster of bright stars on the horizon, "and Sirius, the star at his collar. Then I would always be able to find my way home."

He left the old whalebone in Jeff's hands while he carefully packed the sextant back in its box.

"Ye know, lad," the Captain said, rubbing the polished wooden box, "I expect now you'll soon be getting home ... where ye belong. But I'm mighty sorry you won't be cruising to Hawaii as my first mate. You've turned into a fine young sailor." He spoke with a touch of sadness.

Home. Back there. Mom and Dad. Buddy in a box. Suddenly, getting back to the present — *or is it the future?* —back to his own time, anyway ... didn't seem nearly so important to Jeff. They'd found the *Cerberus.* The Captain was going to be a hero. Surely he could stay in Juneau now if he wanted to. *But can I?*

"You're still going to go to Hawaii?" Jeff asked, handing the pendant back to the Captain. He'd rather talk about *this* present. *It's a lot more interesting than that one.*

"Aye son, I believe I will. It feels good to be back on the water. I guess it's where *I* belong." He smiled up at the night, keen grey eyes searching out Sirius. "I might get me another dog, though. It can get lonely on the way without a friend."

He tilted his head and looked at Jeff. "What about you? Won't you be happy to get home?"

Jeff looked back at the warm, wise eyes and a hideous thought hit him. He felt that icy cannonball form in his stomach again.

The Captain must have seen it in his face. "What is it, lad? What's wrong?" he asked.

Jeff had trouble getting the words out. "When I get home, you'll be ... *dead*. Like my dog Buddy." He felt the corners of his eyes beginning to burn. *Oh great, I'm gonna cry. Some tough sailor.*

The Captain looked at the boy for a moment, than put his arm over Jeff's shoulder and held him tightly. "There, there, boy. I'll not be dead."

The way he said it gave Jeff a jolt. *He means it.* He pulled back and looked up.

"You see, lad, I believe that spirit is a kind of energy," the old man said. "It's in us for a while, and then it goes away to somewhere else. I've always thought it goes to the stars." He looked up. "Dogs have it too, that spirit. I think their spirit goes up there, to Sirius, the Dog Star. I can't imagine anything else that would keep it burning so bright and constant.

"That's where my old Maddie is," the Captain looked searchingly into the heavens. "I catch her playing up there from time to time. And I believe I'll go there, too, when my watch on earth is up. Aye, if I'm to spend eternity, I believe I'll spend it with Maddie on the Dog Star.

"And you see, Jeff, stars don't change like people do. So when you get home to the future," he said softly, his eyes on the boy's, "just look to the brightest star in the sky. That's where we'll be, Maddie and Patsy Ann and me."

And Buddy? "Will Buddy be there, too?" Jeff asked urgently.

The Captain rubbed his whiskers thoughtfully for a moment before answering. "Well lad, he's certainly welcome. But I'm not sure that he's there yet.

"You see, it's a mighty bond, the one between dog and man," the Captain smiled. "Or dog and boy. I have the feeling Buddy's still waiting for you in your world, waiting to be certain that you're all right. When he knows that, aye, then I'm sure we'll see him at the Dog Star. When he's free."

That sorta does sound like heaven. Buddy and the Captain and Patsy Ann and Maddie. Jeff was certain Buddy would like them all. *That's where he belongs,* Jeff nodded to himself. *And I could ask for a telescope for my birthday,* he thought excitedly. *Then I'll always be able to find them.*

He looked up at Sirius, the Dog Star. Then he made a wish. *A wish upon a star. For Buddy.*

Let him be free.

twenty-six

OLD SECRETS

DONG ...

Dong ...

The clock in the wheelhouse was striking. Jeff opened his right eye just enough to determine that it was light out.

Dong ...

Three, he counted.

Dong ...

Four ... five ... six bells ... Silence. A moment or two to think. *Seven o'clock!* And something else. Something about the way *DogStar* moved and ... *Silence, that was it! No engine.* They were at anchor.

He opened both eyes and discovered that he was stretched out on the saloon sofa. He sat up and shot a quick look out the nearest porthole. *Land! And not moving.* They were in a small bay. He didn't remember anchoring. *Must have fallen asleep,* he thought.

A noise made him turn back to the saloon. *Yikes!* Rose sat watching him from the end of the sofa by his feet.

"You snore," she said.

"I do not!" he protested, looking around for support from the Captain and finding him at the galley stove.

But the Captain just raised one thick grey eyebrow and turned back to the pot of porridge he was stirring.

No help there. Jeff shrugged and gave up.

Over steaming bowls of porridge, the Captain explained that after Jeff had fallen asleep last night, he had put into the bay and dropped *DogStar*'s anchor. They would weigh it again after breakfast and should be back in Juneau by late afternoon or early evening.

It hit him again. *We did it! We really did it!* But then the rest hit him, too. *So now it's almost over.*

Rose looked over her spoon at him. "Will you go back to Canada when we get home?" she asked quietly.

Eh? Jeff considered. "Stay here, I'll be right back."

He went forward to his cabin and pulled his watch from the drawer. It still read Tuesday, but now the time was 5:30 p.m. If he was going to make it back in time to meet his parents at Patsy Ann Square by six o'clock, it would have to be soon. *Like, tomorrow!* A strange feeling came over him, excitement mixed with sadness.

Jeff dragged his feet back to the saloon table.

"Well?" she asked.

"Uh … yeah, probably. I guess."

The Captain broke the awkward moment, clearing his throat loudly and announcing briskly, "Well then, let's get this ship under way, shall we?"

THEY HAD BEEN chugging north for almost three hours and the sun was high in the sky when the Captain called Jeff to the wheel. Leaving the boy at the helm, he took his binoculars and stepped onto the deck. He raised the glasses to his eyes and focused on something in their wake.

Looking back, Jeff saw a ship some distance behind them but plainly making better speed than *DogStar*. It would not be too long before the steamer overtook them.

The Captain stepped back into the wheelhouse. "When she's closer, we'll signal her," he said. "I want to put Rose on board."

"No!" protested Rose.

"Aye, girl," the old man said firmly. "You'll be home before the day's out anyway. And she'll get you there hours ahead of *DogStar*," he added, nodding towards the steamer. "There's no need to put your mother through any more grief than we already have."

Jeff looked over at Rose where she sat unhappily on the settee. As much as he wanted time to stop and let him enjoy this perfect morning forever, and as much as he didn't want to see Rose go, he knew the Captain was right. He had a thought. Being the first ashore meant being the first to tell the story. "You'll be able to tell them the news!" he said.

Rose's face brightened a little.

"That's right!" the Captain agreed. "As soon as you land, go to the mayor and tell him we're bringing back Juneau's gold. That should get word around town in a hurry!"

The resentment on Rose's face vanished. "Why, I bet they'll get a parade ready for when you come back into harbour!" she exclaimed.

Kupraenof Queen came readily to a stop when Captain Harper hailed her. After a short discussion, its captain agreed to take Rose on board for the rest of the distance to Juneau. He even offered to let down the *Queen*'s stairs for Rose to walk up "lady-like," as he said. But Rose was happy to climb up the rope ladder that a crewman let snake down the ship's side. *Happier,* Jeff thought, watching her overalls disappear over the rail.

In a moment she was back at the rail, leaning over and waving. "Bye! See you in Juneau!"

The Captain stood at the little outside wheel and put *DogStar*'s engine into gear. She nosed away from the steamer's side. Jeff hauled in *DogStar*'s fenders and watched *Kupraenof Queen* gather way.

IT WAS mid-afternoon when Jeff looked across at the Captain and saw a worried look on the weathered brown face. *Why's he blue? He's going to be a hero.*

His mind ran over the last forty-eight hours. Surely the Captain couldn't get into trouble for letting Jeff leave Juneau if he also brought him back. *No, that isn't it.*

"That magnet still bothering you, Captain?"

"Yes. It is," admitted the Captain. "It's a dreadful thing to set a ship on the rocks on purpose, a dreadful thing. It was just the grace of God that brought the people home safe. They could as easily all have drowned!"

"Do you have any idea who put the magnet there?" Jeff asked. "Why would someone want to throw you off course?"

The Captain stared at the water ahead of them, his eyes looking into the past. He shook his head, "I can't imagine it. There was no-one I would have counted as my enemy."

Lame, Jeff thought, *very lame.* "Somebody must have had something to gain," Jeff insisted. *Follow the money.* It was what Dad always said. He was a lawyer and knew how these things worked.

"But that's the thing, Jeff. No one gained. Everyone lost!" He was thoughtful a moment. "Well, Shrite got most of his loss back from the insurance, but for the rest it was just pure loss."

"Didn't you say that Mayor Shrite was on the ship?"

"Aye, along with five other passengers and the crew," he sighed. "One of them must have slipped the magnet onto the bridge. And any one could have done it. There was a lot of visiting on the bridge, as I recall."

"Maybe there's a clue in the strongbox," Jeff suggested.

The weed-encrusted safe still stood in the middle of the wheelhouse floor. Its fronds of seaweed were curling as they dried and it gave off a rich low-tide smell. The Captain looked at it thoughtfully for a while, then shook his head.

"Captain, *think* about it," Jeff prompted. "Shrite was on the ship. Shrite collected insurance money. Nobody else got a dime. There must be *something* in that strongbox that he wanted to go down with the ship."

The Captain raised his eyebrow. "That certainly makes the most sense." He sighed. "I don't like to open it, Jeff, but we'd better know what we're sailing back to."

Then he nodded at a hatch. "Pull that up, lad, and you'll

find a steel bar on the left side. Bring it out." He tied the wheel off again. "Let's have a look."

Together, they untied the lashing that held the rusted box to the deck and tipped it onto its back. The Captain inserted the flattened end of the steel bar into the corroded seam between the box and one of its hinges. Then he pushed down. The box had probably once been really strong. But seventeen years in the sea had done its work. For a moment, the Captain strained and nothing budged, but then there was a brief shrieking noise and a spray of rusty water flew across *DogStar*'s wheelhouse. The hinge had broken away from the corroded wall of the strongbox.

The Captain shifted position and inserted the bar under the other hinge. It put up more of a fight. But when Jeff added his weight to the bar, it too broke away. After that, it still took some doing to break the door away from the rest of the strongbox. Time and salt water had welded the two together into a solid mass of rust. But after some struggle and several more applications of the iron bar, they finally had it open.

The inside of the box was better preserved. It was laid out with several metal trays that pulled out like drawers. Each drawer had a metal lid that once had been sealed with wire; Jeff could see the rusty lines where the thin metal wires had been eaten away to nothing.

They pulled out the first drawer. Inside were dozens of neat bundles of currency, mainly ten- and twenty-dollar bills. *Pretty wet bills.* Each bundle had a paper wrapper on which the stamp "City of Juneau" could still be clearly read. Some of the wrappers had started to fall apart, but on the whole the money looked like it had weathered almost two decades underwater pretty well.

The next two trays were both much heavier than the first. Each contained a number of leather pouches, tied at the neck. Every pouch also had a cardboard tag tied to it; names were still visible on some of the tags. Jeff looked at the Captain for an explanation.

"Gold," he said. "Dust or nuggets. Some of those bigger ones probably have bars in them."

No wonder that box was so heavy.

The last tray came out with more difficulty. But when it lay on the deck and the Captain opened it, it proved to contain a flat leather satchel almost as large as the tray itself. Jeff could still read the name stamped with gold letters into the black leather: "Shrite Shipping & Brokerage, Inc." Two straps held the satchel closed, ending in small brass locks.

After a moment's hesitation, the Captain pulled out a pocket knife and opened it. With two quick motions, he cut the leather straps and pulled open the satchel. Inside were more bundles of currency, except that all these bills seemed to be hundreds. *This must be Shrite's two million dollars!* Jeff didn't know anyone who could say that they'd seen that much money before.

But something was different about this money. Jeff looked closer. The colour on these hundreds looked way more washed out than the ink on the tens and twenties had. In places, the corners of the bills had softened and crumbled away. Jeff gasped when the Captain reached to pick up a bundle and it fell apart between his fingers.

Ohmigosh! It's phony!

His face ashen under its tan, the Captain closed the leather flap back over the contents of the satchel. They each looked anew at the gold lettering on the outside.

"Shrite!" both said at almost the same instant.

So he's the counterfeiter, not me! That's why he kept trying to get the "plates" from me! And he insured funny money and collected real money ... that's why he sunk the ship! Then another thought hit him. *Rose! We told her to find Shrite as soon as she got to Juneau.*

"My God, lad," breathed the Captain. "We've sent her right into his hands!" He leapt back to the helm and leaned on the throttle, pushing it forward as far as it would go. The note of *DogStar's* engine went from a steady low throb to a high roar and she surged ahead. The Captain unlashed the wheel.

And then, without warning, the roar lost its vigour. The engine coughed and faltered. Its steady pulse fell back to a protracted sputtering that ended in several loud barks and then nothing.

In the silence, *DogStar* drifted softly to a stop.

twenty-seven
DEEP WATER

PATSY ANN'S head came up. Her quick movement caught Snuff Malakov's eye and he looked up from his cards. The only sounds were the usual ones: the distant thump of the rock-crushers at the Alaska Juneau mine, the chuff of a handful of cars and trucks going by outside the Longshoremen's Hall. And anyway, Snuff knew that whatever had caught the deaf Bull Terrier's attention, it was something he sure couldn't hear.

Patsy Ann got up, stretched "fore and aft" and yawned with her customary impressive dental display.

Snuff put his cards down on the table and said, "I'll fold, too rich for my blood. Besides, looks like this'll be the last hand, anyway." He nodded over at Patsy Ann.

"That'll be *Kupraenof Queen*, I expect." Hank Watson glanced into her corner, then back at his cards. "See your dime and call. Two pair, jacks high."

Patsy Ann gave herself one of those truly invigorating nose-to-tail shakes that ended with her little back legs moving so hard they danced right off the floor. Jake Earness beamed at Hank and threw down three sixes and a pair of twos. "Full house." He raked in the fifty cents that lay on the table and pushed back his chair.

Patsy Ann gave a final little shiver to compose herself and stepped over to the door. Snuff opened it for her and the three longshoremen followed her out. Together, they walked the half-block to the wharf.

The three men stopped. Hank put his hands over his eyes and looked down the channel. "Yep, that's the *Queen* alright. She'll be tying up right here, then."

The little white dog kept walking.

"Where's she goin'?" asked Jake.

"You sure that's not the coal boat, Hank?" suggested Snuff. "Be the first time I've seen Patsy Ann get the wrong wharf."

Hank took another look, then shrugged and wagged his head. "Nope, it's *Kupraenof Queen* for sure."

But Patsy Ann didn't stop at the coal wharf either. In fact, she kept right on going past the end of the harbour, picking up speed to a brisk trot when she reached the road that led to the boat basin. At the row of cottages, she began to run, fat little body galloping along in her hurry. At the one with the sweet peas on the fence, she made a sharp, skidding left turn and bolted up the walk. This time, the door was closed.

She barked.

There was silence in the house.

She barked again. There was a sharp, urgent note in her voice. She barked, and kept on barking.

The door opened. It was Sylvia, hair up, wearing a long white apron and holding a paring knife in one hand. A curl of bright red apple peel hung from the apron's oversized pocket.

Her eyes were rimmed in red and her face was tired and lined. "Why, Patsy Ann! What a ruckus. Come on in, then, and have some apples ..." She held the door open for the dog.

But Patsy Ann wasn't interested in bites of apple right now. She danced away from the door, barking, then turned until she was half-facing the road. Eyes still on Sylvia, she barked some more. Sylvia put her head to one side and looked at Patsy Ann. Then she noticed movement in the distance above the dog's head and looked up and out over Gastineau Channel. A ship was heading in toward the harbour.

She looked back down at Patsy Ann. The stocky little dog barked again. A perplexed look crossed Sylvia's face. "Now, why aren't you already down on that dock, girl?" she asked. Sylvia's eyebrows shot up as her expression suddenly changed. "Oh, my! Oh my goodness!" Suddenly she seemed flustered. She took one step toward Patsy Ann, then one back to the door. Then she turned again and looked quickly at the dog and up to the ship. People crowded the deck. Some were waving. Patsy Ann barked again, such sharp notes that they almost hurt.

"Yes," Sylvia said. "All right. Give me a minute." She disappeared into the cottage, leaving the door open behind her.

Patsy Ann put her tail down and sat, pink tongue hanging out. But she stopped barking.

When Sylvia reappeared a moment later, she had taken off the apron and put on a blue hat and was carrying a small blue purse. She set off down the road, walking fast, Patsy Ann trotting at her side.

"Oh, I hope I'm not making a fool of myself," Sylvia said to Patsy Ann as they hurried along. "The cutter won't be here until tonight. It's been driving me crazy and I can't do a thing 'til it comes. Chief Beggs said they'd sent telegrams to Ketchikan and Sitka but I went to the station this morning and no one's answered yet!" Patsy Ann turned her head and managed to slap her tongue on Sylvia's knee as it flashed past.

After that, Sylvia seemed to run out of breath and saved what she had left for half-running the last hundred metres to the wharf. There was a press of people on hand to greet the ship. Without Patsy Ann, Sylvia would have had to push and elbow her way to get to the front. As it was, the little white dog put her thick head down and shouldered a path through the legs, Sylvia following close on her tail.

The *Kupraenof Queen* was just gliding slowly up to the timbered quay. Passengers lined her rail and looked out from many of the portholes that ran in a double row down her side. A crewman stood at a little open door in the rail, holding a rope as thick around as Sylvia's arm. As she watched, he threw it to Hank Watson, waiting on the wharf.

Anxiously, Sylvia scanned the faces at the rail. Then her heart jumped. "Momma!" she heard.

"Rose!" Sylvia cried. "Rose Elizabeth!"

"Momma!" the shout came again. Sylvia's eyes followed the sound to the open door in the ship's railing. A blue-uniformed officer stood there now, waiting for Hank to push the heavy gangway into place.

❖

Sylvia craned and squinted, then called again, "Rose!" In the shadows behind the ship's officer she was sure she'd seen a slim figure with pigtails.

"Momma!" Rose pushed in front of the ship's officer and waved wildly.

It was another ten minutes before Sylvia was hugging Rose to her chest and laughing and wiping away tears and thanking *Kupraenof Queen*'s captain all at once. Patsy Ann danced around them both, darting in to deliver a few strategic licks to Sylvia's damp cheeks and Rose's flushed ones.

Sylvia allowed herself one more hug then pulled back, held Rose by the shoulders and looked at her daughter closely. Rose's overalls were stained with grey and brown patches of grime, but that was usual. Otherwise, she seemed just fine. And her face was alight with suppressed excitement, green eyes sparkling with glee.

"Says she has some kind of big news," the *Queen*'s captain said at their side. "Wouldn't tell us what it is, though. Said it had to wait 'til she got home."

Even as she stood to give the captain an impulsive, grateful hug, Sylvia looked down at her daughter with curiosity.

"Yes, well, anyway." The embarrassed officer extricated himself from the woman and backed away. "Glad we could bring her back to you, ma'am. A good day to you, ma'am!" He tipped his hat and turned back, blushing, to his ship.

For just a moment, Sylvia stood with her eyes closed, whispering something. Then she turned her attention to Rose.

"They didn't kidnap me, Momma," Rose was saying. "I ran away. I'm sorry."

"I know, honey," Sylvia said. "And I didn't really think the Captain had kidnapped you. But you have to promise me never, ever, ever to do that again. You had me worried out of my mind." She looked Rose directly in the eyes. "Promise?"

"I promise," said Rose, her voice serious.

Sylvia shifted on her heels and asked, "So, what's this big piece of news? And where are the Captain and that boy, Jeff?"

Like soda that's been shaken and uncapped, the words came bubbling out of Rose. "We found the ship! The one the Captain lost! Only it's not lost anymore, it's there. And we went aboard and got the safe and all the town's money. And they're on the way back right now, Jeff and the Captain! I'd still be with them, but they made me get on the steamer!"

Sylvia gaped, her mouth opened but no words came out. Finally she said, "You mean the Captain remembered where the gold ship went down?"

"I don't know if he remembered it or if someone told him, but it's there."

"And he and Jeff found the gold and the money?"

"*We* found it," Rose corrected her.

"Oh my," Sylvia said. "Oh my, my." Suddenly she looked skeptically at her daughter. "Really, Rose?" she asked. "This isn't just a tall tale, is it?"

Rose shook her head. "No! Really, it's not! I helped Jeff and the Captain carry the safe back to *DogStar*. I'm supposed to go tell the mayor."

"Well," Sylvia said slowly. "Then all right, I guess we should. And we'd better tell Chief Beggs that you're back, too." She leaned down to give Rose one last, fast hug before the girl could object, then took her hand. "Oh baby, I'm so glad you're home. Let's go see the mayor right now!"

Before they could take a step, a voice from the ship yelled, "There she is!" They looked over.

A silver-haired man was leaning through a porthole a few metres away, pointing with excitement at Patsy Ann. "There's that white dog in the postcard!" he was saying to someone behind him. "Quick, Bess, pass me one of those cookies."

Now the man was holding something in his hand, an almond macaroon by the smell of it. Patsy Ann was on the edge of the quay, looking up at the porthole. The man's hand moved. The macaroon sailed across the space between the ship and the dock. Patsy Ann's head was up, eyes on the spinning white cookie. She jumped to seize it from the air and then ... Then she and everyone else realized that, in her eagerness, Patsy Ann had jumped right off the edge of the wharf. There was a strangled yelp, followed by a resounding splash.

Several other people joined Sylvia and Rose as they rushed over to look down. This wasn't Patsy Ann's first unplanned jump off the dock. She was already paddling energetically for the muddy bank under the wharf, snuffling and splashing with effort and irritation. But she had the cookie.

Rose and her mother watched until Patsy Ann was safe. Then they turned away from the water and started through the crowd.

ONCE PATSY ANN reached the mudbank, she stopped for a minute to shake the sea water from her short white fur and catch her breath. She was still under the wharf, which now stretched like a huge echoing roof over her head and along the shore for a great distance in either direction.

Giving her pelt a final, annoyed shake, she set out along the narrow strip of mud. She knew where a rotting timber in an older portion of the wharf had fallen down and left a gap. If she climbed the embankment at the right spot, the gap was big enough for a dog to crawl through.

It was a white-and-mud-coloured Bull Terrier that finally regained the street. Patsy Ann's nose twitched at the strong odours of dead shellfish, live worms and worse, rising from the high boots of brown mud on all four of her feet. She crossed Egan Drive and headed up Main Street. One or two passers-by stopped to pass her a treat. But quite a few others gave her one sniff and crossed quickly to the far sidewalk.

By the time she reached the Federal Building, the sun had dipped below the summit of Douglas Island across the channel and Juneau's long summer dusk was falling. The hours when the building bustled and buzzed with people were over. The big public doors were locked.

Patsy Ann looked up. The windows of Mayor Shrite's large corner office glowed a warm yellow. Further along the second floor, Henry Burns' window was dark. Patsy Ann trotted around the corner and along the wall to the side door. One sniff told her that Jefferson was long gone for the day.

Plantings of shrubbery stood on either side of the door like sentries. The white-and-brown dog crawled into the shadow of the thickest bushes and settled down to wait.

twenty-eight
UNDER SAIL

THE CAPTAIN emerged, red-faced and grease-stained, from *DogStar*'s engine compartment. "Fuel pump," he told Jeff, spitting into a rag. "I can fix it. But it will take a couple of hours."

A couple of hours! And Kuprawhatever Queen *is already way ahead of us!*

Jeff followed the Captain back to the wheelhouse. Without her engine to push her through the waves, *DogStar* now wallowed in the hollows between them. She rolled unpleasantly and the strong afternoon breeze was pushing her slowly toward a small cluster of islands.

The Captain eyed the sky, then said: "Well, there's no point in drifting when we can sail. Let's get some canvas aloft!"

To the rescue under sail! Cool!

The Captain went forward and set *DogStar*'s small triangular jib. With the two of them hauling on the lines, they made short work of getting up the much larger sail that hung from the shorter of *DogStar*'s two masts. Stout wooden poles kept it spread at the top and bottom. *Gaff up, boom down … gaff up, boom down,* Jeff reminded himself.

Jeff watched while the Captain adjusted the sails, tying and untying ropes to the row of cleats along the back wall of the wheelhouse.

"She'd carry more aloft easily enough," said the Captain, nodding at *DogStar*'s taller main mast forward. "But you'll have to take the helm while I'm below, so we won't press it."

Once the sails were drawing to his satisfaction, he showed Jeff their course and gave him the wheel. *Wow! She feels way different under sail,* he noticed immediately. *Way smoother.*

Captain Harper watched for a minute to be sure that Jeff was going to be all right, then disappeared below. For the first time, Jeff noticed the silence. *It's so quiet without the engine.*

DogStar lifted her forefoot over a wave and sliced neatly down its back, her masts dipping daintily as she came to the trough and started up the next wave. Water foamed along her sides with a soft *whoosh*. The sail over his head fluttered cheekily in the breeze. The rigging they had checked so carefully creaked gently as it took the strain of the wind.

"I think I like this better, Captain," he said, when the old man came up for air and to check on their progress. "Maybe you don't need to fix the engine at all!"

That raised a chuckle from the old man. "Aye, well. We'll see what you say when the sun's setting and there's not a baby's breath o' wind on the water!"

They adjusted the sails and the Captain returned to his labours below.

IN THE END, it *was* almost sunset before the Captain came on deck again, now much more greasy and with dark sweat stains through his grey jersey, to announce that he thought he had the fuel pump repaired. And the wind was indeed failing, just as the Captain had predicted. But when the Captain pressed the starter button, *DogStar's* engine throbbed back to life. Within minutes they were under way, with the wheelhouse floor once again vibrating steadily beneath their feet.

It felt good to be making directly for Juneau at top speed again. But Jeff made himself a silent promise. *When I get back ... OK, if I get back, I'm going to* sail!

twenty-nine

KIDNAPPED

PATSY ANN waited patiently in the bushes outside the Federal Building, paying no mind at all to the tantalizing scents that drifted past her nose. The distant dinner smells of early evening faded into night perfumes of roving cats and hunting owls. The sky overhead went from dove-grey to purple and was working its way toward velvety blackness by the time the door finally burst open.

Chief Beggs' head came out. He held the door half-open behind him and looked up and down the narrow side street. The door snapped shut again. The overhead light went out.

Seconds later, the door opened again.

Shrite charged out of the Federal Building pushing Sylvia ahead of him. A handkerchief was tied over her mouth and she was in handcuffs. "Over there," the mayor hissed, pushing the woman toward a large black car. In moments, she was bundled inside.

"Hurry up," Shrite snarled at the open door.

Out came Beggs with Rose in his arms. Her mouth was gagged but she wasn't in handcuffs. Even through the chief's handkerchief, she was screaming blue murder and above it her eyes blazed defiance. Beggs was having trouble keeping her thrashing arms and legs under control.

He was almost at the car when Patsy Ann shot out of the shadows. Hurling her solid little body into the air like a white torpedo, she slammed headfirst into the chief. Losing both his balance and his hold on the girl, Beggs fell to the ground, arms flailing wildly. Flying out of the big man's grip, Rose landed with a thump in the flower bed.

Beggs' pistol had been jolted from its holster when he fell. As he reached to retrieve it, Rose scrambled to her feet and bolted, yanking the gag from her mouth as she ran.

"Forget the gun," Shrite yelled. "Get the kid!"

But Rose was already gone, dashing down the short side of the Federal Building and around the corner onto Franklin Street, Patsy Ann galloping at her heels. Safely past the corner, Patsy Ann overtook the girl and kept on running, not fast enough to leave Rose behind, but clearly taking charge.

Shooting a look over her shoulder to make sure that Rose was keeping up, Patsy Ann ran along the front of the big Federal Building, across another street and then turned uphill. Soon, both dog and girl were panting hard and beginning to slow down. By then, they had left downtown behind and were among the houses that climbed the lower slopes of Mount Roberts. When finally Patsy Ann stopped, they were in front of a tidy log cabin. It was small but lovingly kept, with hollyhocks bright in the garden and a small verandah with a well-worn porch swing. Light glowed warmly behind the lace curtains.

Rose looked like she was trying to remember something. Then her face cleared and she burst out, "This is Judge Burns' house!" She bent quickly to hug Patsy Ann, whispering, "You're such a clever dog." Then she raced up the steps and pounded her small fist hard on the door.

In a moment it opened and Henry Burns' lean face was looking down at them both with an expression of startled consternation.

"Judge Burns, you've got to help me!" Rose began. "They took my momma!"

Henry opened the door a little wider. "Who are you, young lady?" he asked.

"Rose Elizabeth Baker," she said. "Please, you've got to hurry."

The judge frowned. "But I thought *you* were the one they kidnapped, not your mother."

"No!" Rose said with frustration. "They didn't ... Jeff and the Captain, they didn't kidnap me. I ran away. It's the mayor and Chief Beggs ... *They* took *Momma.* And they have a gun!"

Henry's frown became a look of confusion. He turned to address Patsy Ann. "What on earth is going on?" he asked the dog. "And look at *you,* have you been having mudbaths?"

"She fell off the wharf," Rose said hotly. "Then she rescued me from Chief Beggs. Oh *please,* Judge Burns, won't you just *listen* to me?"

The judge seemed to shake off his surprise. "Yes, young lady, of course I'll listen. But you'd better come inside." He opened the door wide and shot a look at the dog. "You might as well come in too, Patsy Ann. But wipe your feet."

She didn't, but Judge Burns pretended not to notice.

Inside the cozy cabin, the judge sat Rose in a big wing-back chair and let her talk. She told him everything that had happened since she had stowed away on *DogStar*, leaving nothing out.

With every new turn in the girl's tale, the judge looked more alarmed. When at last she was through, he picked up the phone that sat on a table beside him and dialed a number. "Ethel," Judge Burns said into the phone, "get me the duty room down at the base."

Patsy Ann got up and trotted to the door, looking back for someone to open it.

"And hurry," Henry Burns added.

thirty

LOWERING THE BOOM

DEEP DUSK became full night as *DogStar* entered Gastineau Channel. It was flat calm. Clouds hung around the shoulders of the mountains on either side, shutting out the moon and stars. The lights of Juneau made a glittering cluster at the head of the channel, with a scattering of smaller lights reaching out towards them along either shore.

Well, I don't see a parade.

Jeff and the Captain had talked briefly about what they might expect Shrite to do. But they had decided that their guesses were too unsure to make any useful plans. "Just keep your eyes open, lad, and be ready to step lively," the Captain had said.

That's not exactly a playbook, Cap'n, Jeff had thought. But as he gazed forward into the dark, he felt his adrenaline pumping. He felt ready to *step lively* whenever it was called for.

DogStar turned her bow away from the main channel. Ahead of him, Jeff could see the boat basin behind the encircling arms of its twin breakwaters. A green light winked on the tip of the breakwater to the left, a matching red one on the right.

The coloured lights reminded Jeff of something, but he couldn't think what. As he watched, the lights slipped past them to either side and they were inside the basin.

DogStar's engine chuffed softly as they ghosted past a row of fishing boats toward her berth. It was in the darkest corner of the basin. Jeff strained to make out the shadows ahead. *Is there something strange about the outline of the pilings? Is someone hiding there?*

He heard the change in the engine, felt the vibration of the propeller cease, as the Captain dropped *DogStar* out of gear. They coasted forward. *Almost there.*

In the darkness ahead, something glinted.

A dark shape moved away from the shadow of the piling. *It is Chief Beggs, waiting on the dock. And he has a gun!*

"Captain!" Jeff cried out, moving quickly down the deck toward the back of the boat.

"Aye, lad, I see him. We'll turn back and go tie up in town."

The Captain swung *DogStar*'s bow back toward the channel.

A voice came across the water, low but clear, and thick with menace. "I wouldn't do that if I were you, Harper."

Mayor Shrite! A light shone out on the dock, a flashlight. In its beam, a pale face with something funny about it ... *A gag! It's a woman with a gag in her mouth. Where is Rose?* The light flashed off. "Bring that scow of yours back to the dock, Harper," came Shrite's voice again.

"That's Sylvia Baker!" the Captain said. In a louder voice he cried, "All right, Shrite, we're coming 'round. Don't hurt her."

He spun the small wheel and peered into the darkness.

As *DogStar* once again turned her bow toward her own berth, the Captain whispered, "Watch for an opening, Jeff, any opening you can find. If you see one, take it."

As *DogStar* came alongside the float, Beggs shoved Sylvia roughly over the boat's low rail and onto the deck. Then he jumped after her, keeping his pistol leveled on the woman.

Behind him, Shrite heaved a heavy suitcase over the rail. Something inside clanked. His weighty bulk followed. *For a big guy, he sure moves fast,* thought Jeff. Shrite was cursing and breathing heavily. The moment he had his footing, he pulled out a gun and pointed it at the Captain.

"No funny business, Harper. Just turn this thing around and take it back out of here. Nice and smooth and quiet."

The Captain did as he was told. He threw *DogStar*'s propeller into reverse and she backed slowly away from the dock.

Beggs shoved Sylvia Baker into the wheelhouse.

Holy doodle! Gag and handcuffs! But where is Rose?

"Kid!" *Shrite.* "Get back here where I can see you."

Jeff came aft along the side-deck. As he passed the wheelhouse, he glanced in. *OhmiGOSH!* Beggs had freed one of Sylvia's wrists from its handcuff and was busy reattaching it. Only now the pair of cuffs was looped around the railing where the companionway went down to the saloon. For a moment Jeff's gaze met Mrs. Baker's worried eyes looking back at him over the coarse cloth of the gag.

"Move it, kid," Shrite barked. "Come over here, where I can see you." He motioned with his pistol to the strip of deck beside the Captain, between the back of the wheelhouse and the raised roof of the aft cabin.

Jeff eyed the pistol in Shrite's hand. *Jeez, that thing's big. Bigger than on TV. Wayyy bigger.* He stepped warily around the Captain and stood between him and the mast.

Shrite positioned himself on the raised aft cabin roof. He moved his pistol back and forth between Jeff and the Captain. "Turn around," he ordered Jeff.

Jeff did as he was told. Now he was facing forward and Shrite was out of sight behind him. Beggs came out of the wheelhouse, closed the door and came aft. Jeff heard him get up beside Shrite on the aft cabin top. *Great, now we have two guns on us. Some holiday in America!*

"So, it was you," the Captain stated flatly to Shrite.

"You'll be sorry you ever found that ship, Harper."

Jeff's eyes were unseeing, all his attention focused on the sounds coming from behind him, trying to figure out what Beggs and Shrite were up to. They were almost back at the mouth of the basin now. From somewhere out in the channel, a rogue wave caught *DogStar*'s forefoot and she tipped gently into it. Without thinking, Jeff grabbed one of the cleats in the row in front of him for support.

Ohmigosh! He raised his eyes to look up. *Whoa! Be cool now, don't draw any attention to it!*

But, yes, of course it was still up there, right where they'd left it hours ago: the big back sail wrapped around its two heavy wooden poles. *The gaff and the boom.* Altogether, it must weigh a couple of hundred pounds. *Hanging right over the middle of the little back cabin. And all held up by ropes that ... come down right here!* He squeezed the cleat under his right hand. *But which one? Can I really do it without Shrite or Beggs catching on?*

"Listen Shrite, you don't need Mrs. Baker and the boy," the Captain said. "Put them ashore. I'm the one you have a quarrel with."

"Just steer," said Shrite. *Yes! Behind and to the left. Perfect. Now, which rope?* Jeff squeezed his eyes shut for a moment, concentrating. *This one!* The third one over from the mast. *Oh God, let this be it!* His body was between the cleat and the two men. He used only his right hand, the one furthest from them. He let his left hand sit innocently on another cleat, where they could see it.

Don't look down.

His fingers pulled blindly on the coarse new rope. *There!* He had one of its multiple loops off the cleat. He dropped his hand to the cleat's lower horn and began working on the next loop. *How many darn loops?*

Beside him, Jeff felt the Captain go momentarily rigid. He looked up and over at him.

"Eyes forward, both of you." It was Beggs this time.

Jeff obeyed the order. But not before catching the Captain's eye, and ... *Yes, I'm sure I saw it. He's got the play!*

They were almost between the arms of the breakwater now. Jeff felt the tension on the last loop of rope. *This one's it,* he thought. *When it goes, so does the sail. We're going to lower the boom on you, buster!*

He pulled again. It was almost ... *Off!*

"Now!" Jeff yelled, and ducked. Beside him, the Captain shoved the throttle forward, spun the wheel hard and dropped beside him.

Overhead, there was a short rattling rush and the rope whipped past in front of him. Behind them, there was a quick series of thuds and grunts and *DogStar*'s deck lurched under their feet. Something heavy rolled down the cabin top and there was loud splash.

They turned. The gaff and boom and bundled sail rested across Shrite's ample middle on the aft cabin top. He lay without moving, a large gash on the top of his bald pate. In the darkness behind them, they could hear Beggs crying out for help. *DogStar* was turning in place while her engine raced.

The Captain leapt back to the helm. He pulled the engine back down to slow and brought *DogStar* out of her spin. He was just turning her bow back around to where the Chief of Police splashed and begged for rescue when there was a *poof* from somewhere high overhead. A ghastly white brilliance lit up the whole boat basin. *Eh?* Jeff looked up. *Ow!* He pulled his eyes back to sea level. Some kind of flare hung over the harbour, so bright it left squiggly marks in his vision when he looked away.

Things were happening everywhere. Trucks roared along the tops of both breakwaters, headlights bouncing. Men in uniform and carrying rifles pounded down the docks. A siren blared. A great big voice from somewhere on shore said:

"Return your vessel to the public dock. I repeat, return your vessel to the public dock!"

Holy cow, it's the cavalry!

"Get the boathook, lad," the Captain said.

Jeff went to fetch it. On the breakwater, the first vehicle was only thirty metres away now. Rose and Judge Burns rode in the back.

He reached to grab the boathook from its place on the saloon roof. "Look!" he cried, pointing ahead to the dock.

Patsy Ann lay stretched out on the stained black wood of the public dock. Under the icy light of the flare, her white fur seemed to blaze with an otherworldly brilliance. She was licking her paws.

The Captain looked back at Jeff and smiled. "She knew," he said.

thirty-one

A PARTY

HUH? *Whazzat?*

Jeff woke up in his own bunk. But he was cramped. Something was pushing against him, forcing him up against the cabin wall. Something warm, vaguely familiar and ... *dog-smelling! Patsy Ann!* He rolled over and hugged her tight where she lay stretched out like a long pillow.

Beyond the edge of the bunk, he noticed an untidy jumble. *Very unsailorlike*, he thought, and lifted himself to look over Patsy Ann's round shoulders. The clutter was his own clothing. The bottom drawer was pulled open and his shirts, jeans and even his white Nikes, which he hadn't worn since his first day on *DogStar*, were scattered across the floor.

He took Patsy Ann's face in his hands and looked into her beady dark eyes. "Did you do that?" he asked. She washed his face with her warm wet tongue. Jeff lay back in the bunk for a moment, one arm around the dog, and thought about how last night had ended.

The Captain had hauled Chief Beggs aboard, then made him turn over his handcuff key. They'd released Mrs. Baker and promptly put the cuffs to use on the dripping Chief himself. By the time Mayor Shrite was groaning and moaning his way back to consciousness, the Captain had him trussed with enough rope to make a hammock.

Then they'd brought *DogStar* to the dock and for a few minutes it seemed that the whole U.S. Army was there to meet them. Along with Rose and the judge and a short dapper guy who apparently belonged to the U.S. Treasury. *Imagine, a whole department to deal with missing treasure ...*

A million questions were fired at them. Rose and her mother hugged and they both cried. The judge shook his hand and the Captain's hand. Then the little dapper guy shook both their hands too, and congratulated them for "breaking the case." A squad of soldiers came and took Beggs and the mayor away. Then another squad came and took *Cerberus'* rusted strongbox and its contents off for safekeeping.

By the time they had all left and it was only Jeff and the Captain and Patsy Ann on board, the night sky was beginning to lighten over Mount Roberts to the east.

The wheelhouse clock began to chime. Jeff counted. *Four bells.* That made it either six or ten in the morning. Jeff was betting on ten. *Yikes, it's late!*

Jeff climbed awkwardly over Patsy Ann and jumped down onto the cabin's tiny triangle of floor. Among the clothes strewn over the scrap of deck, he noticed his digital wristwatch. He bent to pick it up. Now it said, "5:53 p.m., Tuesday." *Seven "future" minutes to make it back to the ship,* he thought. *Plenty of time.* Patsy Ann climbed down from the bunk with a heavy *thump* and entangled herself in his legs.

The way Jeff felt this morning, he wasn't sure he *wanted* to go back. It might be a lot more exciting to stay right here with Patsy Ann and the Captain and Rose. *We could sail to Hawaii,* he mused, stepping into his own jeans. *I could invest in I.B.M. and make a fortune,* he smiled to himself as he pulled the T-shirt he'd worn off the cruise ship over his head. *And then roll it all over into Microsoft ...* His smile broke into a chuckle.

A bubbling growl came from the companionway leading aft, and he turned. "Patsy Ann!" She had one of his new Nikes in her mouth. Her head was down and she was looking straight at Jeff. He thought he saw smile-wrinkles at the corners of her mouth. When she was sure he was looking, Patsy Ann shook the shoe and growled some more, prancing back and forward in the narrow space. *I know this game!* Jeff laughed out loud and stepped toward the dog. She growled playfully, shook the shoe some more, then turned and ran back to the saloon, Jeff at her heels. The moment they were in the larger cabin, she turned again, laughing at him. *"Come and get it,"* her expression said.

By the time Jeff had wrestled the shoe from her solid jaws, boy and dog were a laughing, tangled heap of legs and arms and tail and fur on the saloon floor.

"Hey there, what's all this?" the Captain's voice interrupted them from the galley. "We'll have no dogfights on *DogStar.*" But when Jeff looked up, he was smiling.

"She musta crawled in with me last night," Jeff started to explain. Patsy Ann settled into a long stretch beside him, grinning with her mouth wide open and panting.

"That so? You're a lucky man, then. I've never known her to sleep in a real bed before." He dropped a spoonful of creamy batter onto the griddle and the flapjack-to-be sizzled at the edges as it settled into a perfect circle. "Judge Burns sent his clerk around three bells ago," the old man said over his shoulder. "Seems there's a civic ceremony out in front of the Gastineau at noon. We're to be guests of honour."

An odd, half-smile played over the Captain's lips. *He's just shaved!* Jeff noticed. "It seems the town's opinion of Old Captain Harper has undergone something of a sea change," the old man said wryly.

Jeff looked down at the shoe in his hand. He looked up at the Captain and their eyes met. He felt something clutch at his heart. But it wasn't the old panic-attack feeling of ice in the chest ... that can't-breathe, can't-think feeling. It was totally different. It was a silent promise, a shared secret of a time they would never lose. He felt his eyes get a little tingly. *But that's OK.*

The Captain winked at him. Then he nodded at the shoe in Jeff's hand. "I'd put those on, lad." He turned back to the griddle and flipped the flapjack. "They look like they came from the moon," he added with that odd half-smile again. "And maybe they do, at that. But I'd guess they're still more the thing for a 'civic ceremony' than rubber boots."

The Captain himself had on his Sunday shoes, a fresh coat of black polish repairing any stains they had suffered in *DogStar*'s temporary flood.

LOW PUFFS of cloud played around the mountaintops, breaking the late summer sunlight into yellow beams that played over Gastineau Channel, the town of Juneau and the green slopes on either side. *Like cosmic searchlights*, Jeff thought, as they walked in single file along the dock: Patsy Ann in the lead, then Jeff and the Captain bringing up the rear.

When the row of cottages came into sight, they saw Rose and her mother stepping out of their door under the curtain of sweet peas. Mother and daughter waited for them at the end of the walk and they all went on together.

Jeff and Rose fell in behind Captain Harper and Sylvia Baker. Up in front, the old man, *who didn't look quite so old in a fresh shave and a clean shirt*, and Rose's mother, *looking much more composed than she had last night*, seemed to find things to talk about.

Behind them, Rose filled Jeff in on what had happened when she and her mother had gone to Mayor Shrite's office. She had barely begun to tell her story when the mayor got up and went to the door. He'd looked out just long enough to send Shirley home, then he had closed and locked the door behind him. When Rose finished speaking, Shrite had called Chief Beggs on the phone and ordered him to come over right away. It was when Beggs got there that they put Sylvia in handcuffs. "They would have put them on me, too," Rose asserted, eyes flashing, "except they only had the one pair." After Rose had given her account to Judge Burns, the judge had called a man he knew at the Juneau U.S. Army detachment.

It was he, it turned out, who had mustered the soldiers.

In return, Jeff told Rose about their discovery of the magnet, and the counterfeit cash under Shrite's name in *Cerberus'* strongbox. Finally they were both caught up, and they lapsed into silence. Ahead of them, Patsy Ann turned up Franklin Street towards the Gastineau Hotel. Suddenly, Jeff felt uneasy, *shy*.

"Rose," he said awkwardly.

"Uh huh." She looked at him, green eyes expectant.

"Umm … It was really nice sailing with you." *More, c'mon guy, more.* "You were great on the wreck, really … I mean … I think you're great … That's all."

Delight mingled with uncertainty in Rose's face. "Do you really have to go back to Canada?"

I don't even know if I can go back. "I … I don't know," he said.

"Do you *want* to go back?" she asked softly.

"Sometimes …" *Not right now.* "Not *now*."

"What are you doing afterward?"

Eh? "Afterward?"

"After the ceremony, silly!"

"Uh, I'm not sure. I … I don't have any plans."

"Want to do something?"

"I …" *What can I say?* "I sure would *like* to Rose, but … We'll see, OK?"

"OK." Jeff felt Rose's hand take his. Her fingers were cooler than he'd expected. She squeezed tightly for a long moment, then let go. *Wow. That was … wow!*

Ahead of them, Jeff saw a crowd of people milling in front of the tall brick Gastineau Hotel. Someone had built a wooden platform right outside the hotel's front door and decked it out in red, white and blue ribbons and streamers. Beyond it, Jeff recognized the tuba from the band that had played at the ballpark on Saturday. In front of the hotel, tables were set up on the sidewalk, with pitchers and covered platters and trays on them. *Awright,* Jeff thought, *now this looks like a party.*

The crowd stepped aside to let the five of them through. It seemed like pretty much the whole town had turned out. Sylvia smiled and waved at Chef Angelo and at Martha and Jimmy, who were both still snuffling into handkerchiefs. Patsy Ann nuzzled Hank Watson's hand in passing and favoured Snuff Malakov with a lick.

Jeff recognized the big burly guy who'd cheated him at Amory's; now he was grinning and nodding his ham face cheerfully. *He still can't stop staring at my Nikes.* There was the beanpole counterman from the Gold Dust Cafe who'd called the police on him. And there was the little jailer with the dark hair! Jeff winked at him.

Awright! Officer McGraw, *saluting,* ushered them toward the little flight of steps up to the platform. *And with a straight face, too.* Jeff couldn't contain a chuckle as he stepped past the man.

Patsy Ann stayed behind while the rest of them climbed the stairs to the little stage. Judge Burns greeted them, wearing a sober black suit instead of his robes and a wide grin on his lean, tanned face. He shook each of them by the hand and showed them to a row of chairs. Then he turned to the crowd and held up his hand to quiet the hubbub of excited chatter.

"Ladies and gentlemen of Juneau," he began, "this is not quite the usual role of a judge." His strong voice carried out over the street. "But due to the, ahem, *incapacity* of our leading civic officials," laughter ran through the crowd, "it is an honour and a pleasure that falls to me.

"Ladies and gentlemen, as many of you already know ..." A voice in the back sang out, "Hooray for Harper!"

The judge continued. "Captain Ezra Harper and Mister Jeffery Kenneth L. Beacon returned to Juneau last night after making a number of very significant discoveries. First, the steamship *Cerberus* has been located and her strongbox has been salvaged, intact." A huge and extended cheer burst from the crowd. After several minutes, it simmered down to a few isolated whistles and scattered applause. "Any of you who had gold on board the ship may attend U.S. District Court at two this afternoon to present your claim." Scattered outbreaks of cheering around the little stage indicated where the fortunate claimants were standing in the crowd.

"Also recovered was one million dollars in cash, the property of the town of Juneau." Less enthusiastic applause. "Which may just help get the budget back in line without our taxes going up again." A heartier cheer. "However, on a more sober note, a number of events in the late hours of last night, as well as certain information and evidence provided by Captain Harper and Mr. Beacon ..." *that'd be the magnet and the leather pouch full of paper mush* "... have led the U.S. Attorney for the Southeast District to lay a number of serious criminal charges against Mayor J. Samuel Shrite and Chief of Police Carter Beggs."

The crowd was quiet, waiting. "Those charges include fraud, kidnapping and assault, as well as uttering, dealing in and making counterfeit obligations or securities."

A satisfied sigh seemed to rise from the crowd as the full extent of the villainy became clear. Sentiments to the effect of "I told you something was up between those two," drifted toward the stage. Henry Burns consulted a note and added, "There will be other charges as soon as we figure out what statute the intentional wrecking of a ship comes under." The crowd growled its disapproval of the dreadful act.

"Meanwhile," Judge Burns beamed, "all charges against Jeffery Kenneth L. Beacon have been dropped and the pledge of the sailing vessel *DogStar* against his appearance in court has been released. Jeffery and *DogStar* are free to come and go as they please."

The crowd erupted again in the loudest cheering yet. Hats flew up. The band struck up a rousing march. Before it could get properly going though, the judge held up his hands for quiet, then spoke again. "Now, Mrs. Sylvia Baker would like to say a few words." He smiled at her as she stepped to the rough wooden podium.

Rose clapped like a mad thing for her mother. Jeff watched as she held herself very straight in her chair, her face flushed and her green eyes dancing over the crowd. *I'm going to miss her,* he thought.

"Ladies and gentlemen," Sylvia Baker began, "I asked Judge Burns if I could speak for a moment just to convey my heartfelt thanks to Captain Harper and Jeff. Last night, they saved my life." She looked back to where they both sat. "Thank you, both of you," she said with feeling. "If I can ever do anything for either of you, I hope …"

"You can come for dinner with me tonight," Captain Harper said in a strong, clear voice before she could finish. *Holy cow! The Captain just asked Mrs. Baker on a date! In front of everybody! Awright!* Jeff beamed, and reached across Rose to clap the old man on the shoulder.

"Why, Captain Harper, I'd be delighted!" The loudest cheer yet seemed to burst like a happy storm over the crowd as Sylvia smiled and stepped back to her seat beside the Captain. It went on for a long time and when it finally ended, the band was doing its best to start up again.

Judge Burns stepped back to the front of the platform. But it seemed the crowd had heard enough. Raising his voice over the buzz of conversation, Judge Burns reminded the folks that "the good hoteliers of Juneau have prepared refreshments for us … and this ceremony is hereby concluded."

A final ragged cheer greeted this last statement, even if no-one much heard the words. There was a sudden rush as the younger and hungrier members of the crowd moved toward the tables.

Judge Burns led their little group down from the platform. Well-wishers flowed around them immediately, pumping Jeff's hand, clapping the Captain heartily on the back, and hugging Sylvia. In seconds, Rose was surrounded by a scrum of other kids her own age. Jeff saw her arms flail as she vividly recounted their passage through Stoney Narrows.

THEN IT happened.

He heard her bark. Sharp. Urgent. Unmistakable. Jeff looked over heads and between shoulders and spotted her.

The stocky white dog stood at the end of the block towards the harbour, looking back. *Directly at me.*

Jeff's heart raced. Patsy Ann was on full alert, broad chest spread and tail sticking straight out. Her ears were up and she was listening to something only she could hear. A ray of sunlight caught her beady eyes. Pinpoints of light danced in her black pupils, like stars in the midnight sky.

With a shock, Jeff recognized the opening to the alley behind her. *A red awning on the right and a green one to the left ... is that it?*

The entrance to the alley was clear. Nothing stood in the way. Patsy Ann barked again. Jeff looked around him; no-one else was paying any attention to her. *Maybe they can't hear her.*

He caught the Captain's eye. *He does! He can hear her.*

Over the heads of the people between them, the Captain called to him: "Aye lad, that's your ship!" *Just a little longer, please ...* "Ye'd best be on your way. It's time ..."

Around him, the crowd's chatter seemed to fade away. No one was talking any less, but they were all somehow distant and remote. Except for the clear grey eyes of the Captain watching him. And the sound of Patsy Ann barking.

But I haven't even said goodbye, or ... "Thank you," he shouted to the old man. "Thank you for everything."

Patsy Ann's barking was sharp, fast and continuous now. Time was running out. *OK, OK.* "I ... Goodbye!" He turned to follow the dog.

"Wait," the Captain called.

Jeff turned back. The Captain reached up to his throat, ripping the bone medallion on its chain from his neck. The old man held the object to his heart for just a moment, then raised it over his head. "Remember," he called out and launched the bone disk into the air over the crowd, its silver chain twisting in the light. Jeff reached out and caught it one-handed as Patsy Ann's barking became almost frantic.

"I'll be seeing you!" The words came from both of them at the same time.

Then Jeff turned and ran. He broke through the crowd and saw Patsy Ann disappear into the alley. He leaned forward and put everything he had into running. Grabbing the corner of the building with the green awning, he swung at full speed into the mouth of the alley. Ahead, he could just see a flash of white. It was very dark between the buildings.

As he picked up speed again, he turned once to look over his shoulder. There was no light there, just a blind brick wall.

Then he was running too hard to think anymore, legs, arms, heart and lungs pumping full out. It was all he could do to follow the blaze of white ahead of him. It seemed always to be just on the point of vanishing entirely around another dark turn in the maze of alleys.

He was dodging breathlessly around corners ... hurdling drifts of trash ... deking past dumpsters. He couldn't see Patsy Ann ahead of him anymore. *I've lost her!*

Suddenly he burst out into bright sunlight, too bright for his eyes after the dark alley.

Jeff tripped and fell sprawling to the ground.

thirty-two

THE PRESENT

"WHERE ON EARTH were you?" *Dad? Is that Dad's voice?*

"Didn't you hear the ship's whistle? We're going to be the last people on board!" *Mom?*

Jeff's lungs burned. He wheezed and gasped, trying to suck enough oxygen into them to stop feeling dizzy. *Am I really back?*

Patsy Ann! He looked around frantically for her. Then he saw her. Or rather, saw her statue. The late-afternoon sun scattered orange and yellow reflections from her bronze flanks. *We didn't say goodbye,* he thought with regret. *But I'll be seeing you, too.*

Another thought hit him. He opened his fist. *Yes! The whalebone oval was still there!* Jeff closed his fingers around it and squeezed his eyes tight shut for a moment in gratitude. Then he stuffed it quickly into his pocket.

He got to his feet and dusted himself off. "I'm OK, I'm OK, really," he said. "I got lost, but I figured out how to get back."

His parents seemed to accept that for the time being, although he caught a furtive exchange of funny looks. It helped that they were in such a rush to get back to the ship. As soon as he was on his feet, each parent took an arm and began hurrying him along the wharf toward the gangplank.

"They used to load coal here, y'know," he told them as they went.

"That so?" Dad looked at him curiously.

Then they were scurrying up the gangplank past the disapproving eye of an officer in starched white shirt and dark blue epaulettes. As they reached the top and stepped down again onto the deck, he spoke into a walkie-talkie.

By the time they stopped and turned to catch their breaths, the gangplank was being pulled away from the side of the ship.

People lined the rails, looking out over the wharf and taking a final few photographs of each other with Juneau in the background. The ship's whistle gave three long, loud blasts, and Jeff felt the steel plates under his feet vibrate gently as the big ship began to move ever so slowly away from its berth.

Idly, he ran his eyes over the backs of the people at the rail. *Eh?* His eyes stopped at a short, slender figure in white painter pants and a striped red and white top. *And pigtails, chestnut-coloured pigtails. Could it …*

"Rose!" He almost shouted it, stepping closer.

The girl in pigtails turned. But it wasn't Rose at all. It was that girl he'd talked to on the ship before …

"Rosemary!" she corrected him. *Still … there was something … something a lot alike about them.*

"Yeah, sorry, I mean Rosemary."

"Oh, it's you," she said, then looked around. "Where's your dog? Didn't you take him to shore?" She didn't say it like it was a crazy thing at all.

"Uh, no, I left him in the cabin." He looked out over the town for a second. *OK, so say something else. She* really *looks like Rose.* "Uh ... How'd you like Juneau?"

Her green eyes lit up. "I loved it! I went to see where my grandma was born."

Huh? Jeff felt a tingling echo of the strange feeling he'd first felt on the far side of the alley. "Your grandma lived here?"

"Uh-huh," said Rosemary brightly. "Just over there." She pointed away toward the right, where a road followed the foot of the mountain along the shore of Gastineau Channel.

There was a full-fledged shiver traveling up his spine now. "Rose ... mary," he added, just in time.

"Yeah?"

"Um, you want to do something afterward?"

"After what?"

"Uh, you know, just later, after the ship leaves. I gotta go to the cabin with my folks first, clean up and stuff. But I'll be back!"

She gave him an odd, *figuring* kind of look out from under her bangs. *She's got green eyes! Bet her grandma had green eyes, too.* Then she smiled. "OK!"

"Great, great. See you later, then."

JEFF CAUGHT another one of those Parent Looks passing between Mom and Dad when he turned back to them. But they snapped smiles into place when they saw him looking.

And on the way back to their cabin, they seemed pleased with themselves, almost giggly, *like they've got some kind of secret.*

Ha! Jeff thought to himself smugly. *If they only knew how big a secret I've got!*

Mom turned the key and opened the door to the Beacons' cabin. Jeff remembered his cramped space on *DogStar* and couldn't help thinking, *boy, is this place plush.*

His eyes went straight to Buddy's brass urn. *Still there!* He felt relief. *I'm home, Buddy. I found out a lot of stuff. I can't wait to tell you.*

Then it hit him. Clear as the bells that tolled out the time on the Captain's ship. Clear as that bolt of lightning down the cliff by the cove. Clear as the light in Patsy Ann's eyes.

"Mom, Dad," Jeff said. "I'm sorry, I'll wash up later. But right now I've got to do something." He picked up Buddy's canister and headed for the door. Halfway there, he stopped and returned for the flowers, not daring to look at his parents. Then he dashed out into the corridor.

As he reached the stern, the big ship was just beginning to gather way, its huge propellers churning the water below him into a green and white froth.

I've got to let him go. He held up the brass urn and spoke aloud. "I know you'll like it there, Buddy ... she's a real nice dog." He felt hot tears on his cheeks but he didn't care. "And I'll always be able to find you ... Always."

Slowly Jeff unscrewed the brass lid. When it was all the way off, he turned the little canister upside down over the rail. White ashes spilled out in a fine, thin stream that fell and fell until it was lost forever in the churning wake.

Jeff's tears were flowing hard now, and when he spoke again, his voice cracked. "Spirit never dies, Buddy, remember that and ... and I'll be seein' you." He hardly got his last words out. Blindly, he threw the flowers out over the water. *It won't ever go back to being the way it was before. I won't ever be the same again.* "I love you, Buddy."

A Bull Terrier barked and his head shot up. *It can't be!* He looked to his right toward the sound. They were passing a marina. With an effort he recognized the old boat basin where he had lived with the Captain on *DogStar* all that time ago. *Until just this morning.*

Then he saw her. *Patsy Ann!* She was standing at the end of the pier, grinning and wagging her tail. *It's her spirit ... she came back to say goodbye.* He felt a surge of joy in his heart.

Then it overflowed. He heard another bark, like Patsy Ann's, only deeper, *more familiar.* Jeff's heart raced and he stopped breathing. Frantically he rubbed tears from his eyes and stared again at the shore. There was a second dog on the end of the pier, standing beside Patsy Ann. Another Bull Terrier, bigger and broader across the shoulders. Wearing a black collar. *Oh my gosh, Buddy's with her! Buddy's going to be with Patsy Ann! Yessssss!*

Something like a dam burst inside Jeff. He was still crying, but his tears felt different. He was grinning from ear to ear. His head felt light. From somewhere far away, he heard barking. Patsy Ann's clear note, Buddy's gruffer one, both sounding happy. Through blurry eyes, he saw the two dogs turn together and run back along the pier. Before they reached the shore they had vanished. *They're going to the Dog Star.*

For a long time, Jeff just stood there. When finally he took a deep breath and turned around, he almost bumped into his parents. *How long have they been here?* "Did you *see that*?" he asked.

Mom wore a big smile and her eyes looked misty. But she didn't answer.

Dad spoke, and he seemed a little misty, too. "That was a very wonderful thing you just did, son," he said, his voice thick. He put his arm around Jeff and hugged him close. *Wow! Aliens have stolen my father.*

"Ken, I'm going to tell him now," Frances Beacon insisted. Her husband nodded in agreement, "Absolutely."

Eh? Judging from Mom's tone of voice, this *sounded* like a good thing.

"Son," she said, "we were going to save this as a surprise for your birthday, but ... Well, we did a little research while we were in Juneau. And a wonderful woman with something called the Friends of Patsy Ann Society told us that the original Patsy Ann's great-great-great-great-great-great," she was counting on her fingers, "great-great-grandchildren will be born in a few weeks. We thought maybe you'd like one of the pups for your birthday?"

Not much! I can always ask for a telescope for Christmas!

PATSY ANN

is a real Bull Terrier who lived in Juneau, Alaska, during the 1930s. Stone deaf from birth, she somehow "heard" the whistles of ships long before they came into sight and would trot purposefully to the wharf to greet them. She became so famous that her likeness appeared on postcards. In 1934, the town's mayor bestowed upon her the title of "Official Greeter of Juneau."

In 1992, on the fiftieth anniversary of her death, a bronze statue of Patsy Ann was erected on the Juneau waterfront. There the little dog sits watching and waiting with eternal patience, forever fulfilling her duties as "Official Greeter."

The authors are donating a portion of their royalties to the Friends of Patsy Ann Society, an organization set up in conjunction with the Gastineau Humane Society to promote understanding of and kindness to animals. Patsy Ann's statue was created by noted artist and dog show judge, Anna Harris.

For more about Patsy Ann, log on to her website:
http://www.patsyann.com

BEVERLEY WOOD is a writer and marketing consultant who worked for twelve years as operations manager at *Maclean's* magazine. She has published articles with *Maclean's*, *Destinations*, *Tribute*, *Pacific Northwest* and *Pacific Rim News Service*.

CHRIS WOOD is a Vancouver-based writer and author. In a career spanning four decades he has written thousands of magazine articles, radio scripts and other stories. In addition to the Patsy Ann series written with his wife, Beverley Wood, Chris is the co-author with Peter S. Grant of *Blockbusters and Trade Wars* (Douglas & McIntyre), a book about popular music, movies, books and television.

Beverley and Chris live in Vancouver in an artist's loft with their Bull Terrier, Cato.

S I R I U S M Y S T E R I E S

by Beverley and Chris Wood Coming Soon from Polestar:

Look for these new adventures starring Patsy Ann

Jack's Knife

Jack Kyle's 21st-century mom wants to break up his friendship with a retired policeman. But when Al McMann is taken to hospital and Patsy Ann spirits Jack back to Juneau, Alaska, in the 1930s, Jack finds himself embroiled in the controversial hunt for endangered whales and in pursuit of a daring bandit. The outcome could change his old friend's life as well as his own.

1-55192-709-8 • Coming in Spring 2005

The Golden Boy

Tomi Tanaka can take almost anything apart and put it back together again. But he can't seem to please his demanding dad. When Patsy Ann visits him, the two travel back to Juneau, Alaska, in the 1930s, where Tomi has a chance to make sense of a puzzling treasure that has the town stumped — and he ends up on the trail of a mysterious missing gold mine.

1-55192-711-X • Coming in Spring 2006